A MUTUAL APPETITE

"Open for me," Burke said against her lips, and she drank in his words.

He tasted of peppermint and brandy and . . . heat; glorious, wonderful, heat. Desire sent honey through her veins, and Cordelia shivered in the warmth of his body heat. No, that didn't make sense, but she could not stop to puzzle it out. She swayed toward Burke, wanting . . . wanting . . . something; she didn't know what. A mewling moan escaped her.

He pulled back a fraction. She followed, eager for whatever came next.

"Easy," he whispered, slowing the pace of his kisses, each a little less fervent. "You have convinced me that you are quite experienced," he whispered, the lie sliding off his tongue with surprising ease, "But now is neither the time nor the place to indulge our mutual appetites."

What was he saying? What did he mean? Cordelia fought to regain her senses. Suddenly the room came back into focus and she realized she'd been kissing a man practically in full view of half the *ton*. Embarrassment warmed her cheeks. "I . . . I . . ."

"Don't worry. No one can see. Your reputation is safe. From everyone except me."

BOOK YOUR PLACE ON OUR WEBSITE AND MAKE THE READING CONNECTION!

We've created a customized website just for our very special readers, where you can get the inside scoop on everything that's going on with Zebra, Pinnacle and Kensington books.

When you come online, you'll have the exciting opportunity to:

- View covers of upcoming books
- Read sample chapters
- Learn about our future publishing schedule (listed by publication month *and author*)
- Find out when your favorite authors will be visiting a city near you
- Search for and order backlist books from our online catalog
- Check out author bios and background information
- Send e-mail to your favorite authors
- Meet the Kensington staff online
- Join us in weekly chats with authors, readers and other guests
- Get writing guidelines
- AND MUCH MORE!

**Visit our website at
http://www.kensingtonbooks.com**

THE NIGHT WE KISSED

Laurie Brown

ZEBRA BOOKS
Kensington Publishing Corp.
http://www.kensingtonbooks.com

ZEBRA BOOKS are published by

Kensington Publishing Corp.
850 Third Avenue
New York, NY 10022

All Kensington titles, imprints and distributed lines are available at special quantity discounts for bulk purchases for sales promotion, premiums, fund-raising, educational or institutional use.

Special book excerpts or customized printings can also be created to fit specific needs. For details, write or phone the office of the Kensington Special Sales Manager: Kensington Publishing Corp., 850 Third Avenue, New York, NY 10022. Attn. Special Sales Department. Phone: 1-800-221-2647.

First Printing: October 2003
10 9 8 7 6 5 4 3 2 1

Printed in the United States of America

One

"I missed him." Cordelia Weston hung the old hunting rifle back on its hook over the fieldstone mantle.

"Oh, my God, you tried to kill him," her sister Emily said, biting her thumbnail.

"If I'd wanted to kill Ernest, I wouldn't have missed," Cordelia said. Not that he didn't deserve to die, but it would be just as impossible for her pregnant eighteen-year-old sister to marry a dead man as one who had fled home to England. "He wasn't on the stage to Savannah. He must have taken another route." She held back a comment on his apparent haste to depart. Recriminations wouldn't help now.

All the way home, Cordelia had tried to come up with an answer to her sister's problem. What they needed was a man. Any man without the current encumbrance of a wife would do, as far as she was concerned. An innocent babe didn't deserve to be born with the stigma of being a bastard. Emily would have to stop her useless hand-wringing and marry someone other than Ernest. Now, all Cordelia had to do was convince her sister.

She poured a cup of coffee from the ever present pot over the fire. Not real coffee, of course. They hadn't had that since the beginning of the war. At least the bitter chicory brew was hot. As she warmed her hands around the mug, she glanced over at Granny sitting in her rocker, winding the same ball of wool. Like Odysseus's wife Penelope, Granny knitted the same scarf all day and unwound her progress each night. Today she seemed to be having one of her good days.

"Are you warm enough, Granny?" Cordelia asked. "Can I get you anything?"

"No, thank you, child. I'm fine."

Cordelia breathed an inward sigh and sank into a chair beside the plank table. When Granny had a bad day, when she had one of her spells, *difficult* took on new meaning. Sometimes Granny just thought she was someone else, but other times she became disoriented and wandered off.

"I'm sure Ernest will have a reasonable explanation when he returns," Emily said. "I know his father was unwell. Maybe Ernest had to return to inherit his title. That must be it. But if that's the case, it could be months and months before he comes back for me, and the baby is due by Thanksgiving. Oh, what am I going to do?" she wailed.

"You could always marry someone else," Granny said.

Cordelia gave her a grateful smile, and nodded in agreement.

Emily sent her a disgusted look. "Even if I would marry someone else, who would that be? Every man from sixteen to sixty is off fighting Yankees." She plopped down into the only other chair. "Crazy old woman," she whispered under her breath.

"Shush," Cordelia said, kicking at her sister under the table. If Granny behaved a bit eccentric at times, that didn't make her crazy. She deserved their sympathy. The war had taken her husband, and she'd watched the main house of their lovely plantation home, Belle Oaks, burn to the ground.

"Why? She doesn't care," Emily said with a sidelong glare at Granny. "That's why we're stuck in this . . . this . . . shanty." She gave an exaggerated shiver of revulsion as she looked around the room.

The small log cabin where they now lived might be rustic, but it was warm and dry on a chilly rainy evening, a fact Cordelia appreciated even if Emily didn't.

Granny pounded her cane on the floor. "There's Mr. Marlin at the General Store. If you marry him, he'll give us credit."

"That sickly old weasel?" Emily gave Granny a look of disbelieving horror. "Not if he was the last man on earth."

"It's a little late to be choosy," Cordelia muttered.

Emily jumped up. "I'll have you know I could've had my pick of any man in Savannah. You're just jealous because you didn't inherit Mama's looks." She flipped a golden curl back over her shoulder. Tipping her head to the side, she put one finger on her chin. "And how many beaus did you have? If my memory serves me correctly it was . . . oh, yes, one."

Cordelia's heart constricted at the thought of her dear friend Travis, killed recently at Shiloh. He hadn't really been her beau. He'd just wanted someone to write chatty letters to him, so she'd given him her favorite red hair ribbon to tie on his sleeve. Poor Travis. She made a mental note to call on his mother later in the week.

Emily put her hands on her hips, accentuating her voluptuous figure, another attribute Cordelia had *not* inherited from their mother. Except she had her mother's hips. Hardly a blessing when she was small and narrow everywhere else. Cordelia had inherited their father's plain light brown hair and ordinary hazel eyes.

Despite their reduced circumstances, Emily had dressed for dinner in a pink ruffled confection, stylish at the outbreak of the war. Cordelia wiped her palms on the dark brown cotton of her day dress. Not fashionable, but practical for chores and chasing recalcitrant bridegrooms.

"Time to set the table," Granny said, and because it was one of the few tasks Emily was willing to do without an argument, Cordelia didn't offer to help.

"When I marry Ernest and we're living in London, I won't be forced to perform menial labor. I'll have an army of servants catering to my every whim," Emily said dreamily as she placed the chipped stoneware on the table.

"In that case, you should go to England," Granny said.

Emily whirled around. "What a wonderful idea." She ran over to Granny and gave her a hug. "Granny, I adore you." With loving care, Emily helped the older woman to the table.

Cordelia tried to ignore the insincere gushing, and spooned a serving of rabbit stew into her bowl. Of course Emily would listen to advice that echoed what she wanted to hear, but why did her sister have to be so impractical?

"There's only one problem," Cordelia said around a bite of cornbread.

"Don't speak with your mouth full," Granny said.

"Please," Emily added with a delicate shudder. She gracefully took her seat. "Did you leave your manners in the barn?"

Cordelia waved her spoon in the air just to aggravate her sister. "A more appropriate question would be, how do you expect to get to England in the middle of a war?"

"Oh, you'll think of something," Emily said, as if such mundane matters were beneath her consideration. "You always manage somehow."

Cordelia propped her elbows on the table and rested her forehead in her hands, her ravenous appetite suddenly gone. She'd done her best to take care of her family in a world turned upside down, but Emily expected a miracle. Didn't she realize the Yankees had all but closed the harbors? Passage on one of the daring blockade runners cost a small fortune, and money was one of the many things they no longer had.

"Maybe Granny will remember where she buried the family silver and her jewels," Emily said. "There's bound to be lots of cash. Not Confederate dollars, either."

"Shush," Cordelia said, peeking at Granny. Mentioning the silver or jewels usually set off one of her bad spells. Beneath the table, she crossed her fingers.

"Do you remember . . ." Granny said.

Cordelia relaxed and settled into a more comfortable position for one of the older woman's interminable stories.

"Do you remember Jebidiah Cosley of Aspen Hill?" Granny asked.

"Of course, I do," Emily said, clasping her hands under her chin in rapturous delight. "I especially recall the last cotillion at Aspen Hill. I wore my silver blue moiré silk with the ecru lace panels in the skirt and sleeves." She heaved a deep sigh. "Forrest Lee was the handsomest man there, so dashing in his uniform he literally stole my breath away. He waltzed with me three times. A sure sign of his intentions."

Cordelia snorted. Where was Forrest Lee now when they needed him? Gallivanting across Georgia in pursuit of honor and glory like all the other men, while the womenfolk dug sweet potatoes to keep from starving.

Granny pounded her cane on the floor to get attention. "I was speaking."

"Yes ma'am," Emily and Cordelia mumbled in unison.

"As I was about to say, Jebidiah Cosley is home on furlough. I hear he plans to ship his daughter and his prize stallion to safety."

If Cordelia had to guess, it would be a toss-up which

mattered more to Jeb Cosley, his spoiled, willful sixteen-year-old daughter with the unfortunate nickname of Precious, or the fractious stallion. Her money was on Thunderation.

"What does that have to do with us?" Emily asked.

Granny shrugged. "Just making polite dinner conversation."

They ate in silence for several minutes. Cordelia pushed the few pieces of unsavory meat and overcooked vegetables around her bowl. Let Emily fantasize about ballrooms and stupid dresses, she daydreamed about food. Roast beef, rare and sliced thin with horseradish sauce. White bread soft as a cloud and spread with strawberry jam. And ice cream. She licked her lips. Creamy, smooth—

"That's it." Emily jumped up and twirled around in the center of the small room, hugging herself. "I have the most marvelous idea. I'll accompany Precious and Thunderation."

"How do you know they're going to England?" Cordelia asked.

"Jeb has relatives in London. A cousin, or a brother, right, Granny?"

"An uncle. Theodore."

"See? Where else would Jeb send his daughter?"

"All right," Cordelia said, "I'll concede London is a logical assumption, but you don't have any money for passage."

"That's the genius of my plan. I'll volunteer to be the dear girl's companion, and Jeb will pay my fare."

"More than likely, he'd ask Cordelia to chaperone Precious," Granny said.

"He only likes her best because that stupid horse of his adores her," Emily said, sticking out her bottom lip. "Did you know she goes to Aspen Hill to visit that beast?" she addressed Granny.

Cordelia could have argued that. She didn't actually go there to just to see Thunderation, but if she was there on other errands, she always made time to stop in and bring him a bit of apple or carrot.

"I should think the fact that Cordelia is a respectable spinster would weigh more in her favor than the regard of a horse," Granny said.

Cordelia cringed inwardly at the term *spinster*, but at twenty-five she was definitely on the shelf. When she had been the age that most young women attended balls and were courted, she was helping her grandmother run the plantation, nursing her ailing mother, and taking care of her younger sister.

"I've got it," Emily said to Cordelia. "You can volunteer to tend the horse on the journey, keep him calm and that sort of thing. Jeb will be thrilled. Once we get to England, we'll stay with Uncle Theodore until we find Ernest, a few days at most. He'll get a special license, we'll get married, and then we won't have to worry about money ever again. You can stay with us, Cordelia, for . . . a while, and then I'll pay your fare home. See? Pure genius."

Her sister looked genuinely happy for the first time in weeks, but Cordelia couldn't go running off to England. She had obligations, commitments. People depended on her. However, she couldn't explain that to her sister without betraying her secret activities.

"We don't know whether Jeb Cosley needs a chaperone for his daughter and a companion for his horse, or not," Cordelia said. "And I can't up and leave everything on a moment's notice."

"You can convince him," Emily wheedled. "I know you can." Tears filled her eyes, her expression forlorn. "If you don't help me, I don't know what I'll do. You'll go with me, won't you? I'll just die if I have to marry anyone other than Ernest."

"There are other people we have to consider," Cordelia said, jerking her head toward Granny. They both turned to look at their grandmother, who had emptied her bowl of stew and now wore it on her head like a cap.

Cordelia stifled a groan. Stressful situations usually set Granny off on one of her bad spells. Obviously, she couldn't be left alone to fend for herself.

Somehow Cordelia would have to convince Jeb that Emily would be a suitable companion and chaperone for his sixteen-year-old daughter. Not an easy task. If it turned out that Cordelia had to go with Emily, they would have to take Granny with them. Cordelia rubbed her temples. Stay or go, both offered the prospect of disaster.

When her family was finally asleep, Cordelia slipped out into the night, the covered kettle of leftover stew in one hand and a bundle of old clothes under the other arm. Without needing the benefit of a lantern, she made her way to their ramshackle barn. She opened the door just wide enough to squeeze through, set her burden to one side, and pulled the door shut, the soft scratch of wood on dirt ominously loud in the still darkness.

She pulled a candle stub and a match from her pocket and set the light on the rail of an empty stall. From the far corner, four pairs of eyes blinked up at her. A man, woman, and two children hunkered in the dark, fearfully watchful.

Keeping her voice low, yet friendly, Cordelia picked up the food and clothing, and carried it to the little group. "Please, eat," Cordelia said. "It's not much, but there's cornbread and stew." The words were barely out of her mouth before they tucked in, the father making sure his wife and children ate first.

Cordelia retreated and stood watch by the door, waiting for the subtle scratching she hoped would come soon. When it did, she opened the door to let Madame Lavonne slip inside.

"I contacted Mockingbird," Cordelia whispered, using the code name even though they both knew his real identity. This way, if the runaways were caught, they wouldn't be able to reveal any information, even inadvertently. "The Quaker will be waiting across the river at one hour before dawn."

Madame Lavonne nodded. "I'll take them across as soon as the moon sets. Rufus says two shipments next week."

Cordelia motioned for the older woman to follow her outside. They found a dry spot under the oak tree and sat. She pulled a napkin-wrapped slice of cornbread out of her pocket and handed it to her friend.

Madame Lavonne broke the golden square into two pieces.

Cordelia refused the offer to share. "I had plenty at supper."

Madame Lavonne ate one piece, her lean, wrinkled brown fingers catching every crumb. She rewrapped the remaining half in the napkin, and Cordelia knew it would find its way into one of the children's pockets before the night was over.

"We might have a problem," Cordelia said. "Emily—"

"I know all about Emily, and the plan to go to London."

"But how? She just—"

"Madame knows many things." The old woman cackled at her own thoughts. She tapped her forehead, indicating the mysterious all-seeing third eye. "Many things."

Madame Lavonne had grown up in New Orleans, daughter of a voodoo priestess. After coming to Savan-

nah, Madame had earned enough money making
charms and potions to buy her freedom. Since then
she'd helped others along the path of freedom in any
way she could. Madame Lavonne always seemed to know
what was going to happen before the event took place.

Cordelia shook her head. "I can't go. Hopefully, Jeb
will send Emily with Precious, and I'll stay with Granny."

"Fate is opening a door for you." Madame Lavonne
smiled, her teeth a slash of white across her mocha
complexion.

"I can be of more use here than in London," Cordelia
said.

"Maybe you should not be so certain. Maybe Fate has
provided a way to contact . . ."

"Go on."

"Never mind," Madame said. "There are too many
Confederates in London just now, lobbying for support
for their cause. It could be dangerous."

"And this isn't?"

"Here, you have friends who would help you."

"Tell me what you were thinking. At least let me make
up my own mind."

Madame Lavonne hesitated before she nodded. "I
have corresponded with several people in London, abolitionists who have donated most generously. I call them
our angels. However, the war has made the transfer of
funds difficult."

"If I went to England, I could contact your friends, and
bring back any donations." Cordelia jumped up, excited
by the opportunity to make a major difference. They
would have money to buy blankets, and shoes, and . . ."

Cordelia's shoulders slumped. "Unfortunately, everything depends on Jeb Cosley."

Madame Lavonne rose from her sitting position with
an ease that belied her advanced years. "I will have a

chat with Mr. Cosley." She chuckled. "A bit of clay, a few feathers, and *voila*, you are packing your bags."

Cordelia shivered in the sudden cool breeze.

"I won't share a bed with you." Emily stuck out her bottom lip. "You smell awful."

Cordelia had returned to the ship's only passenger cabin after settling the horse in his stall below decks, and had walked into the middle of an argument between her sister and grandmother.

She took a deep breath before dealing with the latest in her sister's long litany of complaints. However, in this case, Emily was somewhat justified. Before Granny would get on the ship, she'd insisted on stopping at Madame Lavonne's for a travel charm, which she wore around her neck and which did emit an unpleasant odor. Granny had traded all their household goods, what little they had left, for a number of magical knickknacks.

Cordelia wasn't sure what the other charms were for, or against, because Granny had locked everything in her old travel trunk for safekeeping. Supposedly, anyone who disturbed the lid would be cursed with painful boils. Cordelia didn't believe that, but she suspected the trunk would smell even worse than Granny.

Madame Lavonne had slipped Cordelia three letters and given instructions as to their delivery. Strange directions, but Cordelia hadn't had time for questions.

Emily and Granny traded glares. Too bad Cordelia hadn't thought to ask for a charm to make Emily more pleasant. A very long journey loomed ahead.

"I don't want to share with her, either," Granny said, crossing her arms. "She snores and hogs the covers."

Emily stuck out her tongue before pulling her white cotton nightgown over her head.

"Fine. You and I can share the trundle bed, and Emily can share with Precious." Cordelia looked around the small cabin. "Where is that girl?"

Emily crawled into the larger regular bed and pulled the coverlet up to her chin. "I think she went up on deck to watch."

"Watch what?" Cordelia asked. "The whole point of sailing at midnight on a moonless night is that nothing can be seen."

The ship lurched into motion, and Cordelia doused the lights in accordance with the captain's instructions. No lights. No noise. No passengers on deck.

Sitting on her bed in the darkness, Cordelia expected Precious to return any moment, and she intended to give the girl a stern talking to. She took her duties as chaperone seriously. In the dark, the passage of time was hard to judge, and she couldn't shake the feeling that something was wrong. "I'm going to look for her," she said, standing. She groped blindly toward the door.

"You won't find her," Granny said.

"I know it's dark, but—"

"Ask Emily."

"What is going on?" Cordelia returned to the bed, stubbing her toe on the trundle. "What does Granny mean?"

When her sister didn't answer her question, Cordelia patted the bed until she found her sister's arm and shook her. "I know you're still awake, Emily, because you're not snoring. What is Granny talking about?"

"Granny's crazy," Emily muttered, jerking her arm free and turning on her side to face the wall. "I'm going to sleep."

Something in her manner told Cordelia that Emily was evading the question. "Where's Precious?"

"Emily knows," Granny said, her tone smug.

Cordelia grabbed her sister's shoulder and flipped her on her back. "Whatever it is, you'd better tell me, and right this minute."

Emily sat up. "Oh, all right. Precious doesn't want to go to England."

"She's just a child. Now, where is she?"

"Precious will be seventeen in four months. I think that's old enough to know her own mind."

"Where is she?" Cordelia asked through gritted teeth.

"She got off the ship before we sailed. She's staying in Savannah with Susan Higdon, a dear friend of ours from school, who, for your information, is already putting up her hair and wearing long dresses and she won't be seventeen for eight months. Tomorrow Precious is meeting her fiancé, and they're going to be married, and go to Venice for their honeymoon."

"Who would even think of marrying an underage girl?"

"Lance Daugherty would."

"Lance is a bounder and a cad," Cordelia said as she headed for the door. Poor naive Precious had fallen for the lies of a man known for despoiling virgins and leaving them stranded far from home.

"Where are you going?" Emily asked.

"To find the captain and tell him to turn this ship around."

Cordelia felt her way down the short hall to the half-flight of steps which led up to the main deck. Suddenly a loud screech ripped through the still night. Footsteps pounded across the deck. Were they under attack?

As she popped her head above the deck, a belch of fire flared off to her left. A moment later, the boom of a cannon reached her ears, and the ball whizzed by and plopped into the water ahead of the ship. The Yankees were firing across their bow, the signal to heave to and stand by to be boarded.

Sailors, obviously ignoring the warning shot, rushed to pile on every stitch of canvas available. Someone grabbed her arm and yelled in her ear to get below. She shook him off, but then she was grabbed from behind.

"We're gonna die," Emily yelled in her ear. "The Yankees are going to sink us. I'm too young to die. I—"

Cordelia turned and took her sister by the shoulders and shook her until she stopped ranting.

"Go stay with Granny. I'll be back in a minute."

"Where are you going?" Emily clutched at Cordelia's sleeve. "Don't leave me. I don't want to die alone."

"We're not going to die." She didn't have time to argue. Each second put them farther away. Cordelia turned Emily around and pushed her toward the cabin. "Now go stay with Granny."

On deck, Cordelia made her way past bales of cotton and kegs of molasses. Every inch of space was crammed with trade goods that would bring a premium price outside the Confederacy. Even so fully laden the small ship seemed to fly over the waves. The booming cannon of the Yankee gunboat receded in their wake. She caught up with Captain Moss in the stern of the ship.

"You must turn the ship around," Cordelia said.

"Afraid I can't oblige, Miss. If the Yankees catch us, they'll confiscate my ship and everything on it."

"A young woman's life is at stake." She pulled from her pocket her father's two-shot derringer that she always carried and aimed right between his eyes. "Now give the order to turn around."

The captain's eyes widened, but he quickly recovered his swaggering attitude and laughed in her face. "Even if I did, the crew would mutiny. Not a man here wants to hang as a traitor."

She realized too late the caliber of men she'd trusted with their lives. Captain Moss was known for his daring and maritime skill, but obviously his morals were lacking. With a swift move, he snatched the pistol out of her hand.

"Give that back."

The captain shrugged, smiled a gap-toothed grin. "I'll return your weapon when we reach the Bahamas."

"You, sir, are not a gentleman," she said.

He motioned to one of his men. "Take this woman below and lock her in her cabin." He doffed his hat in a mocking bow. "If you'll excuse me, I have some Yankees to outrun."

Cordelia looked back over her shoulder as the sailor practically dragged her across the deck. The Yankee blockade faded into the distance. She said a silent prayer for poor Precious, and for what lay ahead. Fate had swung a door wide open and she felt destiny rushing toward her at a dizzying, dangerous speed.

Two

Anthony Burke, Viscount Deering, sat in his carriage, staring down at his hands.

"Where to, milord?" the coachman asked through the trapdoor in the roof.

That was the very question that perplexed him. By rights he should head to his usual Thursday luncheon of leek soup and beef pasty at his club, but the missive he'd seen earlier had placed him smack in the middle of a conundrum. Although his position in the Diplomatic Corps had always entailed, to one degree or another, knowledge of Her Majesty's confidential correspondence on official matters, his ethics had never been challenged. Nor had he ever doubted the wisdom of his superiors in the Department. This morning both had been tested, and found wanting.

"Milord? Where to, sir?"

Burke started at the coachman's voice. He dug out his pocket watch and checked the time, finding the tune it played, "God Save the Queen," oddly comforting. The honorable path was obvious. Even though he gave the allegation no merit, his friend deserved to know the circumstances. Once he'd passed along the information, he could return to work with a clear conscience. "Marsfield House," he said. "And don't dawdle."

The carriage soon pulled into Raleigh Square, and stopped in front of the three-story redbrick Georgian mansion. After handing his hat, gloves, and cane to the butler, Burke showed himself into the library. As a long-time friend of the earl, he wasn't required to wait to be announced.

Eight years ago, when Burke had joined the Agency, Marsfield had been his mentor. The secret organization was formed during the Napoleonic Wars to gather information on foreign nationals. Its reach had widened, and its roots ran deep into Whitehall—some even said directly to the Queen. Burke had resigned from the Agency to take his current post in the Diplomatic Corps, a position better suited to his logical, fastidious nature, but he had remained friends with Lord Marsfield and his wife.

"Ah, Burke," Marsfield said. He was a tall man, the silver at his temples accentuating his distinguished bearing. His maroon and navy paisley smoking jacket echoed the colors of the masculine yet elegant surroundings. He stepped from behind his desk to shake hands. "You're just the man I need."

"Sir?"

"Preston here is between assignments and is making a nuisance of himself." Marsfield nodded toward the dark-headed man draped nonchalantly in a maroon leather chair. "Can't you take him off to do whatever mischief it is that young people do these days?"

Burke turned to the man who had been his best friend since boyhood. He had certainly not expected to find Preston here. "I thought you had an afternoon engagement with a beautiful woman."

Preston's dark eyes betrayed no emotion, but his lip

twitched at the corner. He saluted his friend with a near empty glass of brandy. "I do. I'll be leaving soon."

Burke nodded and turned back to Marsfield. "If I might have a few moments of your time, sir. Your name came up today—"

Anne, Lady Marsfield, breezed into the room, pulling on her gloves. "I'm finally ready—oh, hello, Burke dear." She was dressed to go out in a deep green outfit that matched her eyes, her riotous curls tucked neatly beneath a stylish hat with a huge white ostrich plume. Though tall for a woman, she still had to stand on her tiptoes to buss Burke's cheek.

"How are the children?" he asked, with genuine fondness for both the children and their mother.

"Growing daily. I would ask the governess to bring them down so you could see for yourself, but the little terrors are finally taking their naps. I had to read them their favorite books twice."

"Your stories, I presume."

Anne had started to write children's books after her marriage and, judging by the popularity of her Aunt Bunny literary persona, had done quite well.

She grimaced. "It's terrible to have to admit it, but no. Even though he's only four, Stephen favors swashbuckling pirate stories. He loves that strange wooden boat you gave him and drags it everywhere, even to bed."

"Actually, it's a scale model of the *Helene*, a new steamship I've invested in quite heavily. When she's finished, she'll break all speed records set by old-fashioned sailing ships. Steam is the future." He realized he was rambling on about a subject of great fascination to him but of little interest to anyone else. A habit he'd been trying to break. "And Andrea? How is she?"

"She'll be especially disappointed she missed you. She's decided she's going to marry you when she grows up."

Surprised, he blinked. How did a man reply to that?

Anne patted his arm. "Don't be too alarmed. Last week it was the organ grinder in Covent Garden, the one with the monkey that wears the cute little red hat. The week before, it was Preston."

"I was replaced by a monkey," Preston said with an exaggerated groan. He stood and straightened his impeccable gray afternoon coat, its cut and his tie the height of fashion. "Perhaps I should buy a red hat."

She turned to Preston. "Not today. You promised to take me to the new exhibit of fairy paintings at Thorsen's Gallery. Shall we?"

Burke looked at his friend. "You're taking Anne to lunch?"

"See what I mean?" Marsfield said. "He's a bloody nuisance. If he's not keeping me from my work, he's attempting to steal my wife's affections."

Anne made a face in her husband's direction, and Preston looked sheepish. Burke knew Preston had once carried a torch for Anne. Just as he knew she adored Marsfield, and the earl was besotted with her.

"Are you coming with us?" she asked Burke.

"I must offer my apologies. I'm expected back in the office at one-thirty, and I have a matter to discuss with Marsfield."

"Sounds important," she said, one eyebrow raised.

Preston stood up straighter. "If Burke is willing to give up a meal, you can bet it's important."

Anne rang for the butler. "I'll have sandwiches and tea brought in." Then she removed her hat and sat on the beige brocade sofa, motioning for the gentlemen to join her. "This sounds more interesting than paintings."

Marsfield took the place next to her, and Preston resumed his seat in one of the side chairs.

Burke hesitated. "It's a matter of some delicacy, sir."

"I'm among the people I trust most. I hope you feel the same." Marsfield nodded toward the remaining seat in the conversation grouping.

"Of course I do," Burke said, sitting in the sturdy high-backed chair. He swallowed. There was no way to sugarcoat it. "The Diplomatic Office received a message this morning from Alan Pinkerton, head of the Secret Service for the United States Government. It was in a diplomatic pouch but wasn't sealed with an official cache. Usually such letters are requests for public appearances or preferences, invitations, or announcements. I log each arrival, summarize it, and refer it to the appropriate official."

Burke paused for a sip of tea.

Marsfield gave him a look he recognized. "In twenty-five words or less," he said, though not unkindly.

Preston, however, hooted with laughter at the familiar request. Brevity had never been one of Burke's strong points, but he'd been working on it. His current relapse was a measure of how deeply this matter had unsettled him.

"Pinkerton's letter warned that a female Confederate agent is en route to London. He named you, sir, as her primary contact."

"Why would a Confederate agent come here?" Anne asked. "And why in the world would she contact Marsfield?"

Marsfield picked up his wife's hand and kissed her knuckles. A silent message seemed to pass between them.

Burke suffered a twinge of jealousy. Though he'd had several long-term relationships with mistresses, the closeness that the earl and his wife shared had eluded him. He glanced at Preston, who examined his fingernails with studied indifference.

"Shall I explain, sir, or would you rather do the honors?" Burke asked.

A knock on the door changed the topic to inconsequential chatter while the butler wheeled in a cart loaded with sandwiches, an assortment of cheeses, fruit, and sweets, and an elaborate silver tea service. After thanking the servant and informing him that they would serve themselves, Anne excused him.

Marsfield leaned back with his cup of tea. "Perhaps I should explain," he offered. "That way you'll have an opportunity to eat."

Burke nodded, and Anne handed him a plate she had filled to overflowing.

"The Confederacy desperately needs a market for their cotton because the Union has established an effective blockade. England needs the raw cotton to keep her textile industry running. So far Parliament has maintained a precarious balance between the queen's adamant antislavery stance and the interests of the mill owners and workers."

"So the Confederacy would like our fleet to destroy the blockade and reestablish trade," Anne said.

"Exactly," Burke agreed.

"I always said you were a quick study," Marsfield said to her with a knowing wink. "Don't have to draw you a picture."

She slapped his arm and turned to Burke. "Please ignore his teasing and continue. How does this concern Marsfield, other than his vote in the House?"

Burke set his plate of food on the table, for once in his life not the least hungry. "Apparently the female agent has a list of influential peers to either blackmail or bribe into supporting her cause. The letter gave Marsfield as the only known name on the encoded list."

"That doesn't make sense," Preston said. "Marsfield

is hardly a candidate for either blackmail or bribery. His reputation has been beyond redemption since he put on his first pair of long pants, and he doesn't need the money. Not unless Anne has taken to gambling with the same verve she took to shopping."

She gave him a quelling look but remained silent.

"I think there must be more to the story, if it has upset Burke enough to seek me out," Marsfield said. "We can all appreciate his ethical dilemma in revealing confidential information. What did the queen's ministers say?"

"Actually, it was never classified at any level of secrecy, and that in itself is a worry. My superior refused to forward the message, deeming a woman agent not enough of a threat to bother. I disagreed. One tiny spark can set off a large powder keg. He wouldn't relent. Since I strongly felt the situation pointed to a potential danger, I decided to pursue the matter further. When I looked for the letter, it had disappeared, as if it had never arrived. Even my daily log has been expertly altered. All in the space of precisely fifty-three minutes during which I was away from my desk. I fear the conspiracy reaches into the Diplomatic Corps, but I have no evidence, no proof. You have only my word, and, frankly, as I present this, I realize just how bloody bonkers it sounds."

"If you say it happened, then I believe you," Marsfield said. "I trust your memory more than I do my own. No, I think the danger to this country is real. Many members of Parliament have interests in the textile industry, myself included."

Both Preston and Burke admitted they, too, had similar financial investments.

"I agree with your analysis. The situation is potentially explosive," Marsfield added. "If England enters into the conflict on either side, it would have worldwide ramifications. I would have liked to have seen that letter, though. I've corresponded with Pinkerton on several matters of mutual interest, and I'd recognize his hand."

"You think the letter was a forgery?" Burke asked.

"Not really, though I am curious as to why he named me. The letter may have contained a clue. A brilliant man; his mind works in a devious, circuitous manner. Perhaps that's why he's so good at his job. I'll write this afternoon asking him for clarification."

"We can't just sit around and wait for a reply," Burke said.

"No, but right now my hands are full." Marsfield rubbed his chin. "I'd like for you to take charge of this investigation."

"Me, sir?" Burke swallowed. "I'd be happy to help out, but I must remind you I no longer work for the Agency."

"We'll deal with that later. Until we have an understanding of who is involved, I'd like to keep this matter to as few people as possible."

Marsfield rose to pace the length of the room, and the others knew to be silent while he worked the problem over in his head. Finally he stopped and looked up. "How many ships arrive each week from the Confederacy?"

"There can't be many," Burke offered. "After all, isn't that the point of the agent's mission?"

Marsfield nodded and retraced his path, speaking as he paced. "I need someone who has well-honed powers of observation, an excellent memory, and who is a good judge of character to meet those ships and watch for female passengers. I also need someone whose presence won't cause remark."

He stopped again, directly in front of Burke. "With your shipbuilding interests, you have a perfect excuse for observing the activities in the area."

Although Burke knew Marsfield was using manipu-

lating techniques, he was not immune to flattery. It
would mean rearranging his meticulous schedule, and
much last-minute rushing to and fro, which he detested.
Not that he relished hanging around the filthy docks
either, but sacrifices must be made, and a pair of boots
was a small price.

"I'll do my best; however, my regular duties may interfere. If there is a conflict of schedules, the prime
minister's directives must take precedence. Although
quite junior, I am a member of his staff." Burke managed
to say it humbly, but pride swelled his chest.

"I'll talk to the PM and have you temporarily reas-
signed to me," Marsfield said. "Effective immediately."

Burke set his cup and saucer down on the table with
an uncharacteristic clatter. Two things were suddenly
clear. Marsfield, and the Agency, were more powerfully
connected than he'd suspected, and the situation was
more explosive than he had feared.

"What can I do to help?" Anne asked Burke.

He blinked, not sure of what response to make.

"Surely you don't expect me to sit idle, working on my
embroidery?" she asked.

Burke stifled a laugh and dared not look at his friends.
Anne had been known to throw knotted-beyond-repair
stitchery across the room in frustration.

Burke looked to Marsfield, but his one-time mentor
indicated Burke was now in charge.

"Surely, Preston would be—"

Marsfield shook his head as he resumed his seat. "I
need someone with diplomatic experience, and a cool
head. Preston can help, but I expect you to keep him in
line."

That comment earned a raised eyebrow from Preston.

"Now, what's your plan?" Marsfield asked.

"Plan?"

"Come, come. I know you thought about it all the way over here. Right?"

Burke cleared his throat. "Well, I think we should compose a list of probable targets, men with large textile interests, especially those in severe financial distress."

Marsfield and Preston nodded.

"Since no one knows the conditions of every man's pockets better than the marriage-minded mothers of the ton—"

Anne groaned. "You don't have to ask. I'll make the rounds of teas and luncheons to gather the latest information." She dropped her head and covered her eyes.

"Meanwhile, I'll check out the brothels and gaming halls for the latest scandals," Preston volunteered.

"Why do you get the fun job?" Anne asked in a sulky voice.

Preston grinned.

"I'll contact the harbormaster," Burke said to keep the topic of conversation focused and forestall an argument. "I should be able to obtain forewarning of any ship arriving with goods from the Confederacy."

"Good plan. Excellent start." Marsfield stood and slapped Burke on the back. "I have faith in you."

Burke was still reeling. He was back in the Agency, working for Marsfield, and in charge of a major investigation with worldwide ramifications. All in the space of less than an hour. His world had just tilted off-center. Even though he could not have honorably done it, something told him he would have been wiser to have had his usual lunch.

Three

June

Cordelia stood at the ship's railing watching the bustle of the docking procedure with trepidation.

"This is never going to work," she said, tugging down on her skirt, which ended six inches above her ankles. Ruffled pantalets covered her legs and boot-tops, but it had been more than nine years since she'd last worn the juvenile accessory, and they were not as comfortable as she remembered. "We should have turned back when we changed ships in the Bahamas."

"Stop fidgeting," Emily said.

"This dress is . . . I don't like wearing stolen clothes."

"We only borrowed the clothes she left behind. She could hardly sneak off the ship with her trunks. You only have to pretend to be Precious until we find Ernest. A few days at most."

"What if her great-uncle Theodore can tell I'm an impostor?"

"Call him Uncle Theo," Emily said. "He hasn't seen her since she was a baby, remember? Even if her father has sent a description, it would only contain generalities, blond hair, blue eyes, unpleasant manner."

"Don't speak evil of the dead," Granny said, crossing herself.

"She's not dead," Cordelia said.

"Might as well be," the old woman muttered. "She's ruined, and it's the same thing."

"All right," Emily said, throwing up her hands, her voice peevish. "For the last time, I admit I made an error in judgment helping Precious, but if I'd confessed before we sailed, Cordelia would have insisted on going after her. We wouldn't be here now, and I'd have no chance of finding Ernest in time." She dabbed at her eyes with her handkerchief. "I just want my baby to have a father when it's born."

Cordelia wouldn't say so, but she understood Emily's situation was desperate. Her sister's motives, while not exactly pure, were justifiable. Even so, how she'd let Emily talk her into this insane scheme, she'd never know. "Can't we just tell Uncle Theo the truth and throw ourselves on his mercy? Surely he wouldn't turn us out on the street."

"What will we do if he does?" Emily countered. "Why I can just picture dear Granny sitting on a street corner begging for coins to buy her supper." She frowned at Cordelia. "You should be ashamed of yourself for thinking only of your own comfort."

"I'm not, but it's ridiculous to think a woman of my age can pass herself off as a child."

"Sixteen is not a child," Emily said.

"Maybe not to an eighteen-year-old," Cordelia muttered sarcastically under her breath.

"Sixteen is on the verge of womanhood," Emily continued, as if she hadn't heard. "You're near enough in size to wear her clothes, and your hair has lightened nicely in the sun, very nearly blond." She patted her own perfectly coifed golden curls. "The accompanying tan is unfortunate, but we did the best we could to protect your skin."

Cordelia shook her head, the hair hanging loose

down her back, overly warm and bothersome compared to the tight chignon or braids she favored. The sailors must have thought she was crazy, sitting on the deck with a towel over her face while Granny repeatedly poured lemon concentrate on her head. The sun had played havoc with Cordelia's complexion, including giving her ghastly freckles across her nose. They'd tried a lemon concoction on her skin, but it had succeeded only in giving her a rash.

"I think the peachy complexion enhances her hair," Granny said. "And her eyes."

Emily turned to face Cordelia. "They do look . . . blueish. Hazel eyes are so undependable. Just remember to only wear the blue dresses, and don't stand next to anyone in green, or your eyes will reflect that color."

The ship bumped against the wharf, and all three women turned back to the rail.

"I think that's the uncle, Theodore Cosley, Lord Gravely," Granny said, indicating a portly gentleman waiting beside a fine yellow carriage with a crest emblazoned on the door. "Wave to him."

Cordelia raised her hand and wiggled her fingers.

"Not that way," Granny hissed. "If you want this charade to work, you'll have to think like a child."

"I'm on the verge of womanhood," Cordelia said, her tone making it obvious she wasn't thrilled by the prospect of reliving those awkward years.

"The younger you act, the better," Granny said. "At least pretend you're glad to see him."

Cordelia waved her arm over her head.

"They've lowered the gangway," Granny added. "Now, run on down there, eager for a new adventure, excited to be off this old confining ship."

Cordelia shook her head in wonder. All her life, Granny had told her to slow down, don't race, don't

skip, walk like a lady. Now she was saying just the opposite. Cordelia turned and took a few steps. Getting off
the ship had tremendous appeal. Six weeks cooped up
with Emily's primping, and Granny's smelly charms had
taken its toll on her patience.

The gangway gave a little with each step, giving her a
buoyancy her spirits quickly echoed. The voyage was
over, and she'd survived. She smiled and waved, getting
into the act. Waiting out of the way, about ten feet to the
left of the end of the gangway, Uncle Theo waved her
forward and gave her a welcoming smile. She took a
deep breath. In for a penny, in for a pound. Letting out
a whoop of joy, she ran the rest of the way down the
ramp.

She stumbled as soon as she hit dry land. Steel-hard
arms caught her before she sprawled onto her face.

"Whoa, there, girl," the stranger said with a chuckle,
as he set her back on her feet and steadied her.

"What happened?" Cordelia asked his shiny black
knee-high boots. "Why is the ground moving?" She
looked up, past thighs like tree trunks, and faced his
massive chest, covered in a dark blue superfine jacket
and starched shirt with pin-tucked pleats. Her gaze
drifted up to his dimpled chin and clean-shaven cheeks
framed by neat light blond sideburns. Firm, generous
lips quirked in a half-smile, just enough to show a row of
even white teeth. His deep blue eyes sparkled with
amusement. A smiling Viking warrior.

Yet his eyelashes weren't blond like his hair. They were
brown, tipped with gold. As if Freya, the Norse goddess
of love and beauty, had taken a paintbrush and gilded
the very ends. He was Thor, in a cutaway coat and top
hat. The earth seemed to slip sideways, and she grabbed
at his sleeve.

"You haven't got your land legs yet," he said.

"Tell me where I can get some, and I'll trade these limbs in. They don't seem to work anymore."

"Just hang on to me."

His response resonated to her core. This ordinary act of looking at a man, of touching his arm, was affecting her in a manner she had never before experienced. She didn't want to let go of him.

"The feeling will pass in a few minutes," he promised.

Cordelia nodded, but somehow she doubted his words.

"Here, now." The portly gentleman Granny had identified as Theo Cosley bustled up. "Oh, it's you, Deering. I'd heard you'd taken a flyer in the shipping market. Sizing up the competition, eh?" He turned to Cordelia and leaned over to peer at her. "And you must be my great-niece, Precious."

She curtsyed as best she could without letting go of the Viking's arm. "Uncle Theo."

"Sea legs," Deering explained.

"What? Oh, right-o. Guess you two should be properly introduced. Viscount Deering, may I present my great-niece from the Colonies, Sarah Louise Cosley, otherwise known as Precious. Precious, meet Anthony Burke, Viscount Deering."

Cringing at the use of the atrocious nickname, she again tried to curtsy, as would be expected of a young girl meeting an older gentleman—with disastrous results. She stumbled sideways, bounced off pillow-shaped Uncle Theo, and rebounded directly into Deering's arms. He looked down at her with evident surprise.

"Now I know what a billiard ball feels like," she said, and they both laughed, her laughter tinged with embarrassment. Who would have thought the clean, crisp smell of shirt starch could be so sensual? The citrus-woodsy scent of his cologne was ever so appealing. She closed her eyes and inhaled deeply before he set her back on her feet. Uncle Theo gave her a quizzical look, and she remembered she was supposed to be acting like a child, not some love-starved spinster.

"Saving a damsel in distress is the aspiration of every gentleman," Deering said with a gallant bow.

"And deserves a fitting reward. I vote for ice cream." She turned to Theo. "Can we, Uncle Theo? I've heard about a place called Gunter's. I haven't had ice cream for ages and ages." Although she'd brought up the subject with a different goal in mind, her mouth watered at the thought of real ice cream. She'd give her ruffled pantalets for just one small dish. "Can we? Please?"

"Perhaps tomorrow, child. Today we have much to do."

"Promise?" For added effect, she jiggled his arm.

"Yes, yes. I'll take you to Gunter's tomorrow afternoon. I promise."

"If there's nothing else I can do," Deering said. "I'd best see to my business. I'll bid you good-day, Miss Precious." He tipped his hat to her. "Lord Gravely."

Uncle Theo nodded. "Give my regards to your family. And thank you for your assistance."

"Yes, thank you," she echoed. Lord Deering turned and walked away. Some of the sunshine went out of her day.

"Now, didn't you have some baggage?" Uncle Theo asked. "A horse maybe? A companion?"

Between the mesmerizing Viking and the lure of ice cream, she'd totally forgotten Granny, Emily, and Thunderation. Shame burned Cordelia's cheeks as she turned back toward the ship.

Thank goodness her relatives had had enough sense to walk down the gangway at a sedate pace, holding on to each other. In addition, Granny used her cane to steady herself, and they didn't seem to have any difficulty adjusting to land. They strolled the short distance to the carriage.

Cordelia introduced them. "Uncle Theo, this is—"

"Vivian Hathaway," Uncle Theo interrupted.

"Hello, Gravely. It's been a long time," Granny said. "It's Smith now. Mrs. Vivian Smith."

"You . . . you two know each other?" Cordelia asked.

Uncle Theo doffed his hat and bent over Granny's hand in an old-fashioned salute. He straightened, but held on to her hand, looking at her even though he spoke to Cordelia. "Back when the world was younger, before dirt was made, this lovely woman and I were—"

"Friends," Granny said. She snatched her hand back.

"You haven't changed a bit, Vivian."

Granny snorted. "Well, you have." She squinted at him. "Actually, the loss of hair suits you. That Byron mop you favored as a boy never flattered your round face."

Theo bristled visibly. "Still speaking your mind, I see." He turned to Emily. "And this beautiful young woman is . . ."

"Oh, do forgive my lapse of manners," Granny said in a formal tone that clearly pointed to his previous presumptive behavior. "Lord Gravely, may I present my granddaughter, Miss Emily Weston, companion to your great-niece."

"Chaperone," Emily corrected. "As a favor to her dear father."

"Welcome. I'm pleased to have you as my guest. And your grandmother, too, of course."

After the usual introductory chitchat, Cordelia breathed a small sigh of relief. They seemed to be getting along without making any slips that would betray their ruse, although the apparent tension between Granny and Theo worried her. Even though she knew her grandmother could have a sharp tongue, she'd never known her to be outright rude before.

The grooms walked by, leading Thunderation. She directed everyone's attention to the horse in the hope that Emily wouldn't broach the subject so close to her heart, the whereabouts of Ernest and her impending nuptials, before they had even left the docks.

"Isn't he magnificent?" Cordelia asked no one in particular.

"Big," Uncle Theo said.

"Twenty hands high, the chest of a champion and the heart of a winner."

Uncle Theo gave her a quizzical look. "I thought you—"

Thunderation stumbled. "Oh no." Cordelia started forward, but Uncle Theo stopped her by the shoulders.

"Let my grooms handle him. They know what they're about. He'll be fine. Just a little frisky because of the new odors."

"He's been acting like he smelled fresh grass for several days," Cordelia said.

"Once he gets his land legs, they'll load him in that wagon and we'll be off. I've got a nice stall waiting, and a stable yard that will seem like heaven to him after that ship."

Thunderation staggered like a newborn foal. He shook his head and looked down at his legs as if they belonged to some other beast. She understood exactly how he felt. His expression was so comical, she giggled.

Granny and Emily decided to wait in the carriage, but Cordelia wasn't willing to enclose herself in another small space until absolutely necessary. As she watched the grooms walk Thunderation up and down the wharf, she noticed Anthony Burke, leaning half-hidden against a doorway several shops away. Normally a single figure wouldn't stand out on the bustling wharf. Normally

Thunderation would have all of her attention, but her gaze seemed to gravitate to the handsome Viking of its own accord. Somehow she knew she would be able to pick him out of a crowd. He looked directly at her, and a thrill shivered up her spine.

Burke averted his gaze. He hadn't meant to stare. What was it about the chit that kept drawing his attention? Certainly not the schoolgirl outfit with the outrageously large bow at the back of her small waist, or that absurd straw hat which kept slipping off-center. The sprinkling of freckles across her nose gave her a certain country-raised air some might find appealing, but she was much too young, one or two years away from her presentation to society at least.

Bloody hell. He'd never been attracted to innocents, preferring sophisticated women, experienced women who understood and accepted that he would never marry. Yet, he had *felt* her laughter deep in his soul, even though he could not possibly have heard it over the din of the crowded wharf.

He dismissed the silly notion with a shake of his head.

The other woman, Emily Weston, interested him.

On a professional level, he clarified to himself. He'd made a point of lingering nearby long enough to hear the introductions, and a less likely looking *companion* he could not imagine. Only women without prospects accepted such an unprepossessing position. That woman had prospects to turn the head of a monk.

If the Confederates chose a female agent to blackmail or bribe members of the ton, it only made logical sense to select someone beautiful, someone who could wangle introductions and invitations from a gullible, unsuspecting peer. Lord Gravely fit the latter description. The

arrival of his great-niece had inadvertently provided a
cover above reproach.

The woman seemed uninterested in the conversation,
and kept looking around, not like a person taking in the
dismal scenery, but with an air of anticipation, as if she
were looking for someone. Suspicious behavior.

He decided to ask Anne to check out Gravely, and he
would keep an eye on Miss Emily Weston. If she acted in
a manner consistent with her status as a companion, he
would look elsewhere for the suspect. However, without
a shred of hard evidence and despite Gravely's staunch
support of the queen, Burke's gut told him he'd found
the spy.

Cordelia paced the lovely pink and white bedroom.
Not fair. She'd been shuffled off to bed at the unreasonable hour of eight o'clock as a young girl should be.
Actually, that part wasn't so bad. After the six-week voyage, privacy was a luxury and the absence of her vocal
relatives more than welcome. But the early bedtime
meant she missed dining with the *adults*. She hadn't
complained then, because she'd been promised a tray in
her room. Emily, Granny, and Theo had feasted on the
offerings of his excellent cook, the myriad delicious
odors making their way up the stairs to tempt her almost
to drooling. Did she receive so much as a taste? No.
Cook had sent up the standard child's supper of hot porridge and warm milk to help her sleep. Not fair at all. If
Emily expected her to—

A furtive knock sent her stomping to the door. She
whipped it open.

Granny scurried inside, checking to make sure no one
was in the hall before she shut the door. "I slipped out
while Emily's playing the piano. Figured you'd still be

awake, and I thought you might like this." From her pockets she pulled out two napkins, and unwrapped tidbits from dinner. A hunk of bread, a slice of ham and a wedge of savory cheese in one. A crisp red apple, and a cherry tart in the other. From another pocket, she produced a book.

Cordelia hugged her. "Thank you. I was near ready to raid the kitchen."

Granny chuckled. "I have to get back. No telling what those two will mastermind in my absence."

"Uncle Theo and Emily?"

Granny rolled her eyes. "She can't help but flatter him, it's just her way. But you'd think at his age he'd have gained a lick of sense."

"What is it between you and Theo?"

"Haven't got time to explain now. Put a shawl or something on the floor after I leave or the light shining through the crack under the door will invite someone to interfere with your reading." She kissed her granddaughter's cheek. "You're not missing anything downstairs."

After closing the door and rearranging a throw rug to block any light from escaping, Cordelia nibbled as she read *Lucinda's Dishonor* from cover to cover. Her first modern novel. She'd never known such wonderful stories existed and vowed to search the library for more. She laughed and cried with Lucinda, not giving another thought to the people downstairs who held her fate in their incapable hands.

Only the following morning did she learn Uncle Theo had asked Emily to stay on as chaperone and to supervise her lessons. Dear Precious, they had decided together, needed significant *polishing* before she could make her debut in four months, when she would supposedly turn seventeen. Before Cordelia had an opportunity to speak to Emily privately and squash the ridiculous plan, a dancing master had been engaged. By midmorning a daily schedule of painting and music lessons were arranged, and a "decorum tutor" retained for Wednesdays and Fridays. By lunchtime the *modiste au courant* had been summoned to overhaul her wardrobe. Her sister was having too much fun. At the expense of Theo's generous pocketbook.

As Emily blossomed, Granny wilted. In her room, suffering from a severe headache, she declined the promised trip to the ice cream shop. Declaring she was comfortable, she insisted Cordelia should go. The nice upstairs maid, Quimsy, promised to keep an eye on Granny.

Cordelia had been feeling guilty about accepting Theo's generosity and was having second thoughts about the deception. But if she told him the truth, would he eject them penniless into the street with no place to go? What would happen to Granny then? Cordelia couldn't risk it. Finding Ernest quickly was the only solution.

At the ice cream parlor Uncle Theo and Emily were the center attraction, and both reveled in the attention. Theo confessed he'd never had so many young men seek his opinion on such a variety of subjects, and then of course, he must introduce them to his great-niece and her dear friend.

In the course of twenty-four hours, Emily had promoted herself from paid companion to chaperone to dear friend. It wouldn't surprise Cordelia if by tomorrow Uncle Theo adopted her.

Four young men had joined them at the small marble-topped table, and yet Emily hadn't brought up the subject of Ernest. Surely, one of the gentleman must know of him. She tugged on her sister's sleeve. "Ask them about you know who," she hissed. Emily could charm information out of anyone wearing pants, whereas Cordelia usually just bluntly blurted out her question. "Ask them, or I will."

"What is it, my dear?" Theo asked.

Emily patted his hand. "The sweet child is worried about Granny left at home. Why don't you give Precious some money and let her purchase a few treats to take home to her?"

Theo placed several coins on the table in front of Cordelia. "Candy for Vivian, huh? I suggest licorice whips and sour balls."

Emily turned back to Cordelia. "All this adult talk must be so boring to you." She raised her eyebrows and gave Cordelia a meaningful look that said, *Play along, and I'll explain later.* "Why don't you go over to the counter and pick out some sweets?"

Cordelia pressed her lips together. She grabbed the coins and flounced away, her seat immediately taken by another eager young man.

She walked the length of the counter, the very bounty of available treats making it difficult to choose. Vanilla fudge or hazelnut pralines. Chocolate creams and peppermint twirls. Or marzipan in fruit shapes and covered with colored sugars. The glass case ended near the shop door.

Cordelia fingered the letter in her pocket, one of the three Madame Lavonne had given her with instructions to deliver them in person using the password *Archangel.* The first address was a book stall several doors down from Gunter's.

Although they'd planned to shop after having ice cream, she doubted she could convince her sister and Theo to visit the book stall. Emily's idea of shopping consisted solely of objects she could wear. Cordelia worried that in the short day or two it would take to find Ernest, she wouldn't have another opportunity to deliver the

letter. With a glance back to confirm that neither Uncle
Theo nor Emily was paying any attention to her, Cordelia
slipped out the door.

She quickly found the book stall, The Book Nook, and
entered.

"May I help you?" an older man with thick wire-
rimmed glasses asked from behind the counter.

"Yes, please." She looked around and saw no one else
in the shop. "I'm looking for a treatise on the Archangel
Michael."

The man nodded. "Alas, I haven't had a copy for several years. Perhaps something on the Archangel Azrael?"

She slid the sealed white envelope, devoid of an address other than the number one in the upper right
corner, across the narrow slate counter.

The shopkeeper opened the envelope, scanned the
contents, then quickly tucked it into a pocket inside his
worn coat. "How can I contact you?" he whispered.

She gave him one of Uncle Theo's cards. "I'll be at
this address for at least three days. After that, I'll have to
let you know."

The bell over the door tinkled and she whirled
around. Lord Deering entered.

"What are you doing here?" she asked him.

"I believe that would be my question." He looked
around. "Where is your chaperone?"

"I . . . I wanted a book." She grabbed the nearest book
to hand. A slim brown volume. "Emily and Theo are still
at Gunter's. Thank you," she said to the shopkeeper.
"You may put this on my uncle's account."

She made a silent vow to repay Theo for his unknow-
ing generosity.

Burke looked over her shoulder. *"The Iliad,"* he read
the title aloud. "You read Latin?" he asked one eyebrow
raised.

"Oh, I do my best. We do have schools in America." She gave him a superior smile. "Do you come here often?" she asked, then could have kicked herself for not saying something more intelligent.

"Ah, no—that is, I was going to Gunter's myself when I saw you come in here," Burke said. "I expected your chaperone would . . . You really should not be out alone. I'll escort you back to your uncle."

A terrible thought occurred to Cordelia. "Don't tell me you followed me in order to obtain an introduction to Emily Weston?"

"Well . . . I . . ."

"I should have known." The experience was not a new one for Cordelia, but this time it hurt more than ever before. The shopkeeper returned the book to her, wrapped in brown paper and tied with string. She nodded to him and turned to face Burke. "Come on," she said, the resignation in her tone more obvious than she'd intended.

Another customer entered, and Burke held the door for her to exit. At the threshold a whiff of heaven caught Cordelia's attention. She stopped in her tracks. Coffee. Real coffee. Such as she'd not had since the early days of the war, before prices had climbed out of reach. She sniffed. Colombian beans, dark roasted and freshly brewed. She closed her eyes in appreciation, and a tiny moan escaped. "Mmmmm."

"What is it?" Burke asked. "Are you hurt?"

She shook her head. Rushing from the book stall, she followed her nose to the next storefront, a coffee shop.

"You can't go in there," Burke said as her hand touched the door handle.

"Why not?"

"Women and children are not allowed."

Just then a woman wearing a low-cut red sateen dress,

maneuvered her way past Burke with a generous smile. He tipped his hat and responded to her "good after-noon" as he held the door open for her.

Cordelia followed. He stopped her by grabbing her around the waist and twirling her back onto the walk.

"Respectable women do not frequent coffeehouses, and *children* are definitely not allowed."

She faced him with her hands on her hips. "All I want is a cup of coffee."

"It stunts your growth."

She snorted. "I drink coffee all the time at home."

He stared down at her from his six-foot-four height. "My point, exactly."

The heady aroma fed her craving. She wrapped her arms around her waist. "If you bring me a cup of coffee, I'll introduce you to Emily," she promised in a desperate bid.

"I can't leave you standing out here alone," he said, but she could tell he was tempted.

"I'll tell you all about her. Her favorite flower. Her fa-vorite color. I'll answer all your questions about her."

A gentleman stepped around them with a nod to Burke. "Afternoon, Deering."

"Farnsworth." Burke stopped him with a hand to the shoulder. "Begging your favor, old sod. Would you mind bringing me out a cup?" He nodded toward Cordelia.

"I quite understand," Farnsworth said. "I have two younger sisters, you know. I'm at your service. Be right back."

Cordelia danced from one foot to the other as they waited. And waited.

"This is against my better judgment," Burke confessed.

She distracted him from his second thoughts by point-ing to a vendor pushing his cart. "Look, fruit tarts. Doesn't that sound good? I'd like a tart to go with my coffee." She pulled one of the coins Uncle Theo had given her out of her pocket. "Is this enough?"

Anthony Burke indicated that she should put away her money, and stepped into the street to stop the vendor. He hadn't eaten food from a street vendor since his school days, but the apple tarts looked fresh and appealing. He bought two.

Farnsworth returned and handed him a tray with a coffeepot, a large ceramic mug, a creamer, and several lumps of sugar before disappearing back inside the coffeehouse. Miss Cosley—Precious—held a paper-wrapped tart in each hand, her book tucked under her arm.

Burke looked around for a place to set down the tray, and while his head was turned, she darted across the street.

"In here," she called, ducking through an open iron gate.

He followed, but stopped two steps inside the fence. "This is a graveyard."

"With a most convenient stone bench." Precious took the tray from him and set it next to the tarts. She motioned for him to sit on the other end, using the bench between them as a table. After putting a lump of sugar in the cup, she poured with all the aplomb of a countess in her parlor.

"This is most irregular. You can't picnic in a graveyard."

"Why not? Do you think they'll mind?" She waved around at the headstones. "I think," she peered at a nearby inscription, "Mistress Elvyra Minnifer, Beloved Sister, 1736 to 1801, would be glad of the company." She cradled her mug, closed her eyes, and breathed in the aroma. "Mmmm," she sighed, and took a sip. "Wonderful. Would you like some?"

"We should get back to your uncle. You're not too young to be mindful of your reputation."

"Surely my reputation is safe in a graveyard," she argued cheerfully, unwrapping a tart. "These look yummy. Aren't you going to eat yours?" She took a bite, and the sweet, sticky juice ran down her chin.

"Oops," she said with a tiny embarrassed giggle. Tipping her head back to keep the juice from dripping, she searched blindly for a napkin.

Without a second thought, Burke reached over and wiped her chin with his thumb. Touching her was a mistake. Her smooth skin, her warmth were a temptation to linger. The simple gesture became a caress. He wanted to continue to touch her, to—

He jerked his hand away.

"Are you all right?"

"I'm fine," Burke said through gritted teeth. He retrieved his handkerchief and handed it to her, as he should have done in the first place.

Cordelia gave him a quizzical look, then focused her gaze at their surroundings. "In some cultures, feasting among one's ancestors is considered a sign of respect, a tribute that brings good fortune."

"These are not your ancestors."

"They could be." She pointed to a nearby headstone. "There. Isolde Humperdink, Mother of Twelve, 1642 to 1676. She's bound to have hundreds of descendants by now. Poor thing died so young. Probably in childbirth."

Burke stood abruptly. "That is not a subject I wish to discuss."

"What?"

"Never mind. We must—"

"Hey there! What do you two think you're doing?" The curate of the church came running out, waving his arms above his head. "Scat, you hooligans. I'm calling out the watch."

Burke grabbed her hand and pulled her up and out

the gate. She stumbled along behind him, trying not to spill the cup of coffee she still held.

"Slow down."

He shortened his stride, but still she lagged behind.

"Slow down, I said."

He stopped, dropped her hand, and turned. "Any slower and I'd be walking backwards. Do you want to be arrested?"

Anger sparked his blue eyes. Instinct told her that to anyone else it would be a danger signal, but she felt no threat—only a warmth deep inside that could not be attributed to the steaming brew. The hand he'd held, once burning, now felt bereft and cold. She switched her mug to that hand and strolled by him, finishing the last of the coffee.

"They do not arrest young girls," she commented over her shoulder. At least she didn't think they did.

"I see," he said, following her. "I'm to be arrested, while you, who started the whole debacle, simply walk away."

"You exaggerate."

"You twist the facts to meet your convenience."

"That's my prerogative." She almost added "as a woman" but caught the slip in time.

Burke shook his head. "American girls are much different than their English counterparts." His tone did not indicate it was a favorable comparison.

"In what way?" she asked as they walked back to the ice cream shop.

"My sister, Helene, would never think of doing anything as outrageous as that . . . that . . ."

"Debacle?"

"Exactly. She's quiet and accommodating. One can almost forget she's in the room. Of course, she was often unwell as a child." He turned to Cordelia. "I cannot imagine you either quiet or sickly."

"Thank you," she replied, though unsure whether he'd meant it as a compliment. She stopped at the door to the ice cream shop, loathe to end their chat.

Suddenly, whistles sounded and footsteps pounded toward them. They looked at each other and simultaneously dove for the shop door. Blocking each other's way, they missed the man running past, but turned as the watchman chased him shouting, "Stop, thief!"

She looked up to see Burke's comic expression of resignation fade into surprised relief. A giggle burbled up, and even the quick movement of her hand couldn't stop its escape. He chuckled in response, the release of tension palpable. They looked at each other and shared another laugh. She wanted the moment to last forever.

The door opened behind her. "There you are, Precious," Uncle Theo said. He escorted Emily on his arm. "And Deering, too. Ah, what good fortune." He introduced Burke and Emily. "Is your carriage nearby?"

"I beg your pardon?"

"We have just received a message that Miss Emily is needed at home, presumably something to do with her grandmother. However, since we planned to shop after refreshing ourselves, I sent my coach off, not to return for two hours. None of those young pups in there are of any use. Not a carriage among them." Lord Gravely looked up and down the street. "There is never a hack when you need one."

"One won't be necessary," Burke said. "My vehicle is just around the corner and at your disposal."

"Why, thank you, Lord Deering," Emily said, taking his arm and moving off in the direction he'd indicated. "I can't tell you how grateful I am for your timely assistance."

Cordelia was left to follow with Uncle Theo. *Oooh, Lord Deering,* she mimicked her sister's tone in her head. *A big strong man like you helping poor little me.*

Cordelia resented her sister's unconscious flirting because she wanted to be the one to take Burke's arm and walk beside him. In the carriage, Emily sat next to him and monopolized the conversation, asking innumerable questions about London and society in general.

As far as Cordelia could tell, Emily no longer seemed interested in looking for Ernest. She'd landed in a posh position particularly suited to her talents and interests. Emily was just as good at denying reality, in her own way, as Granny was in hers.

Cordelia would have to find Ernest. Quickly. She'd need help, but who did she know? No one other than Theo and Burke. How could she get either man to help her without revealing everything?

Burke's carriage turned into the drive at Theo's house, and she noted the butler, his face more pinched than usual, and the maid Quimsy, her apron twisted in her hands and her cap askew, waiting at the front door. What had Granny done now?

Four

Burke alighted from the carriage first and handed Cordelia down. While he helped the others, she ran up the front steps.

Quimsy grabbed her arm. "Oh, miss. I looked everywhere for her, I did, before I sent the message to the master."

The rest of the group—Theo, Emily, and Burke—gathered by the door.

"She's gone?" Theo asked.

"No, milord." The maid looked at him with relief, as if his appearance solved all her problems. "We found her about ten minutes ago."

"Where is she? Is she all right?" Cordelia asked.

"In the ballroom," the butler said, his expression dour and disapproving. "She—"

Cordelia rushed into the house and up the stairs. She skidded to a halt in the middle of the well-polished floor of the empty ballroom.

"I can't see a thing," Emily said, entering the ballroom on Burke's arm.

"Open the drapes for some light," Burke directed, and the butler scrambled to obey.

The maid came in huffing and puffing behind them. "She's up there," Quimsy gasped, pointing to the musicians' balcony. "She barricaded the door to the stairs and won't open it."

Cordelia spotted her, leaning over the railing. "Come down from there this instant before you fall and hurt yourself."

"Stop," Granny bellowed, pointing at the butler with a long-stemmed rose from the vase in the entryway.

He turned.

"Yes, you," Granny said. "That's enough light."

The butler looked to Theo, and he nodded.

A single shaft of light lit the balcony like a stage.

"How are we going to get her down?" Emily asked in a whisper.

"I haven't the foggiest idea," Uncle Theo said.

"If you have a ladder," Burke said. "I could—"

"O Romeo, Romeo! Wherefore art thou, Romeo?" Granny said, quoting Shakespeare.

"Who's Romeo?" the maid asked. "No one here's named—"

Granny continued Juliet's lines. "Deny thy father, and refuse thy name; Or, if thou wilt not, be but sworn my love, And I'll no longer be a Capulet."

Unexpectedly, Burke stepped forward and recited the next line as Romeo. "Shall I hear more, or shall I speak at this?"

Granny said, "'Tis but thy name that is my enemy; thou art thyself, though not a Montague."

"What are they talking about?" Quimsy asked in a loud voice. "What does she mean she's a cap-o-let? Is that some kind of hat? And is he as balmy as—"

"Shhhhhh," the others said together, having missed several lines of the play.

Granny said, "What's in a name? That which we call a rose by any other name would smell as sweet; so Romeo would, were he not Romeo call'd, retain that dear perfection which he owes without that title. Romeo, doff thy name; and for that name, which is no part of thee, take all myself."

Burke walked to a spot directly under the balcony, yet stayed out of the shaft of light. "I take thee at thy word. Call me but love, and I'll be new baptized; henceforth I never will be Romeo."

"What man art thou that, thus bescreen'd in night, so stumblest on my counsel?"

"By a name I know not how to tell thee who I am. My name, dear saint, is hateful to myself, because it is an enemy to thee. Had I it written, I would tear the word."

Cordelia sniffed, and wiped away a tear as they continued. She had to admire a man who not only quoted Shakespeare flawlessly and with emotion, but who gratified an old woman's whim without being asked. When they finished the scene, she applauded wildly with the rest of the audience.

"Young man?" Granny called down.

"Yes, ma'am?"

"Wait for me in the parlor. I'd like to meet you." She turned away and then turned back. "Theo? Please order tea. I'm rather thirsty." She opened the door to the stairs, then turned back again. "The good black pekoe tea. Not that mediocre blend you served last night."

Cordelia let out a sigh. Granny was herself again. Playing Juliet could be easily dismissed, or at least explained as circumstantial. What woman standing on a lit balcony wouldn't be tempted to utter the famous words? Perhaps no one would speculate on why she'd gone up there in the first place.

"Deering, may I present Juliet, otherwise known as Mrs. Vivian Smith," Gravely said. "Mrs. Smith, this is—"

"Please join us for tea," Granny said, sitting by the table and picking up the pot to pour. "Are you an actor?"

When he replied no, she looked a tad disappointed.

"Really, Vivian," Gravely said in a huff. "If you had allowed me to complete the introduction, you would know this is *Lord* Deering. Perhaps then you wouldn't have insulted—"

"No harm," Burke said. "Actually, I'm a bit flattered. I've not had a chance to test my recitation skills for quite some time. Since my school days, if I remember correctly."

"Sit, sit," Mrs. Smith said, waving him to one of the Queen Anne chairs with the needlepoint roses on the seat.

Burke sat carefully on the delicate piece of furniture, afraid it might collapse under his weight at any moment. He balanced a plate of biscuits on one knee and held a delicate cup and saucer in his large hand. He usually avoided such situations, feeling like a bull in a china shop. His goal had been to observe Emily, not integrate himself into her family, yet here he was, tugged along by strange circumstance.

In hindsight, he probably shouldn't have responded to Juliet's plea, but something in the woman's eyes, a stark loneliness, had resonated in him. He wasn't prone to impulsive actions, having learned early that failure to think matters through logically landed him in trouble. He'd proven his hypothesis once again.

Although the situation looked normal on the surface, tension filled the air like a subtle perfume. Lord Gravely and Mrs. Smith sniped at each other with veiled insults. Emily flitted from one spot to another. Precious huddled in her corner of the sofa, either sulking or simply trying to ignore everyone else. Burke swallowed a big gulp of tea. If he finished quickly, he could make his escape.

Emily jumped up again. "I'm going to play the piano. Any requests?"

Burke juggled cup, saucer, plate, and napkin to stand.

"Sit down," Mrs. Smith said to him. "Just because Emily is hopping around like flea on a scratchy dog doesn't mean you have to keep getting up. You don't see Theo here popping up and down."

"I've got a bad knee," Theo muttered into his cup.

Emily seated herself at the piano positioned near the bay window and shuffled through the pages of sheet music.

Burke sat cautiously. "Mrs. Smith—"

"Please call me Vivian. Such formality seems unnecessary after playing the balcony scene together."

Burke agreed, though he was not at all sure he wanted to be on a first-name basis.

"Do you ride?" Vivian asked.

"Of course he rides," Gravely answered for him. "Silly question to ask an English gentleman."

"Actually, not so much anymore," Burke replied. "I—"

"You'd need a really big horse," Precious said, then looked chagrined.

"My thinking exactly," the older woman said. "Thunderation would be perfect for him."

Precious jerked upright. "That's ridiculous."

Gravely snorted. "What have you got against the boy?" he asked Vivian. "None of my grooms have been able to ride that unruly monster. Even my nephew Jebidiah said he's only good for breeding, and he should know."

"Thunderation needs some weight on his back in order to respect his rider," Vivian said. "Deering here fits the bill."

"Not true. I've ridden him," Precious said.

Gravely looked at her as if she'd just admitted to having four arms.

"I thought you didn't ride anymore," Gravely said. "Your father wrote that you'd absolutely refused to sit a saddle after the accident. When was it? Three or four years ago?"

"I meant when I was younger," Precious stammered. "I haven't ridden, ah, lately."

"Thunderation needs the exercise," Vivian said.

Burke held up his hand. "One moment, please. I'd love to be of assistance, but—"

"Excellent." Vivian put her cup on the tray and stood as if that was the end of the discussion."

Juggling plates again, Burke also stood. "However—"

"Why don't you go to the stables right now? Precious can introduce you to Thunderation, so you won't be strangers tomorrow morning when you take him to Hyde Park for a run. I'd suggest early, before the trails are crowded."

"But—"

"Now if you'll excuse me, I'm afraid all the exertion has brought on another one of my headaches. I think I'll lie down."

Burke was left standing with his mouth open as the older woman swept out of the room.

"Well," Precious said, blinking.

Burke sank into the chair. "Well, indeed."

"Quite a singular honor. Obviously, Vivian thinks a lot of you," Gravely said.

"Just because he quotes Shakespeare does not make him a rider competent enough to handle Thunderation," Precious pointed out.

Burke quite agreed. An image of him sitting in a mud puddle in the stable yard while the grooms pointed at him and laughed uproariously came to mind. He winced.

"Nonsense. He's an Englishman." Gravely stood. "We're born to ride," he added, slapping Burke on the shoulder, causing his cup to rattle dangerously in the saucer.

Burke set his dishes on the tray. "Actually, sir—"

"However, I'd planned on resuming our outing. Precious, dear child, don't you want to shop for anything?"

She shook her head. "Thank you kindly for the offer, but I already owe you—"

"Nonsense. It's my pleasure to buy things for both of you girls. Well, then, while you and Burke get acquainted with Thunderation, Emily and I will finish our shopping," Theo said. "I did say I'd purchase her a new bonnet."

The desultory piano music stopped immediately, and Emily rejoined the group.

Emily gave Gravely a coquettish smile and took his arm. "You're such a dear sweet man to remember your promise." She led him out of the room with haste, as if someone would change his mind if she hesitated.

Precious stood slowly. "If you don't at least try to ride him, Uncle Theo will never let you hear the end of it."

Burke envisioned his name bandied about the gentlemen's clubs, the punch line of a witty anecdote—a fate he'd tried to avoid all his life. Trying and failing was at least marginally acceptable; refusing to try was out of the question.

Nor had he forgotten his mission, or the girl's promise to answer his questions. Unable to follow Emily on her shopping expedition without an awkward explanation, he could at least gather information about her. He straightened his coat.

"I believe we have an appointment with a horse."

Cordelia led the way to Uncle Theo's immaculate stables. She'd visited Thunderation that morning and had been satisfied he was well cared for despite the fact the stable boys and grooms gave him a wide berth.

"The secret to riding Thunderation is to make friends

with him first," she said to Burke. She refused to analyze why she wanted him to succeed where the others had failed. "The secret to making friends is to acknowledge from the start he is superior in all things."

She opened the gate to the large box stall and stepped inside.

Burke hesitated. "Shouldn't you be a little cautious?"

Cordelia laughed as Thunderation nuzzled her shoulder. She dug in her pocket and held out a piece of apple she'd saved for him. "I've known him since he was a colt. Haven't I, boy?" she said to the horse, patting his neck.

"Should I bow before approaching?"

"It couldn't hurt."

He rolled his eyes at her, but he doffed his hat and made a gallant low-sweeping bow. He held it until the horse whinnied, seemingly granting permission to rise.

"Thunderation, may I present Anthony Burke, Lord Deering."

"Your servant, sir."

The horse nodded as if he understood.

Cordelia motioned Burke closer and slipped him a piece of apple. He let the stallion sniff his hand and take the treat.

"Now just talk, so he gets used to your voice," she said.

"What does one say to such a superior animal?"

Burke's obvious appreciation of her favorite warmed Cordelia's heart. "Oh, anything at all. I usually just tell him about my day. The usual sort of things."

"Well," Burke said, "Today I picnicked in a graveyard, performed the balcony scene from *Romeo and Juliet*, and met His Highness here. Quite extraordinary."

"What is your usual day?" she asked.

"Nothing a girl or a horse would find remotely interesting. What about you? How do you like London so far?"

"I haven't seen much."

"You'll have to be sure to see the sights. The Tower, the Bridge. We have wonderful museums and galleries. I hear the Thorsen has an interesting exhibit of fairy paintings. All the rage, you know."

She petted Thunderation. "Doesn't sound like something that would interest Uncle Theo or Emily."

"But you would enjoy it?"

She shrugged, not wanting to show how much she would like it if he were along. "I like learning new ideas, experiencing new things. After all, what's the point of traveling if you don't?"

He nodded. "I haven't traveled much myself. Scotland grouse hunting, but that was a disaster. Wound up with a broken leg."

"I broke my leg once, too."

"The accident? Is that why you don't ride anymore?"

Actually, she'd fallen out of a peach tree she'd climbed on a dare at age ten. For some reason the lies that had rolled so easily off her tongue stuck in her throat when speaking to Burke. "I'd rather not talk about that."

"I understand." He stroked the horse's nose. "You did promise to tell me about Miss Emily."

For a few moments she'd forgotten his reason for being nice to her. Why did all males gravitate to her sister? If Cordelia were a man, she'd be bored to tears in her sister's company before an hour was up. "Her favorite color is pink. Her favorite flowers are pink roses. And her favorite candy is those little pink mint patties. Consistent, if not original."

"What does she like to do?"

"Shop. And dance. The waltz especially. She loves to waltz."

"And you don't?"

Cordelia shrugged. At the time when most young girls

her age were learning to dance and attending their first cotillions, she'd nursed her mother through a long, fatal illness. After their mourning period ended, Emily was of age for her debut, a most successful debut. Cordelia preferred declining dance invitations to stumbling about the dance floor and making a fool of herself. "I've never danced the waltz."

Burke nodded, as if that were normal. "Of course, in London a young girl isn't allowed to waltz until after she has been presented."

Cordelia snorted. She had no expectations of meeting the queen. Especially once Uncle Theo found out the truth. She'd be lucky if they weren't forced on to the very next westward-bound ship in disgrace, or worse, arrested and incarcerated.

"My sister was terrified of her first dance, too," Burke said. "I practiced with her for hours beforehand, so she did quite well."

"You're a good dancer, then?"

"If I tell you a secret, will you promise not to repeat it?" She crossed her heart and spit between her fingers.

"When I was a lad, I was quite clumsy. I grew into my height early and rather quickly, so I never seemed to know where my arms and legs ended."

"Like having sea legs?"

"Not exactly, but that's a good analogy. I broke a number of my mother's valuable antiques, the vase in the entryway being especially vulnerable for some reason. She grumbled every time she had to replace it. After being the brunt of a lot of teasing, a friend suggested dancing lessons might help." He chuckled. "The dancing master nearly fainted, when I announced I would be taking the classes with my sister, Helene. She soon wished for iron clad dancing slippers, but we persisted."

"And it helped?" she asked, knowing it had. Burke

moved with an easy grace and assurance uncommon in most men, much less a man of his size.

He shrugged. "I haven't broken any vases lately."

"Uncle Theo hired a dancing master for me."

"That's good, no?"

Cordelia picked up a brush and ran it along Thunderation's flank. "I suppose. I don't know. I've never danced before."

"Ever?"

She shook her head and turned away. "Emily always made the waltz look like so much fun."

He took the brush from her hand. "I can teach you to waltz. It's not hard."

Leading Cordelia to an open area, he stood about a foot in front of her. He placed her left hand on his right shoulder, rested his hand high on her back, and then took her other hand in his left.

"This is the proper stance, and no matter which way our feet move, we stay in this relative position."

Cordelia's head swam to be so close to him, to be held in his arms. Breathing was difficult, concentrating on his directions nearly impossible.

"Step, slide, and close. Back, slide, and close. Make a box. Don't look at your feet, it won't help. Step, slide, and close."

He hummed "Greensleeves," and she stumbled around the stall with him.

"Let me lead," he said. "I'll give you signals by either pushing or pulling on your hand or by pressure on your shoulder, like this." He pushed on her hand and pulled on her shoulder and they moved in a circle. "But the steps remain the same. Listen to the beat of the music."

She glared up at him. "Humming does not have a beat."

"All right," he said, "but no comments on my singing.

He sang softly in a deep, rich baritone, placing emphasis on the first of the four beats.

She loved his voice, could have listened to her private concert forever. But she hated that he should think her graceless, and closed her eyes in an attempt to focus on the simple steps.

In her mind's eye the stable faded to become a sparkling ballroom, lit by thousands of candles. Her simple, childish muslin was transformed into a midnight blue silk, spangled with starry brilliants and cinched to show off her waist and make the most of her small breasts. A full orchestra backed his voice, and she floated around the glassy floor in his arms. He looked down at her with adoring eyes and she tipped up her chin, ready for his kiss—

He stopped, and she skidded to a halt on the straw-strewn floor, blinking reality back into place. Thunderation poked his head between them.

"I can't decide if he's jealous," Burke said. "Or if he just wants to cut in for the balance of the dance."

"Silly horse," Cordelia said, a bit breathless. She scratched the stallion behind his ears. "Dancing is one thing you can't do."

"I bet he could if he wanted to, couldn't you, boy?"

The horse shook his head up and down as if in agreement.

"I think you've just made a friend," she said.

"Let's hope he remembers that tomorrow morning."

The stableboy came in to feed Thunderation his ration of oats, so Cordelia and Burke moved out of his way. They headed back to the house through the garden, dusky in the late afternoon sun.

"If—when I do get to go to a dance, will you save the first waltz for me?" she asked.

"You're very young, and that's at least a year or two

away. There'll be lots of boys your own age who will line up for that honor. You won't want to be stuck with your word to an old man like me."

"You're not old."

"Much older than you. Besides, in a way, we've already danced together. Your very first waltz."

Cordelia smiled. "Emily once said a woman never forgets the man with whom she first danced the waltz."

"I am honored."

Thinking of Emily reminded her of the reason she'd agreed to accompany Burke to the stables. "I do have another favor to ask of you."

They paused on the white-shell pathway.

"If I can be of assistance, I gladly offer my service."

She was trying to think of the best way to phrase her request when she saw her grandmother sneaking in the garden gate from the alley, dressed in another one of her outrageous outfits. Granny seemed to be wearing pieces of every outfit she owned and looked like a rag woman. Cordelia wasn't going to stop to ask, nor was she going to wait around and let Burke spot Granny. One crazy episode a day was more than enough. Her plan for soliciting his help in locating Ernest would have to wait.

Cordelia grabbed his arm and dragged him toward the house. Quite a feat considering the difference in their weights, but her determination compensated for her lack of size.

"I'll tell you all about it tomorrow," she promised. "Uncle Theo and Emily will be home directly, and you'll want to be gone before then." Fat chance of that, but Burke wouldn't know Emily could try on hats for hours and hours.

He held back. "Perhaps—"

Strange how panic facilitated lies. "If Emily sees you still here, she'll take it as a sign that you're desperate for her attention. She hates a man who is so shallow he becomes besotted easily. It shows a lack of character." Actually, that was Cordelia's opinion, but it worked to get Burke moving again.

"You must act aloof with Emily," she added. "Hard to catch, if you get my meaning." Oh, how wicked of her to mislead him about her sister's preferences. She knew very well Emily quickly lost interest if a man wasn't instantly enamored of her.

Cordelia practically pushed him out the front door. "Thank you for your assistance and for a wonderful day. I loved the picnic, and the play. Thank you for the dancing lesson." She stopped to take a breath, but gave him no chance to reply. "See you tomorrow. Good-bye." She shut the door and leaned against it for a moment. Then she spotted Granny sprinting up the stairs with the agility of a much younger, much healthier woman.

Cordelia gave chase and caught up with her in front of the older woman's bedroom door.

"Granny Smith, what have you been up to?"

Five

Cordelia stopped her grandmother before the older woman escaped into her bedroom. "What were you doing out in the alley?"

"Me?" Granny turned to her with a vacant expression.

"Yes, you. I saw you sneaking in the garden gate."

"I . . . I . . . Do you want your fortune told? I, Madame Callisto, will read your palm. If we had some tea, the leaves would tell your future."

Cordelia thanked her lucky stars she'd gotten rid of Burke in time. At least the familiar gypsy persona was relatively easy to handle, not like some of Granny's other characters.

"A hot cup of tea would be nice, wouldn't it?" the older woman wheedled.

Cordelia worried that if she left, her grandmother would wander off again. She'd found the best method for dealing with Granny's spells was to play along until bedtime. At least Granny stayed put in her sleep. "Perhaps it would be better if you lay down for a nap first. Then I'll fetch us a nice pot of tea with plenty of loose leaves in it."

Madame Callisto looked up and down the hall and motioned for her to come closer. Cordelia leaned forward.

"I went to the apothecary for some ingredients. A love charm for you," the gypsy whispered. "Very powerful."

So that's what she'd been doing. At home, Madame

Callisto made forays into the woods to look for plants for her potions, but in London she would have to visit a shop for the herbs she needed. Granny knew a lot about the healing properties of plants. When she was herself, she made effective teas to cure headaches, indigestion, insomnia, and the like.

"If you sleep with it under your pillow," Madame added, "you'll dream of the man who is your true love. Then if you put the charm in his pocket, he'll fall madly in love with you. Only one piece of silver."

"Thank you, but—"

"Guaranteed to work on that handsome blond giant."

Cordelia was tempted and had to laugh at herself for even thinking of such a thing. Was insanity hereditary? "I don't have a silver coin."

"Yes, you do." Madame Callisto pointed to the pocket of the ruffled schoolgirl's pinafore Cordelia wore.

When she stuck her hand in the pocket, she found the coins Uncle Theo had given her to buy candy, coins she'd forgotten until then. She pulled her hand out and stared at the money in her open palm, three silver coins. How did Granny know?

Madame cackled in glee and snatched them out of her hand.

"Hey, give those back."

The coins disappeared into the plethora of shawls and scarves she wore, and Madame held out a tiny bundle of calico material tied with a red piece of yarn.

"It doesn't stink, does it?"

Madame waved it under her nose. "Sweet spices. Like perfume."

"You said one silver coin," Cordelia said.

"This charm is even more powerful. To last a lifetime. The other one was temporary. Maybe two weeks." She shrugged. "What can you expect for one coin?"

"If I take this—"

"And follow my instructions."

"If I promise to put it under my pillow—"

"Tonight," Granny insisted.

"Will you then lie down and take a nice long nap?"

Granny nodded. "Cross your heart that you'll use the charm?"

What would it hurt? Cordelia had the uneasy feeling she would dream about Burke, love charm or no. She made the motion over her breast, and the promise seemed to satisfy Madame Callisto, who yawned and stepped calmly into her bedroom.

Cordelia wandered down the hall toward her own room, the empty evening to be spent in the nursery with only a book for company stretched ahead. Being treated as a child had a few advantages, but an active social life wasn't one of them. If she could induce Burke to help find Ernest, her days of imprisonment in ruffled pantalets would be limited. Then the problem would be how to meet him again as herself without rousing his suspicions.

That was a hopeless line of thinking. Once she found Ernest, she would have to tell Uncle Theo the truth, and then she and Granny would go home. She would never see Burke again.

A tear slid down her cheek, but she dashed it away. Unattainable wishes were for fools. She was a practical, responsible adult even if she was dressed in a stupid pinafore and had an eight o'clock curfew. She had to act on behalf of Granny and Emily, who seemed incapable of caring for themselves. Cordelia threw the love charm across the room.

Then she remembered her cross-your-heart promise. She scrambled to retrieve the bundle and placed it under her pillow.

* * *

Burke lost his hat, a recent acquisition that had set him back an unreasonable fee, but he barely gave it a second thought. He was flying. At least that's what riding Thunderation at full gallop felt like. Flying free as if he were weightless—a sensation he hadn't enjoyed since he was a lad. The usual thoroughbred belonging to the members of the ton had seemed too frail to handle his adult bulk. He'd been afraid he'd snap their delicate legs. Thunderation had legs of iron. Despite a sedate start, the stallion had been eager to run and seemed to barely notice the burden he carried, so Burke had given him a free rein.

After a circuit of the park, he slowed the horse to a brisk walk. Thunderation was barely winded. Burke patted the horse's neck.

Marsfield, on a chestnut gelding, and Anne, on a sweet dapple gray mare, pulled their mounts alongside.

"Exceptional horse," Marsfield said after the usual greetings. "Yours?"

"I wish. He's magnificent. A gait like a rocking chair. If I'd known they bred horses like this in America, I would have developed an interest in importing the animals long before this morning."

"From America, you say? Any particular region?"

Even Marsfield's penchant for steering the conversation to the topic of his choice failed to irritate Burke on such a fine day. "Yes, now that you mention it. That's why I invited you to meet me on the trails."

"I knew something was up as soon as I read your message," Marsfield said.

"As you requested, I've continued my observation of any likely suspects. However, I'm fairly certain Miss Emily Weston is not the woman agent as I originally suspected."

"Really? Why?"

"I don't wish to flatter myself by saying this," Burke said, "but I should think a certain degree of intelligence would be a requirement for an agent. Miss Emily does not seem to be . . ."

"You wouldn't be the first man fooled by a woman," Anne said. "We're taught early to play to a certain role."

"I don't think Miss Emily is pretending."

"Now I'm flummoxed," Marsfield said.

"Sir?"

"Well, I've had each of the previous female passengers trailed. Mrs. Mary Micheff is in Hampstead visiting her sister Patricia. Mrs. Linda Lee is in Devon with her daughter Katie to evaluate the first of several finishing schools they are considering. Mrs. Violetta Greene is the stage name of one Agatha Pringle, who, after just four nights under the lights at the Stanford Musical Theater, left for Paris in the company of the so-called Count DuBarge. I could continue through the list. Every woman passenger whose name you've given me has left London as quickly as possible and is exactly where she's supposed to be."

"Have you considered the woman may be disguised as a boy?" Anne flashed a mischievous grin. "It's not unheard of, you know."

"Humph!" Marsfield frowned.

"Don't mind him. He's still upset I fooled him into thinking I was a boy for so long," she explained to Burke.

"Only because you never allow me to forget," Marsfield grumbled. "And, yes, Burke did think of it. No young men or boys have disembarked as passengers."

"What if she worked her way across as a sailor?" Anne asked.

"That would be difficult considering the confines of a ship," Burke said, shaking his head. "I'm sure we're look-

ing for a woman. Did anyone meet the ship yesterday
since I could not?"

"Preston handled it," Marsfield said. "The only female
on board was the captain's wife, and they plan to return
to sea as soon as they can load the return cargo."

Burke nodded. "I checked the manifest. Machine
parts bound for New England."

The conversation lagged as they met two riders coming
from the other direction and passed with polite greetings.

"Then our best suspect is still Miss Emily Weston,"
Burke said. "I'll continue to observe her." He cleared his
throat. "I'm ashamed to admit I've failed to remain discreet. I'm not unknown to the woman. The . . . the
family assumes I'm interested in courting Miss Emily."

"Are you?" Anne asked.

"Good heavens, no," Burke said.

"An excellent ruse," Marsfield said. "How better to
track the woman's movements than to play the lovesick
swain?"

"Perhaps we should invite Lord Gravely and his guests
to dinner," Anne said. "Sort of a welcome to London. Introduce them to a few people. I'll send our regrets to the
Jamesons for tonight, and we'll have them over right
away."

"Lord Gravely's great-niece is but a child."

"That's perfect. She and Andrea can have their own
get-acquainted supper in the nursery."

For some reason Burke couldn't picture Precious at a
knee-high table surrounded by dolls. "Miss Precious is
not . . . well, she's a good bit older than Andrea, and I
suspect girls age more quickly in America."

Anne raised her brows, and he felt compelled to continue.

"She's . . . precocious. Mature, in a way I can't quite explain."

"Well, she's grown up in the middle of a war, hasn't she?" Anne said. "Poor dear. None of us can really understand what something like that does to a child. I'm even more determined to meet her, and help her adjust to her new home."

"Now, Anne, she's not a stray kitten," Marsfield said.

"I know, but I'd like her to feel she has friends. Especially if her companion turns out to be the foreign agent, she'll—"

"All right." Marsfield threw up his hands, and his horse skittered sideways in confusion. He brought the animal under control.

"Something simple, I think," she mused. "I'm sure Letty and Timothy will join us with little Timmy."

"You might want to pass on this invitation," Marsfield said as an aside to Burke and gave an exaggerated shudder. "Young Master Timmy takes after his grandmother, Lady Asterbule."

Anne gave him a look and he subsided. "Very well," she agreed without him saying another word. "But only because it's important for Burke to be there so he can be paired with Emily, not because—"

"We don't even know if they'll accept. They may already have an engagement," Burke pointed out, glad for the chance to interject some logic. "Isn't tonight awfully short notice?"

"Not really," Anne said. "I mean, they only just arrived. How many invitations can they possibly have?"

Burke turned to Marsfield. "Are you sure this is best? You've always recommended remaining detached from a suspect, keeping a distance."

"I meant an emotional, intellectual distance. You are doing that, aren't you?"

"Of course, I am." True, concerning Emily. However, he was forced to admit to himself, he was strangely drawn to

Precious. And to the grandmother. At least the fact that he felt drawn to the grandmother as well gave him hope that his interest in Precious was only that of a friend. He would have to maintain what detachment he had left.

Although he already knew the answer, he had to ask: "Then you suggest I continue the ruse? Pretend to court Miss Emily?"

Marsfield shook his head. "This is your investigation. You do what you think is best."

"Your advice would be welcome."

"Then I suggest you do whatever it takes to conclude it successfully."

Burke had been afraid he would say that.

Cordelia had risen well before dawn, not a surprise considering her early evening. She'd watched from the window, hidden by the lace curtain, as Burke had mounted Thunderation and ridden off like a splendid warrior headed for battle. Did Vikings even ride horses? Surely they must have if they fought on land.

She ruthlessly squashed the thrill the sight gave her. She had decided on a plan to find Ernest, and she would follow it through.

When Burke returned from his ride, she'd already sent word to the stable to ask him to meet her on the verandah overlooking the garden. She loved being outside in the early morning when the world seemed fresh and the day full of possibilities. She sipped her hard-won coffee. The cook had been horrified at the very idea of serving a child "that nasty brew," but she'd finally succumbed to Cordelia's pleading, peppered as it was with blatant flattery.

Burke walked up the garden path, dusting off his breeches and straightening his tie. Oh, the way he moved.

Gave her a thrill just to watch him. She could well imagine him pacing the deck of a Viking ship, his eyes reflecting the sky and sea, his gaze focused on the distant horizon. She blinked as he approached. She needed her wits about her. A lock of his wind-tossed hair fell over his forehead, and her hand itched to comb it back. As if reading her thoughts, he reached up and brushed it aside.

After a cordial greeting she invited him to join her. He hesitated at the bottom of the three steps that led to the broad covered porch and demurred.

"I've just come from the stables. I wouldn't want to offend."

"My sensibilities are not that delicate. You forget I was born on a plantation where we raised horses."

"The coffee does smell delicious. Is Miss Emily about?"

Cordelia held back a snort. The only time she'd seen Emily rise before noon in the last four years, the house had been on fire. Literally. Yankees had torched their plantation home in the early hours of the morning, and only Granny's quick actions had saved everyone. She plastered a sweet smile on her face. "No, I don't believe I've seen her yet this morning."

"Perhaps you would pass along a message?"

She nodded, with as much graciousness as she could muster.

"Thank you. Some friends of mine, Lord and Lady Marsfield will be sending around a note inviting your household to a small dinner party this evening. I wanted to add my encouragement that you accept. I think you will all enjoy the company."

"Will you be in attendance?" She tried to make the question sound casual but wasn't sure she succeeded.

He gave her a curious look. "Yes. I'm also invited."

"Then I'm sure Emily will be pleased." She poured him a cup and indicated a seat across the table.

"I'd like to thank you for introducing me to Thunderation."

"It was Gran—Mrs. Smith's suggestion."

Burke nodded. "You're the one who formally introduced me, and I think that made a difference."

"I take it you had a good ride."

"The best. You're really missing something by not riding him."

Oh, didn't she know it. What with the voyage, it had been almost two months since she'd flown free over the fields, the wind in her hair. She wasn't about to allow those months of suffering to be in vain.

"I invited you here for a specific reason," she said. "I have a favor to ask of you. There's a certain gentleman in London I'd like to locate." At his look of surprise she continued before he could decline. "A friend. I met him last spring and promised to look him up if I should ever come to town."

"Why don't you ask your uncle?"

"Well, you see, Uncle Theo is quite busy, and I've already imposed upon his hospitality. I wouldn't think he knows all that many young people, and I thought you might even know my friend Ernest. That's his name, Ernest Truebrill, Baronet Dandridge, although he might have inherited his father's title by now."

Burke looked at her, suspicion in his eyes. "Miss Precious, I couldn't do anything your uncle would disapprove of. Surely this man isn't . . . he isn't a love interest, is he?"

"Oh, no. Nothing like that. He was always a perfect gentleman to me." That, at least, was the truth. Ernest had been overly polite to her and Granny, which was why they'd never questioned his attention to Emily until it was too late. Cordelia's sincerity must have been reflected in her tone because Burke visibly relaxed. "He lent me a book, and I'd like to return it."

"I would gladly perform that errand for you. Perhaps with an appropriate note—"

"I would prefer returning it in person, properly chaperoned, of course. I simply need your help finding his direction."

"The name doesn't sound familiar. Did he say where his family is seated? A county? An area?"

"No, now that I think on it, he didn't. He did mention several times a house in London. Quite large, from his description. Built from an unusual yellow marble with columns in front, if I remember correctly. Designed by Christopher Wren. I specifically recall him mentioning that, because at the time I was reading an article on the Greek Revival style in the *Architect's Digest*."

He raised his brows. "Unusual reading material. For a young girl, I mean."

She realized she'd just made a major faux pas and tried to cover her slip of the tongue. "My father had—has a subscription to the monthly magazine." Actually, she was fairly certain Jeb Cosley had not the slightest interest in anything other than horses, the same as her grandfather. James Weston, her father, had enjoyed varied intellectual pursuits. He'd been headmaster of the prestigious Savannah Academy before the war. Cordelia and Emily had moved back to their grandparents' plantation when their mother became ill.

"You're interested in architecture?" Burke asked.

"I'm told all areas of study are beneficial to the mind." Cordelia forced a shrug. "Mostly, there was a dearth of new reading material. The war, you know. I'm sure that issue was months old before I saw it."

"Well, that particular house shouldn't be too hard to find. I'm not acquainted with all his buildings, but Mr. Wren's work is well documented."

"Wonderful." She said it, but she didn't feel it. As

much as she wanted to find Ernest, once that was accomplished, Burke would no longer come around to see Emily, and then Cordelia wouldn't see him either.

"The best place to start would be the Hall of Records, but it won't open again until Monday morning."

Her heart sang. As it was only Saturday morning, that gave her almost two full days rife with the possibility of spending time with him. "I appreciate your assistance."

"On one condition: that you tell your uncle before you try to contact this friend."

She nodded. That promise was easy to make. Once they found Ernest, telling Uncle Theo the whole truth was the first thing she intended to do.

"What are your plans for the day?" he asked. "I thought perhaps you and Miss Emily would like to take in some of the sights this afternoon. I would gladly act as your tour guide. Perhaps the Crystal Pavilion from the Exhibition? There's an indoor arboretum with plants from all over the world."

"That sounds lovely." Even if they would have to take Emily along.

"What sounds lovely?"

Burke stood and Cordelia turned at the sound of Granny's voice, and then she wanted to drop through the floor. Her grandmother sauntered onto the verandah carrying her old knitting bag and wearing a sheet wrapped over her simple day dress, the voluminous linen tied and knotted to resemble something an ancient statue would wear.

"Who is this handsome young man? A caller for Cleopatra so early in the day? I'm flattered."

"Don't you remember Lord Deering?" Cordelia asked, in a desperate attempt to jar Granny back to reality. "You met yesterday."

"I'm expecting a delegation of Romans. Are you a Roman, perhaps?"

"Lord Deering has invited us—" Cordelia stopped as she saw Burke salute, right hand fisted over his heart in the traditional manner of the Roman centurions. "Anthony Burke, Citizen, at your service."

"Anthony. I like that name."

"Meeting you, Your Highness, is a childhood wish granted. May I say, your reported beauty—"

"Well," Granny interrupted him. "You know how it is with royalty. A queen is always young and beautiful to her adoring subjects."

"Then you must count me among yours, because I was about to say your reported beauty does not do justice to your presence."

Granny nodded in a most royal manner. "I thank you for your flattery. But, Anthony, in spite of your pretty words, I must point out that you are not properly attired to attend the Queen of the Nile." She sat in a wrought-iron chair near the railing, dug in her knitting bag, and pulled out another bedsheet. "Here you are, and one for you, too, child."

Cordelia took the sheet and wanted to use it to cover her head. "Please, Gran—"

"Aren't you mixing the Romans and the Greeks?" he asked cheerfully as he wrapped the length of white material around his waist and threw the long end over his left shoulder.

"One is much like the other to me," Granny said with a languid wave of her hand.

"Ah, but it's the Romans who will attack you at Actium," he warned.

"I have heard that rumor myself," Granny said in a conspiratorial tone. "Not to worry, I'll take my royal barge and rout them at sea."

Burke gave her a worried frown and shook his head. "Perhaps, that's not the best tactic to—"

"Shhhh."

"Good morning," Uncle Theo called from the door. "I thought I heard voices." He turned to say over his shoulder, "I'll have my breakfast out here."

"Shhhh," Granny said again. "It's Octavian. I don't trust him."

Cordelia turned to Burke. "Didn't you say earlier you had an appointment elsewhere and had to leave immediately?"

He looked at her as if she was the balmy one. "No. Not at all. May I have more coffee, please?"

She'd offered him a perfectly good excuse to escape and he'd ignored it. No, rebuffed it, as if the idea was distasteful. Well, then he deserved whatever he got for being foolish. With a smile full of pity and a small shake of her head, she poured him another serving.

"What ho?" Uncle Theo said. "No one told me breakfast was a costumed affair." He indicated for the butler to set the tray on the table and ordered more coffee and food for everyone else.

"Beware of Romans bearing gifts," Granny said to Burke in a stage whisper.

"I thought that was Greeks bearing gifts," he answered back in kind.

"The Queen of the Nile does not like to repeat herself." Granny glared at him. "Handmaiden!" She pointed imperiously at Cordelia. "Tell our young warrior what I said earlier."

She wished she could just stand up and walk away, but she couldn't. What would Uncle Theo do if she wasn't here to protect Granny? For her grandmother's sake, she would play her part. "Greeks or Romans, they are both the same to her," she said, but she couldn't muster much enthusiasm.

"In the future, pay attention or you'll lose your warrior status."

"Actually, I'd prefer to be a patrician. I don't really think I'm centurion material."

Granny looked him up and down, frankly assessing his attributes. "You are definitely a Roman warrior."

"A Viking warrior," Cordelia corrected, then felt her cheeks flame. What had possessed her to blurt out her private fantasy? She buried her face in her coffee cup. When she peeked at Burke, he had a small, bemused smile on his face, and seemed not to be paying attention to her. Perhaps, he hadn't heard.

"Ahem!"

Everyone turned to Uncle Theo, and Cordelia sent him a grateful smile.

"In the present company, my attire seems quite inadequate." He patted his napkin, spread across his ample belly. "With only this, I feel quite naked."

"Oh, for Pete's sake." Granny reached into her knitting bag and drew out another bedsheet.

Uncle Theo jumped back when she tossed it to him. "Ho? What? Whew, you scared me there for a minute."

"What did you think it was? An asp?" Granny asked, acid in her tone.

"I wouldn't put it past you. What else have you got in there?" Uncle Theo asked.

"Wouldn't you like to know?" she said, scooting the bag closer to her chair and planting her feet on top of it.

"Not really. Quimsy told the housekeeper, who told the butler, who told me about the curse on your trunk." Uncle Theo shuddered. "I'd prefer to do without boils, thank you very much. Though I do wonder why you're carrying around my good bed linens."

"If I ever get locked in my room, I can tie them together and shimmy out the window to freedom."

"We would never lock you in your room," Cordelia said, horrified that her grandmother could even think such a thing.

Granny patted her hand. "I know, child, and I thank you. Without your support, I couldn't do all the . . . outrageous things I do."

Uncle Theo snorted. "That's one word for it." He stood and wrapped the sheet around himself. "Didn't they have pins or brooches or something to hold this together," he dithered, trying the material one way and then another. He finally tucked the end into his collar like a big napkin and returned to his seat.

"Well, I, for one, think you're all marvelous," Burke said. "I never know what to expect when I come here, and I'm never disappointed. Certainly never bored."

"I'll drink to that," Uncle Theo said, raising high his cup of tea. "To the demise of boredom."

"Hear, hear," Granny and Burke chorused, raising their cups.

Cordelia raised her cup, too, but she didn't agree. A little normal boredom would be a welcome change.

She hoped Burke had warned his friends before they'd issued the dinner invitation, or else Lord and Lady Marsfield could well be in for an unpleasant surprise.

Six

"We have to talk," Cordelia said, entering her sister's bedroom and sitting in the chair by the desk.

The room, bigger than hers, was sumptuously decorated in deep emerald velvet and gilded accessories. This was the second room assigned to Emily. The first, on the fourth floor with the servants, she'd claimed had been drafty. Unhealthy for someone of her oh so delicate nature. Ha! Emily had the constitution of a draft horse and had never been sick a day in her life. But she'd complained so prettily to Uncle Theo, he'd moved her to the present room temporarily. Cordelia expected it would take dynamite to extricate her.

"Look at all these invitations. And two nosegays." Emily had her loot spread around her on the bed, and her breakfast tray on her lap even though it was past eleven o'clock. She sipped her hot chocolate. "Lord Wilcox sent the violets. So sweet."

"Who?" How could Emily have admirers on their third day in town? It defied logic.

"Wilcox. The red-haired gentleman at the ice cream parlor."

"Oh. Mr. Droopy-eyelids."

"I dislike that childish habit you have of naming people after their faults."

"I'm supposed to act childish. It was your idea, remember?"

Emily ignored the jibe. "He's the heir to an earldom. His family is in here." She pulled a slim volume from beneath her pillow. "I found it in the library."

Cordelia blinked. That her sister had found the library was astounding, that she'd read a book voluntarily even more so. She scooted her chair closer to the bed. "Is Ernest listed? Maybe it will help us find him."

"No. There's a Dandridge, but it isn't Ernest. Must be his father or grandfather. The book is over forty years old." Emily handed over the book. "Granny is in there, though. She and her twin sister, Auntie Genevieve."

"Really? Where?"

"Page one eighty-seven."

Emily took a tiny bite of toast as Cordelia found the place.

"I never knew Granny's family was so well-connected," Emily said. "We're related to royalty, no less."

"That means nothing to us. We're Americans." Cordelia closed the book and tossed it back on the bed.

"We're in London now, and here, it's important. It means we'll be welcome in the best homes."

"Right now, I'm only concerned about one particular home." Cordelia took the invitation out of her pocket. "This came to Uncle Theo about half an hour ago by messenger."

Emily took the creamy white envelope with the distinctive hawk crest in the corner. "I just love invitations." She shivered. "The anticipation is so delicious."

"Just read it." When Emily hesitated, stroking the fine vellum stationary, Cordelia blurted out. "We're all invited to a small, informal dinner party tonight at the Marsfields, Lord Deering's friends."

"Oh, him." Emily dropped the envelope onto the velvet counterpane without opening it. "They're probably as dull as he is."

"He is not dull."

"Handsome, I grant you, in a rugged, overgrown sort of way. Quite stylish in his dress. But, really, he has no social skills whatsoever. Can't hold a candle to Wilcox for witty repartee."

"Who?"

"Wilcox. Lord Wilcox."

Cordelia shook her head and spread her hands palm up.

"Mr. Droopy-eyelids," Emily ground out between her teeth.

"Oh, now I know who you're talking about."

"I do wish you would listen to me when I speak."

"And I wish you would pay attention to the important matter of finding Ernest. Uncle Theo has accepted, and we're going to this dinner tonight, and you're going to be nice to Lord Deering and his friends."

"Lord Wilcox has invited me, Granny, and Uncle Theo to his box at the theater."

It did not escape Cordelia's notice that Emily was now calling him *Uncle* Theo, an honor that usually conveyed familiarity and affection. "I'm sure Theo will send his regrets, if he hasn't already."

"I haven't been to the theater in ages." Emily stared off into space. "It's bound to be so much grander than the Savannah Opera House. I wonder if Uncle Theo will change his mind."

If Cordelia didn't get her sister off this tack, she would be spending another lonely evening in the nursery instead of meeting Burke and his friends. "You'll look so grand in an evening dress years out of date. One that is getting tight in the waist, I might remind you."

Emily nearly dropped her cup. "Dinner parties are not unappealing. Who else is invited?"

"Other than Lord Deering, it doesn't matter. He's the one who will find Ernest for you."

"You didn't tell him—"

"Of course not." Cordelia related the excuse she'd concocted.

Emily set her tray aside and swung her legs over the edge of the bed. "That's an excellent ruse. We have time to shop for new gloves before we have to begin dressing."

"Lord Deering is waiting downstairs to escort us to the arboretum."

"That's a collection of plants, right? How utterly boring."

"You will be kind to him. Remember, he—"

"He's going to find Ernest. I've got it. I'm not a simpleton." Emily rummaged in her wardrobe and pulled out a pink muslin day dress, matching hat, and a lemon yellow pelisse. She rang for the maid to help her dress. "Are you going to wear that?" she asked, indicating Cordelia's dress with a nod.

"My choices are somewhat limited," Cordelia said, not even trying to keep the sour tone out of her voice. The sailor dress, white stockings and ankle-high boots, appropriate for an afternoon outing, were particularly unflattering to her figure. The big bow and streaming ribbons at the back of her waist did nothing to disguise her unfortunate hips. Not only did she look childish, but she looked as if she needed to push away from the table a little sooner and a little more often. Unjustly so, considering how limited her diet had been lately.

"You'll need a hat," Emily said from behind the dressing screen decorated with peacocks.

"Downstairs, with my white kid gloves," Cordelia said, remembering the silly straw boater with yet another ridiculously large bow and streaming ribbons attached.

If she ever had a daughter, she would never force her to wear bows.

Burke strolled down the last row of foliage with Miss Emily on his arm, bereft of another topic of intelligent conversation. The woman at his side was no help. If she had any interests, he had yet to discover them. Not books. Not philosophy, nor any of the sciences. Most certainly not botany. Despite the envious glances from other gentlemen they passed, the afternoon left him feeling rather flat.

Precious, however, seemed to be having a grand time. She practically skipped ahead of them, stopping and bending over to read aloud the plaques, doing a respectable job with the long Latin names. She sniffed the blossoms and touched the petals and leaves.

"I think this one is my favorite," she said, as Burke and Emily caught up to her. "I love the fuzzy foliage."

Burke read the identifying plaque. "The *Begonia astorium*, discovered by Sir Nehimiah Astor on his last foray into the jungles of South America, 1855 to 1858."

"Just imagine what he must have gone through to find this," Precious said. "He left his home, family, and friends. Suffered deprivations and discomfort. Risked disease and even death. What is it that makes a man go on an expedition like that?"

"Insanity," Emily answered.

"I suppose naming a species is a form of immortality," Precious said, answering her own question.

An interesting observation. Burke had never thought of it quite that way before. "Perhaps the pursuit of knowledge is its own reward. The thrill of being the first."

"That's a man for you," Emily said with a frown. "A

preoccupation with being first. I should think a better
goal would be to strive for being the best."

"Why, Emily," Precious said, "you just made an acute
philosophical observation."

"I did?"

"Yes. I'm proud of you. Those dinner discussions with
Father . . . that you described having with your father,
must have sunk into your brain after all."

Precious laughed with delight, and the sound seemed
to lodge itself in Burke's chest, creating a warmth. He
rubbed the spot over his heart. Indigestion, he told himself. Heartburn of the ordinary sort.

"Well, don't get excited," Emily said. "Not only was it
unintentional, I'll do my best not to repeat the dubious
achievement."

"Perhaps you would like some refreshment," Burke
said. "I noticed a lemonade concession outside."

"Why, Lord Deering, you must have read my mind,"
Emily said. "I am positively parched."

Burke indicated the exit and took Emily on his right
arm and Precious on his left. In fact, a number of food
vendors had set up booths outside the Crystal Pavilion.
While Emily contentedly sipped a glass of lemonade,
Precious practically danced from booth to booth tasting
one of everything. Burke found her enthusiasm delightful and rather contagious. She rhapsodized over the
bite-size meat pasties. After eating half an ear of corn,
she licked the melted butter off her fingertips. The pastry wrapped sausage on a stick was undoubtedly her
favorite. When she placed her lips around the thick
sausage and moaned her appreciation of its flavor, Burke
could watch no longer and turned away, searching for a
distraction.

He found a perfect one.

"Look. A carousel. Let's ride."

"Not me," Emily said. "Going in circles makes me dizzy."

Precious simply shook her head, the last of her sausage otherwise occupying her mouth. She dragged her feet as she followed him and Emily to the ticket booth.

"It is exactly what you need," he said to Precious. "A carousel horse is the perfect first step to conquering your fear of riding." A break from her company was exactly what he needed.

"Go on," Emily urged. "I'll wait right here for you two."

"What if I get dizzy or sick?" Precious asked. "What if I fall off?"

"You won't," Burke reassured her and purchased two tickets.

Cordelia relented. Even riding around in circles on an inanimate wooden horse had appeal if Burke was at her side. He took her hand to steady her as she stepped up onto the base of the carousel.

"Which one?" he asked with a encouraging smile.

She chose the palomino with the red-painted saddle because it was next to the white charger she'd picked out for him to ride. He lifted her up to the back of her horse. Suddenly eye to eye, he hesitated for a long second with his hands on her waist. Her gloves were still in her pocket and she longed to touch his face, to feel the warmth of his skin. She grabbed for the pole in a desperate move to keep from slipping her arms around his neck and jumping into his embrace.

He cleared his throat and backed away a step, a confused look on his face. "There you go." He took the tickets from his pocket and stuck both of them in the bracket on the horse's head. "Have fun."

"Wait a minute. Aren't you riding?"

He hopped down to the ground. "I think it would

be . . . better if I watch with Miss Emily so she isn't left standing alone." He waved as the carousel started in motion.

Oh, he couldn't leave Emily to wait alone, but he could plunk Cordelia on a wooden horse and leave her to ride all by herself. Have fun, indeed. She clutched at the pole as if it were a certain somebody's neck. Up and down and around. As the carousel made a complete circuit, Burke and Emily came into view. Someone might say they made a beautiful couple. Both tall and blond. Someone might say that. Not Cordelia. He waved and she offered him a grim smile.

Precious didn't seem to be enjoying herself. Burke leaned to the left to catch sight of her as she came around, taking a step in his worry. Was she so afraid of horses that even the tame carousel terrified her? As she came into view, he waved and offered her an encouraging smile. She didn't remove her hand from the pole to wave back. He took another step to the left.

Cordelia closed her eyes so she wouldn't see them together, but that accentuated the movement, and all the rich foods she'd consumed flip-flopped in her stomach. Opening her eyes, she focused on a spot between her horse's ears, but as the herd of wooden animals made another circuit, Burke came into view again. Frowning, he resembled even more the fierce Viking warrior she had named him. How she wanted to jump down, run to him, and confess everything. That she wasn't a child, that she was a woman, with a woman's heart and longings. She caught sight of Emily, and noticed the slightest bulge just below her waist, not so much that anyone else would see, but Cordelia did. Her sister needed her to maintain the masquerade until they found Ernest. Cordelia clutched the pole and stayed in her seat.

Poor Precious. Burke berated himself for putting her through this torture. She was so terrified she had the pole in a death grip. Her slim fingers were turning white with the force of her stranglehold. He stepped to the left to catch sight of her as soon as possible. Should he try to jump aboard? Should he ask the ticket man to stop the carousel? She came into view again, and he noticed slightly less tension in her shoulders as she went by. He stepped to the left again, eager to see if she had relaxed any more. That was more like it. She was waving— timidly, but waving all the same.

Cordelia tried to direct Burke's attention back to Emily. He had strayed rather far from her side, and that redheaded man from the ice cream parlor had joined her sister. "Over there. Mister Droopy-eyelids," she called to Burke.

The calliope music drowned out most of her words, but he was glad to hear she thought it was nice. He nodded and waved back. As she came around again, he realized she was pointing at something. He turned in time to see Miss Emily pass a redheaded man a note that he put in his pocket without reading. Very suspicious behavior. Burke turned and stalked to her side, wanting to get the man's name before he could flee.

Cordelia lost sight of them for a few moments. Emily should not be encouraging the attentions of Mr. Droopy-eyelids when she was engaged to Ernest. Did her sister want the reputation of a trollop? If only Burke would in-

terrupt and send the redhead on his way. As the horses
made their slow way around, she moved in her seat as if
urging a real mount to greater speed. When the circuit
completed, she breathed a sigh of relief as she watched
her gentleman Viking come to the rescue. Not hers, she
corrected herself. A friend. He was only the friend of a
young girl.

As Burke approached, the redheaded man paled, making his freckles stand out like wine droplets splattered on
a damask tablecloth.

"Oh, there you are," Emily said, without an iota of
discomposure. "Do you know Lord Wilcox?"

As she made the introductions, Burke reconsidered
his analysis of Emily. Did she know he'd seen her pass
the note? Her cool behavior under the stress of the current situation gave credence to his first impression at the
wharf. Earlier that day, she'd let an intelligent sentence
slip from between her ruby lips, leading him to think it
was possible she kept more secrets hidden behind the
shallow facade she presented so well.

Wilcox stammered an excuse and left in a hurry.

Burke set Emily's hand on his arm, and turned to watch
the carousel as it slowed to a stop. Precious jumped off the
platform and ran toward them with a radiant smile.

Despite his reason, Burke found the precocious girl
delightful. Her joie de vivre, her laughter, her . . . He
reluctantly made a resolution. For his own peace of
mind, he would have to switch assignments with his
friend. After meeting at dinner tonight, Preston could
pretend to court Emily.

Preston, with his dark looks that the ladies seemed to
find irresistible, would be better at courting Emily. He
only had more experience. The small scar over Pre-

ston's left eye gave him a sardonic mien that had in-
trigued the girls even when Preston and Burke were
boys. He'd told everyone it was from a sword fight. True,
in a way. Burke had given it to him in one of their mock
battles with wooden swords at the age of eight. Girls had
found it so attractive that Burke had once asked Preston
to hit him in the head with a stick.

With Preston taking over his duties with Emily, there
would be no more need for Burke to see Precious. That
would be for the best. He ignored the hollowness that
washed through him at the thought.

He would do one last favor for Precious, but after he
found Ernest so she could return his book, Burke would
say his good-byes. She upset his world, caused dissatis-
faction with the status quo, made him feel its lack of joy
and laughter, something he'd never noticed before.

He even toyed with the idea of asking Marsfield to release him from the assignment, but returning to his
former position, which he had once liked and been so
proud of, no longer held any appeal. Nothing in his life
was the same as before.

As he handed Emily and Precious into his carriage
and gave the driver directions to Lord Gravely's home,
his thoughts were in a tumble.

"You're awfully quiet," Precious said. "Is anything the
matter?"

"What? Oh, no. I suppose I'm fatigued, that's all."

She looked at him as if she didn't believe him, but she
didn't say anything further until they were at her door,
when she and Emily both thanked him most graciously
for the afternoon.

"We'll see you tonight?" Precious asked.

"Yes, yes. I'm looking forward to introducing you to my
friend's little girl. Andrea is quite charming. I'm sure Miss
Emily will find my friend Preston interesting. He traveled

with Sir Burton, you know. Oh, no, you wouldn't know that, but he did." Burke knew he was babbling because he was upset, but he couldn't seem to stop. So he did the next best thing. He bowed and left as quickly as possible, dreading the evening to come.

If he could, he would send his regrets and have dinner at his club. However, pretending to court Emily had paid off. He'd seen her pass a note to Wilcox, widening the scope of the investigation.

In addition, he wanted the evening to go well for Precious, although he had no idea when or why she'd become important to him. He cared for her. Like a sister. Not like he loved Helene, but that was probably because the two girls were so very different. Like he cared for Andrea, the child of his friends. But not exactly. Because he'd known Andrea since the day she was born, had reluctantly held her in his arms when she was only a few hours old. No, he wanted Precious to succeed, wanted his friends to like her because . . . because he cared about her. Circular logic frustrated him to no end.

Cordelia's nervousness escalated as she bathed and dressed for the evening in a frilly confection of sky blue organdy with white silk ribbons tied into the inevitable large bows. What she wouldn't give for the opportunity to wear a dress appropriate for her age. She wouldn't even care if it wasn't the height of fashion, if only it had a flattering waist and a skirt that went all the way to the floor. But she would wear a bow every day for the rest of her life if only the evening ahead would go off without a hitch.

"You look very sweet," Granny said, as they waited in the parlor for Emily and Uncle Theo.

"Thank you," Cordelia said with a grimace that made her grandmother smile. "You look very nice yourself."

"This old thing," Granny said, patting her best silk dress from before the war. "I feel like a gray ghost. I always preferred bright colors, but your grandfather, rest his soul, never liked me to stand out. Putting myself forward, he called it."

Cordelia had never been close to her stern, austere grandfather. He'd always seemed to look at her with censure in his eyes, as if she were guilty of something, though she never figured out quite what.

"You never did tell me, how did you and Grandfather meet?"

"That's a long story, and not terribly interesting." Granny looked up at the clock. "We're already running ten minutes past time to leave."

"Not really. I told everyone six o'clock instead of seven because I knew Emily would be at least a half hour late." Being late for a small dinner party was not only rude, one risked the meal being ruined. As this was the first non-porridge dinner she was to have in days, Cordelia wasn't taking any chances.

"Did you love Grandfather?" Cordelia asked, then thought better of such an impertinent question. She didn't want to set her grandmother off into one of her spells. If she did, they would have to cancel the evening. "My apologies. I'm sure it's none of my business."

Granny looked at her with an assessing gaze. "That depends on why you're asking. I have no intention of baring my soul to satisfy anyone's prurient curiosity, not even yours. That said, if you have a genuine question, I'll answer as best I can."

"I guess what I meant is, if a woman marries without love, can she ever be truly happy?"

"Love isn't a guarantee of happiness." Granny patted her granddaughter's cheek. "And an arranged marriage is not doomed to misery."

"Your marriage was, wasn't it? Miserable, I mean."

Granny hesitated. "Your grandfather was not an easy man, and we saw the world very differently. If I'd known beforehand how things would turn out, I might not have accompanied my twin sister to her new home where I met and married your grandfather. However, I had your mother, and she gave me enough joy to sustain me. We lived just a few miles from your Great-Aunt Genevieve and her boys, so I had a full, active life. I don't regret any of my actions."

Cordelia heard the catch in her grandmother's voice and knew she lied.

Granny smiled sadly. "Well, maybe one or two regrets. It's hard to reach my age and not have a few."

"Not have a few what?" Uncle Theo asked as he entered the parlor, resplendent in a colorful waistcoat embroidered with every species of bird known to man and probably a few mythical ones.

"Regrets," Granny said. "I count that vest among my few."

Uncle Theo smoothed the material over his girth. "Absolutely grand, isn't it?" He held his coat wide so Cordelia could see it better. "Vivian here made it for me when we were younger. I was quite the bird fancier then." He turned from side to side, pointing to and naming several of the species, and giving their distinctive calls.

"I'm surprised you still have it," Granny said, though Cordelia could tell she was pleased.

"I had my tailor let it out in the back an inch or two."

"Or six," Granny said.

He tugged on it, and a button popped open.

"You should have gone for eight," Granny said with a falsely sweet smile.

Cordelia hid a grin. So Theo and Vivian had been more than friends all those years ago. A woman didn't make an intimate gift for a man, nor spend that many hours on fancy needlework unless she had deep feelings. What had happened to separate them? How did Granny wind up marrying someone else an ocean away?

"I'm here," Emily said, sweeping into the room and making a pirouette in the center so everyone could see and admire her favorite rose silk evening dress. She'd removed the large artificial flowers that dated the dress. She'd added a sweep of lace from the waist to one shoulder just like the picture in the latest *Ladies Home Companion* she'd bought on their first shopping trip. Her hair was pulled back into a cascade of golden curls from the top of her head to the nape of her neck. Tiny pink rosebuds from Theo's greenhouse formed a fragrant tiara across the crown of her head.

"Enchanting," Uncle Theo said, with fervor. "Absolutely ravishing. Makes me wish I were twenty years younger."

"Forty years," Granny said, standing and wrapping her shawl over her shoulders. "Let's go before he starts making bird noises again."

Cordelia followed them out the door with her fingers crossed.

Seven

Despite Cordelia's best efforts to leave early, Uncle Theo's coach pulled into Raleigh Square at the last stroke of seven, and he raised the knocker on the double front door of Marsfield House at five minutes past. They handed over their wraps and hats to the butler, who informed them they would be dining al fresco.

Cordelia's breath caught when Burke arrived to escort the party through the main hall and out to the beautiful garden. Although he was excruciatingly correct in his clothing and manners, his hair was just a bit windblown, giving him a rakish air that caused her heart to skip a beat.

The lady of the house met them on the verandah, and after introductions, Anne hooked elbows with Cordelia for the short stroll to the gazebo. Marsfield escorted Granny on his arm. Burke followed with Emily, and Uncle Theo brought up the rear.

"My dear, Precious, you aren't at all what I expected," Anne said. "You're hardly a child at all."

"I'm on the verge of womanhood."

Anne laughed and she leaned closer to whisper. "Does anyone even know what a verge is? All I remember is being treated as a child, yet being expected to act like an adult."

"Exactly," Cordelia said. Already she liked the tall, slim

plainspoken woman in the stylish green dress. "Without the advantage of either. Awkward at best."

"Well, hopefully you'll feel at home here. The evening is to be very casual, *en famille* with a few close friends."

Two small children came running around the corner of the house, screaming and giggling, chased by an astonishingly handsome man.

"These are *mes enfants terrible*," Anne said. She introduced them. Stephen bowed; Andrea introduced her doll, then curtseyed; and Preston raised a dark sardonic eyebrow.

"I resent that implication," Preston said.

Cordelia caught his eye, and she had the sudden feeling he saw straight through her disguise.

Preston bowed over Cordelia's hand. "Whatever Anne or Burke has told you about me, let me assure you, I am worse."

She felt the warmth of his lips through her thin white cotton gloves and a shiver of unease traveled up her arm.

Preston looked up at her, the expression in his chocolate brown eyes saying he was aware of her reaction. He leaned in closer. "And also much, much better," he said, his whisper meant for her ears alone, his voice deep and breathy.

Cordelia snatched her hand back and felt a blush stain her cheeks. "Pleased to meet you," she stammered. Preston was dangerous to anyone wearing skirts, even short skirts and pantalets.

Burke stepped forward, as if to protect her, and she breathed a sigh of relief. Nothing bad would happen to her when Burke was at her side. She laid her hand on his arm, and the strength she felt beneath the cloth gave her the confidence to continue the evening.

Emily elbowed her way forward for an introduction

to Preston, and she oozed charm and sophistication. Cordelia made a mental note to keep an eye on her sister, now paired with Preston, as they continued to stroll through the garden. Emily was in enough trouble already.

In the gazebo, a round table had been set for six with linen tablecloths, bone china, crystal glasses, and silver candelabra. A second, smaller, square table had been set for four with dishes designed to be appealing to, and safe for, children.

Anne apologized to Cordelia for assuming she would be more comfortable at the smaller table. "I will have the tables reset immediately."

"Please don't bother," Cordelia said. "In truth, it's fine." She chose a chair at the smaller table at random and sat.

Anne seated the children, Stephen to Cordelia's right and Andrea across the table. To Cordelia's surprise, Lord Marsfield took the fourth seat at the children's table.

"I'm here for your protection," he explained. "These young hooligans know they'd better behave." He gave each of his offspring a fierce look, which didn't seem to upset either one.

"Burke tells me you went to the Crystal Pavilion today," he said to Cordelia with a genuine smile. "Do you have an interest in botany?"

"I want Burke to sit with us," Andrea said, clapping her hands.

"Burke. Burke," Stephen echoed.

"Now—"

"It's all right, sir," Burke said, stepping forward. "I'd be pleased to be seated at this table."

Marsfield hesitated, then rose.

"Truly, sir. I'd prefer it." Burke sat in Marsfield's place.

"You children behave now," Marsfield said with another stern look.

"Yes sir," both Burke and Cordelia answered. Andrea and Stephen giggled.

"Isn't Burke nice?" Andrea asked Cordelia. When she nodded, the little girl added, "I'm going to marry him when I grow up."

Cordelia relaxed.

"Boat," Stephen said, looking around with panicked expression.

Burke found the toy under the boy's chair and set it on the corner of the table.

"Is that a steamship?" Cordelia asked.

"Yes," Burke responded with a surprised smile. "It's a scale model of the *Helene.*"

"I thought I recognized the general shape from an article I read in the *Scientific Journal.*"

"Another of—"

"My father's subscriptions," Cordelia completed his sentence with a laugh. "Need I add I enjoy reading?"

"I can read," Andrea said, and the conversation took a short tangent while Burke asked about her lessons.

"Helene? That's your sister's name, right?" Cordelia asked as roast beef and vegetables were served. She silently blessed her hostess for not serving her the same plate as the children, tidbits of the adult meal and the inevitable bowl of porridge.

Burke nodded. "I was given the honor of naming the ship, though I'm not sure my sister is flattered. When the *Helene* is launched in two months, she'll be the fastest ship ever to cross the Atlantic, cutting the sailing time by half."

"As someone who has recently spent a miserable amount of time on a ship, I find that possibility fascinating."

"You do?"

"Just think of the implications. Steam travel will revolutionize industry. Overseas mail in weeks instead of months. We once had to wait almost a year for the replacement part for a clock. And trade? The exotic will become readily available. Spices and perfumes. Aromatic woods and oils." She realized she'd taken over the conversation. "Pardon me. I do tend to go on when I get excited."

"That's quite all right," Burke said. "I feel the same." He smiled at her. Suddenly, he looked away, clearing his throat. "What would you want, if you could have anything from a faraway country?" he asked the children.

"A kimono," Andrea answered immediately. She turned to Cordelia and explained in a very grown-up tone, "That's a Japanese dress. Preston went on expedition with Sir Richard Burton, and sent me dolls from all over the world. The one from Japan is my favorite because she has a kimono and funny shoes. I don't play with her too much because she's delicate."

"How about you, mate?" Burke asked Stephen.

"Do they have boats in Japan?"

"Yes they do, but you have the whole world to choose from. Africa, Australia, Alaska?"

"I like boats," Stephen insisted.

"Then a Japanese boat for you," Burke said, ruffling the boy's hair. He looked at Cordelia. "And you, Precious? What is your exotic desire?"

"Oranges."

"Not silks from China? Rubies from India?"

She inclined her head. "Not that I don't value and enjoy fine things, but you only gave me one choice, right? And if that's the case, then I choose oranges."

Burke leaned back in his chair and sipped his wine. "May I be presumptuous and inquire why?"

"The answer is hardly worth the effort."

He encouraged her to continue with a nod and wave of his glass.

"My father used to take me to the market in Savannah, and as a special treat buy me an orange. I remember thinking it was like holding the sun in my hand, like eating sunshine." She shrugged. "Our diet has been somewhat limited lately."

"If Precious wants an orange, then I want one, too," Andrea said.

Cordelia caught snippets of conversation from the larger table, but other than noticing that Emily sat next to Preston, she paid them little attention. Once she thought she caught Preston staring at her, but she dismissed the notion. Obviously a man of sophisticated tastes, he wouldn't find a schoolgirl the least bit interesting. Still, he unnerved her. She was thankful for Burke's solid presence nearby.

Though served on a plate with designs from the Aunt Bunny series of children's books, the roast beef was succulent, and the vegetables tender. She had no call to feel self-conscious when Burke was eating his dinner off a plate bearing a picture of a duck wearing a mackintosh and carrying an umbrella. She was a bit startled when she reached the bottom of her mug of watered wine to find a ceramic frog staring back at her. Her tablemates had obviously been waiting for the moment, because they laughed in delight.

Cordelia thoroughly enjoyed dinner. In many ways, it reminded her of family dinners when she was young, before her mother got sick, before the war.

Over a tasty trifle for desert, Cordelia noticed her sister's chair had somehow slid closer to Preston's.

"La, how you go on," Emily said to him. "Such flattery is bound to go to my head."

Cordelia agreed.

Anne excused herself from the table and came over to pick up Stephen, who was already nodding off. "I think

I'd better get these two up to bed." She held her hand out for Andrea.

"I want Precious to tuck me in," the little girl said.

Cordelia stood immediately. "I'd love to," she said. "Emily can come with us." Before her sister had a chance to decline, she added, "It will give you a chance to fix that bit of hair." She made a little motion toward the back of her head and frowned.

Emily jumped up, touching her hair in several places. "If you'll excuse me."

They made quite a parade. Anne leading with a sleepy boy in her arms. Cordelia and Andrea skipping along holding hands. And Emily following in their wake, trying to keep up so as not to get lost in the large house and yet checking in every shiny reflective surface for the fault with her hair.

Emily and Cordelia admired Andrea's doll collection while Mayberry, the children's governess, changed the little girl's clothes. Anne excused herself, saying she wanted to get the boy into his pajamas before he was completely asleep, and she continued on into Stephen's room next door.

Andrea climbed into her bed and pulled the covers up over herself and her doll.

"If you don't mind," Mayberry said, "I'll help Lady Marsfield and then I'll be right back."

"That's fine," Cordelia said. "We'll wait here with Andrea."

"Will you sing me a song," Andrea asked as Mayberry left.

"Emily will," Cordelia said, before her sister could sneak away. "Her voice is much nicer than mine. Now, close your eyes."

Under Cordelia's watchful eye, Emily sang three songs

before the child fell asleep. She motioned for Emily to step away.

"What was that about?" Emily whispered. "There's nothing wrong with my hair."

"You need the practice," Cordelia whispered back, nodding toward the sleeping child. "Thanksgiving and the baby will be here before you know it."

Emily waved off Cordelia's concern. "You worry about the baby too much."

Cordelia grabbed her sister's arm. "I have to worry because you don't. I'm doing everything I can to find Ernest. The father, in case you forgot."

"How could I?"

"Burke has promised to help me. It's him you should be nice to, not his friend, the London Lothario."

"All right, all right. I'll be nice to him." When Cordelia didn't let go of her arm, Emily asked, "What else do you want from me?"

"Just remember. I'm here to find Ernest so the baby will have a father before it's born, not to gather more beaus for you. At the very least, I expect you to help me."

Mayberry came in the door, and the sisters left after wishing her a whispered good night. They had just rejoined the party in the garden when Granny and Uncle Theo announced they preferred not to prolong the evening, and the gathering broke up early. In the carriage on the way home, Cordelia realized Granny had behaved normally. She gave her grandmother a hug. As far as Cordelia was concerned, the evening had been a success.

Burke sat in the large maroon leather chair in Marsfield's library, warming a brandy glass in his palms. "Well, what did you think of Emily?"

"I'd rather talk about Precious," Preston said, sipping his brandy.

Burke glared at him, before turning to Anne. "What's your opinion? Did you notice anything suspicious about Emily's behavior?"

"Nothing," Anne said. "She's either very smart and very good at her job, or she's innocent."

"I agree," Marsfield said.

Burke nodded, agreeing with their assessment. "We'll continue watching as before. Something is bound to slip soon."

"Now can we discuss Precious?" Preston said.

"Why?" Anne asked. "I found her delightful."

"Me too," Marsfield added.

"If you ask me—"

"Which we didn't," Burke said.

Preston continued in spite of Burke's thinly veiled warning. "If that girl has never been out of the schoolroom, I'll eat my hat."

"You're confusing Emily and Precious," Burke said.

Preston gave back his hard glare of earlier. "I'm never confused about women."

Andrea came running into the room. "Mommy, Mommy." She crawled up into Anne's lap.

"Hello, Pumpkin. What are you doing out of bed? I think all the other little six-year-old girls in London are sound asleep by now. Where's Mayberry?"

"She's asleep in the chair by Stephen's bed. Mommy, can I get a baby?"

"Well, sweetie—"

"Precious is going to get a baby. Can I have one, too?"

Anne motioned for the men to stay out of the conversation. "Why do you say that?"

Andrea tucked her doll under her arm. "I closed my eyes like Precious told me, but she didn't say I had to go to sleep, so I stayed awake. Mommy, what is Thanksgiving?"

"It's an American holiday. In November."

"Do 'Mericans get presents at Thanksgiving?"

"I don't think so. Why?"

"Precious is getting a baby at Thanksgiving. That's what she said." Andrea furrowed her little brow. "First she has to get married, doesn't she? Mommy, do we know Ernest?"

At the sound of breaking glass, Burke looked down at his hands in surprise. His brandy glass had splintered into a thousand pieces.

Eight

"Stop fussing over me," Burke said as Anne dabbed iodine on the tiny cuts on his hands. "It looks worse than it is." One minute he'd been holding his glass of brandy between his palms, and the next, it had disintegrated into bloody shards when he'd involuntarily fisted his hands at the sudden realization of the truth. Precious was going to have Ernest's child.

His hands convulsed again.

"Relax. I'm almost done. I've gotten out all the glass and you don't need stitches. I'm just glad Marsfield had the presence of mind to step into Andrea's line of sight and bundle her off upstairs before she had a chance to get hysterical at the sight of so much blood."

"My sincere—"

"Stop apologizing. Accidents happen." She pulled a roll of gauze from her basket of medical supplies.

"Of course I'll replace the carpet, whatever the cost."

Anne waived Burke's offer. "We put everything of value into storage until the children are a bit older," she said.

Marsfield explained. "I hated growing up not being able to touch anything, always being terrified of breaking something."

Burke nodded. If only his mother had had the same good sense, he would have been much happier as a child.

"How are the hands?" Marsfield asked.

"I'll be fine, sir."

Anne finished wrapping his hands and stood to gather her supplies. "No serious damage. However, I'll want to look at those cuts tomorrow and change the bandages."

"I'll be busy tomorrow," Burke said, without looking her in the eye.

Marsfield returned to his seat by way of the decanter. Handing Burke another glass of brandy, he said, "Drink this one."

"I'm sorry," Preston said.

"You called it right," Burke admitted, carefully balancing the glass between his bandaged hands.

"Now just a minute," Anne said. "You shouldn't make judgments based on the word of an impressionable six-year-old."

"Calm down," Marsfield said. "I'm sorry to have to say it, but I believe Andrea's story. She mentioned Thanksgiving as the due date, and I don't think she's ever heard of that particular holiday before tonight. I questioned her again upstairs, and she gave the same answers. When she makes things up, the story changes with each telling."

Anne shook her head. "That doesn't mean—"

Burke cleared his throat. "Yesterday Precious asked me to help her find someone she met last spring, a friend, someone who came home to London quite recently. She said she wanted to return a book she'd borrowed, and though I offered to run her errand, she insisted she had to complete the task in person. At the time, I didn't think it significant." He took a gulp of his brandy. "That man's name is Ernest Truebrill."

An audible gasp was followed by a long silence.

"Oh, Burke . . ." Anne extended her hand, letting it drop limp into her lap when he didn't take it.

No wonder he'd sensed a maturity in Precious he couldn't name. She wasn't an innocent girl, but an experienced woman. He downed the rest of his brandy in one gulp.

"And have you found this Truebrill fellow?" Marsfield asked.

"Not yet, but I will." He had no doubt of that now. He would find Ernest Truebrill if it was the last thing he ever did.

"Preston and I will help—"

"Thank you, sir, but I'll do this myself."

"Burke, you're not thinking of . . . ?" Anne's hand went to her throat. "That won't solve—"

"I don't intend to kill him," Burke said. Beat him to within an inch of his miserable life maybe, but not kill him, even though the scum of the earth deserved it. "At least not before he marries Precious." He stood and headed for the door. "I need some air."

"Good idea," Preston said, jumping up and following him. "Let's go have a few drinks, maybe gamble a bit, find some—"

Burke turned and placed his hand on Preston's shoulder. "Not tonight. I appreciate the offer, but I think I'd rather be alone."

"You know where I am if you need someone to watch your back."

"Thanks, mate."

"Don't do anything foolish, my friend."

Burke nodded.

He walked, hoping to dull the anguish. He walked through the worst parts of town, practically begging someone to attack him for his fat purse, or his fine coat, or his expensive boots. Though he boxed several times a week to stay in shape, he'd avoided violence all his adult life, fearing the strength of his fists should he lose control. Tonight he wanted a fight, wanted to feel the slickness of bloodied flesh beneath his bare knuckles. He ripped off the bandages in preparation, but even the most desperate of thugs must have sensed the blood-lust in him because they all gave him a wide berth.

So he walked alone, without direction, without destination.

He'd never been much of a drinking man, but he stopped here and there along the way for an ale, another brandy, a whiskey, whatever was available. Instead of dulling the agony and fogging his brain, the alcohol seemed to make his thoughts clearer.

Most surprising to him, the revelation about Precious didn't change the way he felt about her. He still got a warm feeling when he recalled her laughter or her smile. Burke realized he cared for her in a way he'd never felt about anyone else. Was that love? Hell if he knew. He'd always figured he was too rational, too logical to ever fall in love.

His best friend, Preston, fell in love several times a year, so he should know what it felt like. He'd never described it as gut-wrenching pain. Euphoric, transcending, and empowering were the words Preston used to describe love. Burke felt none of those. Therefore, using deductive reasoning, he was not in love, could not be in love, but he did care about Precious. So he walked, and found himself across from her house.

If he cared about her, the best he could do for her was the last thing he wanted to do, find Ernest and bring him to her. He wrapped his arm around the lamppost and leaned against the cool metal.

Cordelia awoke in the middle of the night, sitting bolt upright in bed, automatically reaching for the pistol she kept under her pillow before she realized she was no longer in the little cabin in Georgia. She was at Theo's.

Safe. Light from the nearly full moon streamed in the window, and the clock showed it was well past midnight. She lay back down.

Whatever nightmare or noise had disturbed her, she was wide awake and couldn't go back to sleep. After tossing and turning for a few minutes, Cordelia decided to go down to the kitchen for a cup of warm milk. She rose and put on her robe and slippers. On the way to the desk for the lamp to light her way, she glanced out the window and stopped in her tracks.

She would know him anywhere, pick him out of any crowd. What was Burke doing out there? He was standing, slumped. Was he drunk? Foolish man. Standing there like that, he was easy prey for footpads or thieves. What if he had already been attacked? What if he was hurt? She grabbed the lamp and flew down the stairs.

Because the household residents were all inside, there was no footman asleep by the door waiting to open it. She set the lamp on the table in the entryway, grabbed the first cloak she touched, and slipped out the front door even as she swung the wrap around her.

Holding the cloak close to keep from tripping, she ran down the front steps and across the empty street.

"Burke? Are you all right? What are you doing here?"

He blinked down at her. "I believe that is my question, young lady." Despite his state, his words were clear, his enunciation precise. "What are you doing out at this time of night?"

He tried to straighten up and stumbled. She slipped under his arm to steady him. She smelled alcohol and cigar smoke on his greatcoat.

"Come inside and I'll get you some coffee."

"I don't want coffee," he said. "It'll stunt my growth." Throwing his head back, he laughed at his own joke as if it was the funniest thing he'd ever heard.

"Shhhh. You'll wake everyone in the neighborhood." She had one arm around his waist, but pushing and pulling with all her might, she failed to budge him. "You have to move your feet and help me. Or would you rather we stand here all night?"

"You should not be out in the night air," he said. "It's not good for you, or . . ." He straightened up. "I will escort you to your door."

"Thank you," she said, without letting go of him. She steered him in an almost straight line across the street.

At the steps he hesitated, but she'd already found the key to making him do as she wished. "Come on," she urged. "Help me up the stairs and into the house."

"At your service," he mumbled.

Once inside, she spun him a quarter turn, the highly waxed floor aiding her task. "Please, may I have your arm into the library. It's dark and I'm afraid I may stumble."

"Never fear, my lady." He slapped his fist to his chest, nearly unbalancing them both. "Your Viking warrior is here to protect you."

So he'd heard her comment the other morning on the verandah, and remembered what she'd said. Her cheeks heated, but she concentrated on steering him into the library. Only a single stream of moonlight came through the almost closed drapes, making the room near pitch dark. Once she had him positioned with the sofa behind his knees, she gave him a push and he fell backward, taking her with him.

She struggled to rise, impossible with some of her robe and cloak trapped beneath his bulk.

"Be still for a minute," he said, his voice low and soft. With one hand he guided her head to his chest and cradled it there. "I have something to say, and it will be easier for me if I'm not looking at you."

She stilled in trepidation.

"Precious . . ."

Oh, how she wanted to hear him whisper her true name. She blinked away the moisture from her eyes.

"I know about the baby," he said.

She popped her head up to look at him, but the light was in her eyes, only reflecting the top of his blond head, his face hidden in shadow. She didn't want him to judge Emily harshly. "Burke—"

"It will also be easier, if you don't speak until I'm done."

He stroked her cheek with the lightest touch, surprising considering the size of his hands, but somehow not unexpected. Ever so gently, he urged her head back down to his chest. The warmth of his body drew her like a comforting fire on a winter's night, and she snuggled into his arms.

"I care about you," he continued. "I want you to know that whatever happens, I'm your friend."

His heartbeat thundered in her ear, like primitive jungle drums, setting her pulse racing. The echo of his deep voice in his chest fascinated her so, she barely registered his words.

"You asked me to find Ernest, and I'll do that for you. But I want you to consider an alternative."

She turned her head, burrowing into his shirtfront for a whiff of his woodsy cologne and the clean smell of soap and shirt starch and . . . something else. Distinctly him. Undeniable, and definitely sensual. Wonderful.

"Although he is the biological father, perhaps he is not the best choice."

Tentatively, she laid her hand on his chest, tracing the shape of his muscles with her fingers. Growing bolder as she heard his breath catch.

"I love children, and since, for reasons I would rather

not discuss, I'll never have offspring of my own, I am willing . . . I know I'm making a muddle of this." He took a deep breath. "For the baby's sake, I offer my name, myself, my—"

"You what?" Cordelia sat up so fast, the clasp on the cloak ripped and the three buttons on her robe popped loose and scattered across the floor. She jumped up and glared down at him.

"I offer to be the father—"

"In one breath you say you care for me and the next you offer yourself to be the father?" she asked, emphasizing each word. "Like . . . like some pagan sacrifice on the matrimonial altar?"

Befuddled, Burke stared up at her. A warrior goddess in a thin nightdress. In her anger, he recognized a glorious woman full grown. Highlighted by the shaft of moonlight, her eyes flashed and her breasts heaved. His body reacted, rising to full awareness, saluting her unique beauty.

This was the woman he wanted to bear his sons, give birth to his daughters. His mother's hurtful words rang in his memory, and pain wrenched his gut. He would not have children.

The logical, rational part of him fought for control, warned him not to do something he'd soon regret. But he missed the comfort and rightness of her sweet body next to him, close to his heart. He wanted to hold her. The need to touch her skin became a physical ache. Hungry for the taste of her lips, he opened his arms. "Precious," he whispered. *Come to me,* he willed.

Cordelia stepped back a pace, distance her only defense from the naked desire clearly written on his face. But Emily was the one who had what he wanted, the one who needed a decent father for her baby. Burke would make a marvelous father.

Anger surged through her at the unfairness of life. Burke deserved a house full of big, beautiful children. A veritable Viking horde of little blond boys in short pants and little blond girls in ruffles and ridiculous big bows. Cordelia wanted to be their mother. Unfair, unfair, unfair. The man her heart had chosen wanted to marry Emily. Not Cordelia. She wanted to rant and wail and throw things, but she couldn't.

Because of Emily and the baby, she couldn't.

"I think you'd better leave," she managed to choke out, wanting him gone before her anger and frustration manifested itself in tears.

He stood and held out his hand. "Precious . . ."

She forced herself to take another step back, and jammed her fists on her hips. "Don't you *Precious* me. You're drunk and you have no idea what you're saying."

"I'm not that drunk. Your baby needs a decent father. I'm offering to—"

"It's not *my* baby." Cordelia staggered back another step. Burke thought she was expecting, not Emily. He was offering to marry her, Cordelia, or rather, Precious. She squashed the tiny thrill the thought gave her. As soon as he sobered up and realized Emily was the one who needed a father for her baby, he would change his mind and offer for her.

Burke blinked and shook his head. "All right, I offer to be the father of *the* baby."

"I'm not the one you want."

"I'm very serious about this."

Her eyes watered. She had to get away from him. "Fine. I'll consider your offer to be sincere and I'll talk to Emily for you." She stalked to the door and threw it open. "Now go home, or to your club, or wherever it is you English gentlemen go to sleep it off, but go."

He lumbered toward her, inebriation robbing him of

his usual easy grace, and for some reason that angered her more.

"Can't we—"

"No." She turned from him and fled into the entry-way, cursing herself for not bringing her derringer from under her pillow. She looked around the entrance hall for anything she could use to threaten him into leaving. The vase of roses? No. She pulled open the drawer in the small table, looking for a letter opener, a . . . she found a loaded pistol, apparently kept there against robbers and thieves. Burke followed into the entrance. She whirled around and pointed the pistol at him. "You will go. Now."

He stumbled and looked around.

"What are you waiting for? If you think I don't know how to use this—"

"My hat. I know I had a hat." He patted his pockets as if he thought to find it there.

His confusion was so comically pitiful, her heart went out to him, threatening to rob her of her sustaining anger. She steeled herself. Only a foolish woman would find such bumbling appealing.

"Out. Or you'll be looking for your . . ." The barrel of the pistol wavered up and down as she looked at him from head to toe and back. Several vital body parts occurred to her, and her cheeks burned with the direction of her thoughts. She snapped the pistol upward. "Or you'll be looking for your head."

Burke stared at her for a long minute. "I will return tomorrow for an answer." Then he turned on his heel and left.

Even if Emily didn't think Burke exciting, would she take him up on his offer? He was handsome, and titled, and would be rich when his steamboat project was completed if he wasn't already. Emily's dream match.

Cordelia slumped, her arm falling boneless to her side. She would not let herself cry. Tears were a waste of energy better spent dealing with the situation the best one could. The last few years had taught her that lesson, the hard way.

Suddenly she realized someone had removed the pistol from her nerveless fingers. She spun around.

"Oh, Granny. What are you doing here?"

Granny turned her head and said, "Theo, see the boy gets home safely."

"Uncle Theo, too?" Suddenly the oddity of the situation hit her. "What are you doing down here? How long have you been standing here?" She looked around in embarrassment.

"Not long. Theo and I were playing chess in his study when we heard a noise and thought it was a thief or burglar. We came to investigate."

"Does this mean you and Uncle Theo are reconciled?"

"Certainly not. At our age we tend to nap in the afternoon and therefore need less sleep at night. Chess is simply a quiet method to match wits, though in Theo's case it's barely worth the effort."

"But you're dressed," Cordelia said.

"Well, we weren't playing chess naked."

"I meant you're dressed to go out."

"We came down the back stairs and in the front door to surprise the burglar."

"I didn't hear you come in."

"I can see why," Granny muttered.

Cordelia covered her face with her hands.

"Oh, stop that. Theo didn't see anything, and it will take more than a little snuggling to upset me. Now, let's get you upstairs to bed. Everything will look brighter tomorrow."

Cordelia allowed her grandmother to escort her to

her room, but she didn't believe a word she said. Nothing would ever look bright again. "I don't like London anymore. I want to go home."

"Yes, dear, but we have a few things to do first."

Cordelia nodded. Even though Granny didn't know about the letters, it served as a reminder to Cordelia that she still had her errands for Madame Lavonne to complete. She still had two more letters to deliver, and had been remiss in completing her important tasks.

"Once Emily is married and settled down, we'll leave the city," Granny said. "Maybe we'll go to Paris for a while. Or Italy. I've always wanted to see Rome."

"We don't have any money." Cordelia climbed into her bed.

"Don't you worry. Everything will work out."

"What if we can't find Ernest? What if Burke—"

"Now there's no sense borrowing trouble." Granny pulled up the covers and kissed her forehead.

Cordelia nodded. She had enough troubles of her own without worrying about Emily.

"Here's a little good luck charm," Granny said, tucking a tiny ball of calico fabric tied with red yarn into her hand.

It looked suspiciously like the love charm she'd purchased from Madame Callisto a.k.a. Granny just the other day, and she said so.

Granny chuckled. "Sometimes luck and love are one and the same. Sweet dreams, my dear."

Cordelia didn't see how a bunch of herbs were going to help, but she didn't want to hurt Granny's feelings. "Thank you," she whispered, closing her eyes even though she knew she'd never fall asleep. Left alone, she gripped the charm tightly. So far the love charm had been a disaster, and she needed more than a little luck. She needed a plan.

Determination renewed, she rose once again, and splashed her face with cool water from the washstand. Finding paper, ink, and pen in the desk, she listed everything she could remember about Ernest. Anything that could be used to help locate him. The sooner the better.

Nine

Cordelia closed her hymnal, and as the choir sang the final benediction of the Sunday morning service, she whispered to Granny, "I'm going to speak to the organist."

"Why?"

"I'd like to . . . to tell him how much I enjoyed his solo," Cordelia said for lack of anything more imaginative. She could hardly tell Granny that the organist was the intended recipient of the second letter from Madame Lavonne.

Granny raised her eyebrows, but after a moment's hesitation she nodded. As the crowd filled the aisle, Cordelia fought the tide rushing toward the exit and reached the steps leading up to the organist's perch as he finished the last strains of the recessional.

Cordelia looked at her program for the organist's name. "Mr. Fletcher?"

The young man looked down at her with a surprised expression. "Yes?"

In order to pass him the note, she needed to get closer to him. Even if he descended the stairs, there were still a number of people in the sanctuary of the church. She wanted to finish her errand quickly, and in private, before Granny came looking for her. "May I come up? I'd like to see your organ."

"Well, ah, yes, I suppose so." The man blushed to the edge of his receeding hairline.

Cordelia climbed the eight steps to the small area that contained the five-tiered keyboards of the huge pipe organ.

"How can I help you, miss?" he asked.

Mindful of her mission, Cordelia worked the password into the conversation. "You play beautifully. Like an archangel."

"Thank you. I did my best on such short notice. I didn't find out the regular organist was sick until last night. I would have done better if I'd had more time to practice the selections."

"I think you did quite well. I had hoped to meet the regular organist to . . . to ask about music lessons."

Mr. Fletcher gave her a toothy grin. "I give private lessons. Very nice private lessons."

Something in his tone made Cordelia edge toward the stairs. "I don't think my uncle would approve. When will the regular organist return?"

Mr. Fletcher took a step toward her, very close in the small space.

"Never mind," Cordelia said, turning and running down the stairs.

"Thursday-night choir practice," he called after her. "Unless she's still sick. Then I'll be here."

Cordelia knew she would have to come back. She said a fervent prayer for the regular organist's recovery.

Burke woke with a groan, the sharp sunlight piercing his eyelids like red-hot needles. He rolled over, pulling the blanket over his head.

"Good morning, Sleeping Beauty. Or should I say good afternoon," Preston said in a voice entirely too chipper.

"Go away," Burke mumbled.

"Rise and shine. You're wasting the shank of the day."

"What time is it?"

"Two o'clock in the afternoon."

"Get out of my house and let me die in peace."

"Difficult, old boy, since this is my house."

Burke struggled to a sitting position, blinking Preston's small but elegant parlor into focus. Even though Preston spent much of his time traveling, he refused to stay at his family home and kept the stylish townhouse for when he was in London. Scattered around the gold and green room were souvenirs from his expedition days with Sir Burton, a tiger-skin rug, crossed samurai swords over the mantelpiece, a Tibetan throw made from yak hair on one of the side chairs. Not at all like Burke's simple utilitarian furnishings in his wing of the house that he shared with his mother and sister.

"How did I get here?"

"You refused to go home, so Gravely brought you here."

"Gravely? Where did I meet up with him?"

Preston shrugged. "No clue. You showed up at my door not too long after I got home. Must have been one-thirty or so. But that's past, and we have an errand today, so drink this." He removed a tall glass from the tray on the table next to him, leaned forward, and handed it to Burke.

Burke sniffed the glass and jerked his head away from the dark, vile-smelling liquid. He moaned with the throbbing of his brain sloshing around within his skull. "Are you trying to kill me?"

"That's the best hangover cure known to man or beast. My man Kelso's private recipe."

"What's in it?"

"You don't want to know. Trust me, old friend, and just drink it down all at once. No use prolonging the agony."

Burke trusted that Preston knew more about hangovers

than he did, so he held his nose and chugged the entire glass. He looked down at the unfamiliar nightshirt and then searched the area around the sofa. "Where are my pants? And my shoes?"

"Upstairs in the guest room." Preston stood, smoothing his immaculate waistcoat. "Kelso brushed and pressed your clothes, working half the night so you would look presentable when you exited his domain. Then he realized you couldn't possibly be seen leaving in broad daylight wearing evening clothes without damaging his reputation as a valet of the first water, so he fetched a change for you as well as your shaving gear. As soon as you're washed and dressed, we're off to see Harry Linchford. I sent a note around for him to expect us at three-thirty."

"Linchford? As in Sniffles Linchford? Good Lord, whatever for? Haven't seen him since Eton, and can't say as I've regretted it a bit. Always sick with some dreadful disease like the Black Plague or the Red Death."

"Yes, I'd assumed he'd died of terminal hypochondria by now, but when I asked around the club this morning, his name came up as a Christopher Wren scholar. Apparently he developed a real passion for architecture."

The word passion sparked a vague memory. Burke had a sudden sick feeling that he'd forgotten more than a few drinks. "Did I . . ."

"Yes, you told me everything about Ernest Truebrill, ad infinitum, ad nauseum, until about three in the morning when you finally finished off the last of my best brandy, which I hold you accountable to replace, and collapsed right where you're sitting. Since there was not an icicle's chance in hell of me dragging you upstairs, I threw a blanket over you and warned the servants to stay clear."

"Did I . . ."

"You have Kelso to thank for insisting you not sleep in the clothes he wanted to clean. It took the two of us and a brawny footman to get that nightshirt on you, and, believe me, I will never undertake such a task again."

"Did I . . ."

"Yes, and I agree Truebrill's house is the fastest way to trace him, but I decided not to wait until the Hall of Records opens tomorrow, and looked for other avenues to obtain the same information."

Burke was already beginning to feel better. At least physically. "Hardly logical," he muttered.

"Personally I like the word inspired." Preston shrugged. "What can I say, I'm impatient. And since the cad skipped town once, I don't want to give him another chance."

"What I need to know is, did I really go to see Precious last night? I vaguely remember—"

"As to that, I can't say one way or the other. I hope not. Since she is so close to Emily, it would have been a stupid move to tip our hand with so much riding on this case."

"I don't remember talking about Emily. Just . . . just the baby." Burke let his head fall into his hands.

Preston patted him on the shoulder. "One step at a time, friend. Let's find Ernest first, then worry about what happens after that." He tugged twice on the bellpull to summon his valet.

Burke nodded and stood, amazingly steady, all things considered.

Kelso arrived with a robe over one arm and a tray with a steaming cup of coffee in his hands. "Good afternoon, Lord Deering," he said, his funereal voice and solemn face belying his cheerful words.

"You should bottle that cure, Kelso. You could make a million pounds a year." Burke donned the robe.

"I'm pleased you found it effective," Kelso said, bowing without spilling a drop of coffee. "However, the cure must be mixed fresh and drunk immediately or it will turn rancid."

"Not that anyone could tell," Burke muttered under his breath as he took the proffered cup of coffee.

"A valet's recipes are passed down from father to son. I once was offered two thousand pounds for my black shoe polish formula but had to refuse."

"That's a small fortune," Burke said.

Kelso shook his head sadly. "Well, I know it. But my family has been in service for six generations, and my father would spin in his grave if I went into trade with the family secrets."

"Well, should you ever tire of Preston here, you'll certainly find a welcome on my staff."

"Thank you, sir. Working for his lordship has been rather tame of late."

"Ho, Burke, you'll have to go far to entice Kelso to employment. He became addicted to the thrill of foreign travel when we were with Burton. A tiger ransacking our tent in India. Tarantulas in our shoes in South America. Leeches in the laundry water in Africa. Quite the thing, eh?"

"Yes, milord. I certainly miss the excitement," Kelso said, the same unvarying undertaker's tone to his voice.

Preston nodded with a rueful smile.

"When you're finished with your coffee, Lord Deering, I have prepared a hot bath with Epsom salts to remove the balance of the toxins you ingested. After that, a dose of my energizing tonic, and I predict a complete recovery."

Burke drained his coffee cup and replaced it on the tray.

"As long as it tastes better than the cure."

"Gooseberry-flavored, sir."

"Then lead on to the prescribed treatment." Burke

hesitated by the door and turned around to face his friend. "Perhaps we should take along some tonic for Linchford. You know, to smooth over any difficulties."

"Surely, you don't expect problems from Sniffles the Scholar?"

"The object of a man's passion is irrelevant. Danger is an inherent possibility when intense emotions are involved." As Burke said the words, he realized how close to home the truth struck. A warning he must remember to heed.

Cordelia sat at the desk in the parlor and gripped her pen with fingers stiffened by anger. "Think harder, Emily. Surely you must remember something Ernest said that would help us find him."

Emily sat on the sofa and yawned delicately behind her handkerchief. "We've already been over this a thousand times. In the cabin. On the ship. Now here. I've already told you everything."

"None of this is useful. Did he mention his father's name? The name of his estate?"

"We did not spend our limited time together talking about his father."

"Obviously."

Emily rose and stalked to the other side of the desk. Laying her palms on the wood, she leaned halfway over the barrier. "What was that snide comment supposed to mean?"

Cordelia stood. She also leaned across the desk, stopping with her face inches from her sister's. "If you'd spent more time talking about normal, reasonable subjects, like a man's family or his home, we wouldn't be in this mess."

"If that's what you talk about when you're with a man, it's no wonder you're an old maid."

"Better a spinster than a—"

"Girls, girls," Granny said from her seat near the fireplace, the grate empty in the afternoon sunshine. "It upsets me so to see my sweet girls argue. Now come sit down, have some tea, and let's discuss this like rational adults."

Cordelia straightened and took a deep breath. The last thing she needed today was to upset her grandmother. She realized a good portion of her anger resulted from Burke's offer of marriage, something she hadn't even mentioned to Emily yet.

So she followed Granny's instructions and sat on the chair across from Emily, who resumed her seat on the sofa. Cordelia spread her list on her knee. After several hours of deep thinking last night and the current interrogation, her list of known facts about Ernest seemed distressingly inadequate.

"Thank you," she muttered as Emily handed her a cup.

"Now, let's take stock," Granny said, adjusting her glasses on her nose and reaching for the list. "We have a description of his house, and Lord Deering has promised to pursue that tomorrow at the Hall of Records. We have the name of his tailor and where he bought his boots, hats, and gloves."

"That's helpful, isn't it?" Emily asked.

"Maybe," Cordelia reluctantly conceded. "The shop owners would have his address for a delivery or a bill, but whether or not they'll divulge that information is another matter."

"We'll have Theo pursue that," Granny said. "Perhaps he buys at the same shops and knows the owners."

"Uncle Theo? What will we tell him is the reason?"

Granny stared down at her hands. "Due to circumstances," she said with a quick peek at Cordelia, "it became necessary for me to tell Theo the truth."

"Oh no," Emily cried, covering her cheeks with her hands. "Now Uncle Theo hates me."

"He doesn't hate any of us," Granny said. "He understands and is determined to help any way he can."

"Thank goodness," Cordelia said. "I've had quite enough of being sixteen again." As soon as she said it, she realized the implication. What would Burke think when he found out she wasn't Precious?

"Oh, you'll still have to pretend to be Precious," Granny said, giving Cordelia a significant look. "I didn't tell him about you, but after last night, Theo needed to know Emily is the one who is expecting. He only knows Emily and I came to London to find the father of her baby."

"Last night?" Emily asked. "What happened last night?"

Granny turned to Cordelia, leaving it up to her to explain. As much as she wanted to avoid the issue, Cordelia told her sister of Burke's visit, leaving out the fact that she'd been lying in his arms at the time he made the offer to become the legal father of the baby.

"Oh, pshaw," Emily said. "If I wanted to marry someone other than Ernest, I could certainly find someone better than him."

"What's wrong with him? You should be flattered that a handsome, titled—"

"Boring, uninteresting—"

"Fascinating, noble man would be willing to sacrifice—"

"Did he say marrying me would be a sacrifice?" Emily said, her tone indignant.

"No. I—"

"Girls, please," Granny interrupted.

"Oh, now I see," Emily said, sitting back in her seat

with a chuckle. "You're sweet on Burke and want him for yourself."

Cordelia shook her head.

"You're afraid I'll take him away from you."

"No," Cordelia said, the lie coming easily to her lips because she knew her sister could have any man she set her mind to, and she didn't want her going after Burke just to prove it once again. "He's simply an honorable gentleman worthy of respect."

"And you . . . respect him a lot."

"That is not—"

"Then what is your point?" Emily said with a knowing smirk.

"You and Ernest, and anything you can remember to help us find him."

"I'm sure you talked about something besides fashion," Granny said. "Ernest must have had other interests."

"Of course. He was a veritable font of information on the current rage of the ton's fashionable elite. Spirituality and fairies, for example."

"Did he mention any particulars? A name? A place?" Cordelia prompted.

Emily shrugged. "I wasn't really listening. A load of hogwash, if you ask—"

"Don't mock what you don't understand," Granny said.

"Anything else?" Cordelia asked before the focus of the conversation drifted again. "Any other topics?"

"Egyptology," Emily said. She shook her head and waved that subject away. "I'm not sure if that was his interest or mine."

"Yours? Since when did you—"

"It was right after one of Granny's Cleopatra days, and

I guess it was on my mind, that's all. Ernest did have an interest in horses, especially racehorses."

"Finally, something of value. A clue we can use," Cordelia said.

"Theo mentioned this morning there's a race next Saturday," Granny said. "Willingham Downs, and I believe Theo reserved a box some time ago. Half the ton will be there."

"That's next week. I was hoping to do something productive today," Cordelia said.

"It's Sunday. A day of rest." Granny said.

"I know the perfect activity for a beautiful Sunday afternoon. A nice carriage ride in the park," Emily said, as she stood. "What shall I wear? My lemon muslin, I think, because it will go with my new bonnet."

"That's another thing," Cordelia said. "I don't think you should be accepting gifts from Uncle Theo." She intended to pay Theo back for his hospitality, someday, somehow. Her sister kept running up the tally of indebtedness.

Emily looked at her as if she'd just dropped in from the ceiling. "I should think you of all people would want Uncle Theo to be happy."

"Of course, I do, but—"

"Well, he told me it gave him great pleasure to buy me a new bonnet. Are you calling him a liar?"

"No, but—"

"Are you saying I'm the liar?"

"No, but—"

"Well, then I don't understand your objection to me accepting a bonnet as a present from him. I'm only trying to make him happy in my own small way. Really, Cordelia, sometimes your selfishness astounds me."

She gave up. Arguing with her sister was an exercise in futility. Emily's world would always revolve around herself.

"Now, if we're going for that drive, I'd better change." Emily gave Cordelia's outfit a significant look.

She still had on the white organdy dress and lace pantalets she'd worn to church that morning. "If you want my company, you'll take me as I am." Organdy ruffles or sailor suit, one schoolgirl dress was as dreadful as another.

"Bring my knitting and shawl with you when you come back down, will you, dear?" Granny asked.

"Aren't you coming with us?" Cordelia asked as Emily left.

"I think not. My rheumatism has been acting up, so I'll just sit here by the fire and knit."

"There isn't any fire," Cordelia pointed out. "It's quite warm today even for the middle of June."

"Maybe for you young people. Just wait until you're my age. Well, maybe my shawl will be enough. Go along and have a good time. I'll be fine."

"I'd rather not leave you alone."

"You can't let Emily go out unchaperoned, and there's a house full of servants if I need anything. I expect Theo will be home shortly."

She caught a sparkle in her grandmother's eye before the woman looked away. So, Granny wanted a chance to be alone with Uncle Theo. Cordelia decided the carriage ride should probably be a long one, at least an hour or two. She only hoped she could put up with Emily's limited topics of conversation for that length of time without strangling her.

Maybe Burke would call, and Granny would send him on Thunderation after the carriage. Cordelia lost herself in the memory of the magnificent warrior atop the worthy steed. In her daydream, Burke caught up to their carriage, and he pointedly ignored Emily.

* * *

"Are you sure Linchford is in?" Burke asked as Preston's carriage pulled up to the address. An eight-foot-tall wrought-iron fence surrounded the modest bungalow, and an overgrowth of thornbushes filled the small yard. "The house looks deserted."

Preston consulted his notebook. "This is the correct street and number. I sent around a note, so he should be expecting us."

They alighted and made their way to the front door, where they waited an inordinately long time for their knock to be answered.

"Can't say what I expected of Old Sniffles, but it wasn't this," Preston said, looking around with disdain. He pulled out his watch. "Perhaps—"

"We'll wait," Burke said. The information Linchford hopefully possessed was too important to miss. Burke by-passed the discreet knocker and pounded on the door with his fist.

Within a minute, the door opened a crack. "What do yer want?" a gruff voice asked.

Burke pulled himself to his full height and shot a menacing glare at the one eye peeking out of the slim opening. "We have an appointment," he said in a tone that implied threat of bodily harm should such rudeness continue.

The door creaked open on unoiled hinges.

Burke and Preston were shown into Linchford's study by a sour, slovenly housekeeper who warned them not to expect tea.

"You won't be here long enough," she added with a cackle, leaving them at the open door.

Burke stepped through first. The floor-to-ceiling shelves were packed with books two-deep, crammed in every which way, as well as architectural models of all sizes and made from every conceivable material. A large table dominated the room, stacked with more books and rolls of drawings. Linchford stood behind the table, hunched over a drawing, peering through a large magnifying glass.

"State your business," he said. "I have little patience for foolishness."

"Good day to you, too," Preston said. "Thank you, we're quite well. Yourself?"

Linchford looked up, his one eye huge through the glass. "One's health, or lack thereof, is no joking matter." He straightened with a groan. "I'd ask you to sit, but, as you see, I designed this room with no chairs, specifically so guests would not linger. I have much more important matters to attend to, and I despise inane chitchat."

"Is all this on Christopher Wren?" Burke asked, his arm encompassing the room. "Impressive."

"The greatest architect the world has known. I am but a humble admirer and collector of his drawings." Linchford bowed as if to an altar of Wren's construction. "Now, since I'm sure this isn't a social call, I'd prefer you get to the point. I have much work to do and so little time left, what with my poor health and all."

"I'm sorry to hear your health isn't what it should be," Burke said.

Linchford nodded. "What is it you want? No, let me guess. You've had a gentleman's disagreement regarding something to do with Wren, and you want me to settle it. Right?"

"Actually—" Burke started to explain, but Preston cut him off.

"Absolutely right. Amazing. How did you guess?"

"That seems to be the only reason anyone seeks me out these days. Though they do say, a man with one foot in the grave can see things others can't."

Burke shifted his weight, anxious to get to the point,

but Preston was on a roll. Burke knew from experience to trust his friend's instincts.

"I've heard that, too," Preston said, his eyes wide. "I expect since it's common knowledge, it must be true."

"It is true," Linchford said. "I'm proof. I use that special sight in my research. That's why my book will be the definitive work on Wren, the man and his work. If I can only finish it in time," he added, shaking his head.

"When you do—finish, that is—let me know. I have a contact or two in the publishing business."

Linchford ran around the table and grabbed Preston's hand, pumping it up and down. "Thank you. Thank you."

Preston rescued his hand and directed Linchford's attention to Burke. "If you'll answer our questions, we'll let you get back to your important work."

"Yes, yes. So much research yet to do before I can even start writing."

Preston nudged Burke, telling him without words to hurry up before they lost Linchford altogether.

"Ahem," Burke said. "We saw a house the other day. Can't remember the address. I said it was obviously a Wren design, but Preston insisted it was not."

"If you can't remember the address," Linchford said with a shrug. "I don't see how you expect me to be of any help."

"The building was made of an unusual yellow marble, columns in the front. A large family residence."

Linchford screwed up his face and scratched his head. Then he scratched his chin, then pulled his ear as he looked around the room as if the other men were no longer there, all the while muttering to himself. "Perhaps . . . yellow marble, you say? Maybe . . . no, he said a family residence. Hmmm." He climbed a few rungs up the library steps and chose a book from the upper shelf.

He leafed through it, not actually looking at the pages, and still talking to himself.

Burke took a leery step toward the door. Old Sniffles had gone completely around the bend.

"I've got it," Linchford hollered. He jumped down with a whoop and spun around in the middle of the room.

Burke looked toward the door, judging how long it would take to reach it.

"Aha." Linchford dove under the table and came up with a large portfolio. "It's in here. I'm sure of it." He cleared a space on the table with a sweep of his arm and flopped the folder open. "There." He motioned them over to the table. "Yellow marble. Columns. An early design, not known by many. Not one of his best, but, then, all of his work has a certain brilliance."

Preston leaned over the drawing, and Burke looked over his shoulder. The address seemed to leap out at him. Fourteen-twenty Fortescue Square.

"It doesn't say anything about the owner," Burke said, unable to hide his disappointment.

"The owner? Hey, what's going on here?"

"That's the other half of the bet," Preston said. "I have twenty quid that says the owner is an Italian who rents it to a former French madame."

"You said a gentleman's disagreement. You never said anything about a bet. I do not participate in gambling matters," Linchford said, pulling himself to his full height of five foot three. "Good day, sirs."

"It's not really gambling," Burke explained. "Since there's no way Preston can be right, it's really just teaching him a well-deserved lesson. Right?"

"I stand resolved," Linchford insisted.

Burke nodded. He pulled the bottle of Kelso's tonic from his pocket. "I understand perfectly. I had brought this as a thank-you gift, but . . ." He placed it on the table. "I don't suppose you'd consider it a trade?"

"What is it?" Linchford asked.

"Oh, just some of Kelso's tonic," Burke said with a shrug. "Quite energizing."

"You didn't," Preston said, leaning over and reaching out, as if to grab the bottle. "You promised never to tell anyone."

Linchford snatched the bottle and scurried behind the table. He pulled the stopper and sniffed the tonic. "Who's Kelso, and what's in it?"

"My valet," Preston answered, his tone reluctant.

"Professional secret," Burke said. "But we can both swear to its efficacious properties."

"I'm not swearing to anything," Preston said. "Give it back." He whirled to face Burke. "You know it's dangerous. If he takes too much, he'll be storming the walls of the nearest brothel, wearing out three, four, even five girls."

"I'm sure we can trust him not to take more than the recommended dose of one spoonful."

Linchford nodded vigorously.

Preston shook his head. "He doesn't settle gambling debts, remember. We don't even know if he has the information."

"I have it," Linchford cried. "I do have it." He cradled the bottle of tonic against his bony chest with one hand, while he dug frantically through a stack of papers with the other. "Here. See?" He laid the paper on the table and stepped back out of reach.

Burke hesitated. He realized a vague, unformed hope had hovered in the back of his mind. A hope that he could honestly tell Precious he'd done his best, but Ernest was nowhere to be found. So much hinged on the information contained on that single page. He swallowed, and stepped forward to read. "Fourteen-twenty Fortescue Square. Owner . . ." He hesitated to get his voice under control. "Major Randall Truebrill, Third Baronet Dandridge, retired."

He turned and left the room without another word.

Preston took the reins from Burke's numb fingers and set the curricle in motion. "Where to?"

"Fortescue Square," Burke said.

"Are you sure? Randall isn't exactly Ernest."

"Could be a legal name. Could be his father. Everything else fits." He couldn't think beyond that.

"We could wait until dark, grab him, and put him on a ship bound for China."

Burke shook his head.

"Don't let your well-developed sense of honor get in the way of your happiness. He doesn't deserve it."

Burke rounded on his friend. "I'm not doing this for him."

"I know. You're doing it for her."

"Cut through Hyde Park," Burke said, indicating a right turn with his hand.

"It'll be packed this time of day."

"Still faster than going around."

"Are you in that much of a hurry?"

Burke nodded. "I have to do it quick, before I change my mind. Before I decide to get on that bloody ship to China myself."

Preston gave the horses the signal, and the matched grays turned into Hyde Park in perfect step with each other.

Ten

"You don't have to flirt with every man we pass," Cordelia hissed to her sister. She just wanted to get through the afternoon without a disaster, but Emily attracted attention wherever she went.

"It's only polite to return a friendly greeting." Emily smiled and nodded to the occupants of a similar open landau pulling off the lane to park in the shade. "What a wonderful idea. Driver, pull over."

"No," Cordelia said. "I don't think—"

"There's Lady Marsfield and the children. We should pay our respects. Look, she's waving to us. If we don't stop, she'll think we're cutting her."

Unfortunately, Cordelia couldn't argue with Emily's logic. "Let's not stay long." At least in a moving carriage, her sister's sphere of contact was limited.

"Why are you being so disagreeable? You're acting as if I'm making you late for a romantic assignation with a fantastic man or something," Emily whispered as the coachman jockeyed the carriage into position.

"Common sense can hardly be termed disagreeable."

As soon the carriage stopped, Emily stood. "Since when do good manners contradict common sense?"

Before the coachman had a chance to jump down and open the door, two young gentlemen performed the duty. Cordelia recognized Mr. Droopy-eyelids and Mr. Twitchy-nose from the ice cream parlor.

"Why Lord Wilcox and Lord Digby, imagine meeting you here," Emily said, holding out her dainty hand. "You remember my dear friend Precious Cosley, don't you?"

Both gentlemen nodded but barely looked her way as they handed her down from the carriage after Emily. They then jockeyed for position beside her sister, each trying to be on Emily's right side and thereby have the honor of her hand on his arm. Mr. Droopy-eyelids won. Cordelia started down the crushed-stone path toward Lady Marsfield at a brisk pace, but soon had to pause and wait for the others to catch up.

"Let's walk a little faster, shall we?" Cordelia said in a falsely sweet tone.

Emily trilled an equally false laugh. "The young are so impetuous," she said to her escorts. "It's much too warm to rush. You may run ahead if you want to, Precious. I'll keep an eye on you from here, but do try and remember you are among the ton now. A certain curtailment of your usual boisterousness is appropriate."

Cordelia fought the urge to stick out her tongue. Her behavior was not in question. Emily was the one not acting like an engaged woman supposedly in love with the father of her baby. Rather than make a snide comment, Cordelia turned and stomped away, refusing to imagine what remark her sister made that caused her admirers to guffaw. She plastered a smile on her face as she approached the Marsfield party.

"Good afternoon, Lady Marsfield." Cordelia curtseyed.

"Hello, Precious. How lovely to see you again." Anne introduced the woman standing with her as her sister Letty, and pointed out her nephew Timmy playing with Stephen and his boat at the edge of the Serpentine. "Andrea was hoping to see you again soon." Anne linked arms with Cordelia and walked with her toward the shade of a nearby tree where Andrea and Mayberry sat on a blanket surrounded by a number of dolls and assorted miniature dresses, hats, and other accessories.

On the way, Anne whispered, "I just want you to know I understand, and I'll always be at home for you if you need to talk." Anne patted her arm. "About anything at all."

Cordelia hadn't the slightest idea what Anne was talking about. "Thank you," she said as they approached the governess and her charge.

"Look, Precious," Andrea said. "This is my Spanish senorita."

Cordelia looked at the doll and wondered how she could tell. Black hair painted on a porcelain head and a bare cloth body gave little clue as to the doll's nationality. "Perhaps you should put some clothes on her," she said, kneeling on the edge of the blanket. "She might feel better meeting a stranger if she had some clothes on."

Anne laughed. "For some reason, Andrea is compelled to undress every doll and switch their clothes around, mixing them up into sometimes quite amusing outfits."

Cordelia absently picked up a doll and a red cotton dress. When she noticed the worried expression on Andrea's face, she looked to the governess.

"Miss Andrea has everything laid out where she wants it," Mayberry explained, and then went back to her embroidery.

Cordelia nodded and put the items back exactly where they had been.

The small party was joined by Emily and her escorts, and as the talk centered on ordinary topics like the unseasonably warm weather, Cordelia's attention drifted.

A good portion of the ton seemed to be strolling about the paths, or seated on benches or blankets in the shade, or making the circuit of the park in their carriages. Anne's sister, Letty, and Emily became instant friends due to their common interest in fashion and gossip. They decided to fetch lemonade for everyone from a nearby vendor. The two young men gallantly offered to escort them and carry back their purchases. Preferring to have a few moments to speak to Lady Marsfield, Cordelia declined to accompany them. She hoped, by subtle questioning, to gain information about Burke. Unfortunately, as they left, a friend of Anne's approached to discuss an upcoming benefit concert they chaired together.

Stephen and his cousin Timmy caught Cordelia's eye. Along this section of the Serpentine, a foot-high brick wall edged the water right next to the wide path of crushed stone. A perfect place for young boys to sail their toy boats. Probably the very reason Lady Marsfield had chosen the spot.

Some instinct prompted Cordelia to stand when the two boys began to argue over who could hold the string that kept the boat from floating away. Timmy tugged hard enough to break the string. Free from its tether, the boat drifted away. From the look on Stephen's face, she knew without a doubt he intended going after it.

Cordelia stood and ran toward the boys before the thought fully formed. Her heartbeat thundered in her ears like heavy footfalls. She reached Stephen just as he got one leg up onto the brick barrier. Grabbing him around the waist, she lifted him up off the wall and swung him back down to the ground.

"No swimming today, young—ooff!" Something heavy slammed into her shoulder. The wall hit the back of her knees. She tipped backward into thin air. Despite windmilling her arms for balance, she flipped heels over head into the water.

Burke reached out to stop Precious, but the organdy skirt he grabbed ripped away in his hand. Discarding the flimsy material, he jumped over the wall to save her. Midair he realized his mistake, and twisted sideways to avoid landing on her. Instead, one foot hit the slick, muddy bottom at an odd angle, and he sat down in the water next to her causing a tidal wave to wash over her.

"What did you do that for?" she sputtered, pushing her wet hair out of her face.

The water was only about two feet deep, and though it came just to the middle of his chest, it lapped at her delicate shoulders.

"Are you all right?" he asked.

"I'm fine. Just a bit more damp than I expected."

"My apologies," he said, and offered her his still dry handkerchief from his breast pocket. "I saw Stephen heading for the water and ran after him. Unfortunately, I didn't expect you to have the same idea. I couldn't stop quickly enough to avoid hitting you."

A crowd of curious onlookers gathered.

Precious struggled to stand, and Burke jumped up to help her. He quickly noticed that her white organdy dress, what was left of it, and her white undergarments had turned almost transparent from being wet. He pushed on her shoulders and knocked her back into the water.

"Hey! What was that—"

He stepped between her and the crowd. "Your dress," he whispered.

She looked down, then hunkered lower in the water.

"What am I going to do?" She peeked to the side, around his legs, but despite the crowd, her sister was nowhere in sight.

"Here." He stripped off his coat and held it like a privacy screen. She stood and stepped toward him, the wet material clinging to her slim figure that was not at all childish in form or proportion. The sight gave the term "sheer perfection" new meaning, he thought. As she turned and put her arms in the sleeves, he wrapped his coat around her shoulders.

He helped her over the wall. Though he knew he would never forget the vision of her rising like a nymph from the water, his reason insisted on pointing out that her present "delicate condition" probably accounted for the mature curves of her body.

Anne pushed to his side and cuddled Stephen in her arms. "Thank you, thank you both," she said, over the boy crying about the fate of his boat. She let go of her son long enough to give them each a one-armed hug. "You saved my baby's life." Tears sparkled in her eyes.

The crowd applauded.

"Not really," Cordelia demurred. "We just saved him a dunking." She tugged Burke's coat tighter around her.

Before Anne could start blubbering full force, Burke said, "We should get Precious home as quickly as possible."

"Oh, yes," Anne said. "Here I am making you stand there all wet."

"I want my boat," Stephen wailed.

Andrea, Mayberry in tow, wiggled to her mother's side. "Can I go swimming, Mommy? Precious went swimming. Why can't I?"

Anne quieted her daughter.

"Where's your carriage?" Burke asked, looking down at Precious. She looked like a half-drowned kitten. He fought the urge to take her in his arms.

"I can't leave without Emily. She's—"

"We'll see she gets home safe and sound," Anne said. "Burke, you take Precious home right away before she catches her death of a cold."

"Shouldn't she have a chaperone?"

"Goodness sakes, Burke," Anne said with exasperation. "She's a child, and this is an emergency. Take Preston's curricle."

Burke looked over the heads of the crowd. "Where is he?"

"Preston went after Stephen's boat as soon as he saw you were both fine. He said he'd meet you at Gravely's later with the surprise package, whatever that's supposed to mean. Now, go, go, before she catches her death."

Obviously, his friend intended to continue their errand to Dandridge's house to fetch Ernest. Perhaps it was for the best that Burke wouldn't have a chance to meet the bounder before presenting him to Precious. Better for Ernest's health, if not for Burke's satisfaction.

"May I escort you home?" he asked Precious, offering his arm with a formal bow.

Cordelia gave him a grateful smile for acting as if her standing around soaking wet and wearing his coat was nothing out of the ordinary. Although she knew she should wait for her sister, he offered her the opportunity to escape. A tingling thrill of expectation surfaced at the thought of being alone with Burke, even for a few minutes, even in a carriage in full public view.

She nodded and laid her fingertips on his forearm. His coat hung from her shoulders like a heavy blanket, and the wet hem slapped at her calves. Beneath her droopy lace pantalets her stockings sagged around the tops of her half-boots. Every step squished or squashed or made a sucking noise. She raised her chin and smiled. How utterly grand to walk at his side.

The crowd parted in front of them, and his presence at her side gave her confidence. She followed his lead and nodded politely to the smattering of applause.

When they reached the vehicle, she hesitated.

"Don't worry about the seats," he said as if reading her mind. He handed her up. "This curricle has seen worse than water, believe me."

She sat and pulled the ends of his coat over her knees. "It's very nice. Comfortable."

He reached under the seat to pull out a satchel and then a plaid blanket. She noticed the satchel had his initials on a brass plate by the leather handle. Why would Burke have luggage in Preston's carriage? She would have asked, but his wet, white shirt clinging to the planes of his sculpted chest distracted her attention.

He shook out the blanket and tucked it around her. The touch of his large, strong hands, even through several layers of material, caused goose bumps to rise on her arms. She folded her hands in her lap, gripping her fingers to keep them from trembling.

He climbed in and took up the reins.

"Preston is quite proud of his curricle. Mine isn't as new, though I happen to think it's more comfortable. I personally think of a carriage as transportation, not as a status symbol." He clucked his tongue and snapped the reins gently, setting the matched pair of smart gray horses into motion at a sedate pace.

The presence of the satchel between their feet nagged at her. Was he leaving London? She couldn't restrain her curiosity. "Are you going on a trip?" she asked.

"No. Why do you ask?"

She indicated the satchel with a nod of her head.

"Oh, that," he said, giving an embarrassed chuckle. "I'm forced to admit I didn't make it home last evening and stayed at Preston's house."

Glad he hadn't gone to another pub, or—heaven forbid—a gambling house or brothel, she turned away to hide her smile.

He cleared his throat. "As long as we're discussing last night . . ."

"I'd rather not talk about that right now." A woman liked to look her best when she told a man he couldn't possibly marry her sister because . . . well, just because he couldn't. In spite of the fact that she loved being with him, she suddenly wanted the ride to end.

"I understand your reluctance, however—"

"Are you aware people are staring at us?" she asked. "Perhaps you could drive a little faster?"

Startled, he looked around as if seeing the road for the first time. The open style of the curricle left them in plain sight and as they approached the edge of the park, they were definitely the center of attention. Though only a few rude people pointed and laughed out loud, others stared, and some hid their amusement behind their handkerchiefs or fans.

Burke combed his hair back with his hand. "I guess we are quite a sight." He snapped the reins and the horses responded by quickening their pace. "It's all my fault and—"

"Do you think we'll start a fashion?" Cordelia asked. "By next week, all these people could be wandering around soaking wet." She waved her arm encompassing the entire park. "Muddy hems will be all the rage."

He looked at her and shook his head. "Where do you get such outrageous ideas?"

But he smiled, and it transformed his face, replacing the fiercely scowling warrior with a mischievous young Thor. Her pulse kicked up, pacing the smart clip-clop of the high stepping horses.

"It's not outrageous. Gran—Vivian told me that in her younger days, girls dampened their gowns to make them hang properly."

"But muddy hems?" he asked, one eyebrow raised. "The maids and valets of London will have apoplectic fits."

"Oh, not just any mud will do. To be truly fashionable, the hem must have a good thick coating of the mud to be found only at the bottom of the Serpentine in Hyde Park. We cannot have the servants dragging the ton's laundry in any backyard or alleyway."

"Of course not. What of the adage cleanliness is next to godliness?"

"You think our new fashion will be risqué?" She pretended to think on the matter, scrunching her brow and tilting her head to the side. "I guess I'll just have to pass then. Gran—I mean, Uncle Theo would be quite upset if I did anything considered improper."

"It's a bit late for that," Burke mumbled, as he directed the horses to turn the corner.

Cordelia looked around, aware her disheveled appearance had not escaped public notice, even on the quiet residential street where Uncle Theo lived. Not a stranger to the tags *tomboy* and *hoyden*, she sighed. "I guess you're right."

He pulled the reins and the carriage stopped. Turning to her, he said, "I'm sorry."

A footman came down the stairs, opened the carriage door, and let down the step for Cordelia to disembark.

"One moment," Burke said. "Considering all that has happened, I think we should talk. Privately," he added in a whisper.

"Perhaps later." Cordelia escaped from the carriage before the desire to stay near him overrode her better sense. She paused only long enough to say, "Thank you for bringing me home," before scrambling inside the house.

Burke could not leave. He wanted to make sure Precious understood she had an alternative, before Preston arrived with that bounder Ernest. Burke followed her up the front steps and inside the still open door.

Vivian Smith stopped him four feet into the entryway with her cane pointed at his chest. "I believe an explanation is in order, young man."

"That's what I've been trying to tell you," Precious said.

Vivian directed Quimsy to escort Precious upstairs, then turned to Burke with an expectant expression.

"I take full responsibility for this unfortunate—"

"It's not his fault," Precious yelled from halfway up the stairs, resisting the maid's determined attempts to bundle her away. "It was an accident."

"I'll listen to your story as soon as you are decently dressed," Vivian said.

Precious ran up the stairs, calling, "I'll be right back."

"Well?" Vivian said, turning to him with a stern glare.

Burke related what had happened in the park. "I brought Precious home as quickly as possible. Emily should be along shortly."

"I see. Lord Gravely is to return at any moment, and I expect he'll want to speak to you."

"Yes ma'am." If Precious still refused his proposal, perhaps Gravely could encourage her to at least consider the option. If their carriage ride became a scandal, Gravely might well force the issue. Burke would much rather have Precious agree of her own volition, for her own sake and the good of the child. A stray thought nagged at the back of his brain, but it was like trying to catch a will-o'-the-wisp. Did it have to do with the baby or Precious? Well, if it was important, it would come to him.

"I would like to speak with Lord Gravely when he arrives."

"I'd invite you to tea, but . . ." Granny eyed the puddle his wet shoes were making on the black-and-white tiled floor.

Burke backed several steps toward the door. If he went home, he might miss Preston and Ernest. Sending for his valet and dry clothes would probably take too long. Then he remembered the satchel in the carriage. Evening wear was hardly appropriate for tea, but it was better than dripping wet. "If I might impose upon your hospitality for a room, I have a change of clothes—"

Vivian gave him a speculative look. "Do you always take spare attire to the park?"

"No." He gave a small, embarrassed laugh, and an abbreviated explanation. He also told her of Preston's errand. If all went well, she could expect two more for tea.

"I see," Vivian said. She hesitated for a moment before calling the butler to fetch his satchel and show him upstairs. "I'll meet you in the garden in half an hour," she said. "It looks to be a most interesting afternoon."

Eleven

Cordelia fumed with impatience. Quimsy had insisted she take a hot bath or she would catch her death. Cooperation was quicker than a protracted argument.

"Is the carriage still out front?" she asked.

"The footman took it around to the stable," Quimsy answered, pouring another bucket of warm water over Cordelia's head.

Cordelia smoothed back her wet hair and used a cloth to dry her face. She hated having someone attend her in the bath, hated wearing a bathing chemise, but that was appropriate for a young girl. "Then where is Lord Deering? I know Granny wouldn't let him sit in the parlor all wet. Why is he still here?"

"I'm sure I don't know, miss."

"What did the footman say when he brought up the hot water? I saw you two whispering together."

"Lord Deering's been shown to a guest room. That's all I know." Quimsy held up a bath sheet and Cordelia wrapped herself in it. She stepped behind the dressing screen.

"And?"

"The butler carried up a bag for him. That's all I know."

Cordelia dried off and put on a fresh chemise, stockings and pantalets. She threw on a robe and sat at her dressing table. "You've been downstairs twice," she said, jerking a comb through her tangled hair. "What else have you heard?"

"You must think I'm a terrible gossip, to be asking me all these questions."

"I'm depending on it."

"In that case," Quimsy said, taking the comb from Cordelia's hand and smoothing out her long wet locks. "Mrs. Holbrook, the housekeeper, says your reputation is in tatters and your chances on the marriage mart are already ruined—"

"That's ridiculous. First, I'm not on the marriage mart. Yet," she added, mindful of her disguise. "Second, I only prevented a little boy from falling into the water, hardly a ruinous activity like dancing too many times with the same man or, heaven forbid, baring my limbs in public."

"Cook agrees. She says it won't matter because you haven't had your presentation yet. Until you do, you're still a child, and getting wet in public is frowned upon for a child, but not ruinous."

"Presentation?"

Quimsy nodded. "To the queen. That's when you'll be considered grown up, marriageable."

"I won't be here long enough to be presented."

"Don't say that. The staff is looking forward to the Season, with young people in the house. Balls and parties. Weekends at the country house."

"I don't understand," Cordelia said. "Won't that be more work for all of you?"

"Of course. But Dorcas, who's been in service here since Lord Gravely was young, said she once made ten shillings for doing little extras like bringing a breakfast tray or fixing a hem. At a single country party. Imagine that. She said with my talent for fixing hair, which she doesn't have, I could make double that."

Cordelia could argue about the talent for fixing hair, but she remained silent. There would be no country parties, or balls. As soon as Emily married, she and Granny would leave London and return home.

"I'm more concerned about what is happening now," Cordelia said.

"Lady Vivian sent Fred, the underfootman, after Lord Gravely. Miss Emily is in the parlor with Lady Marsfield, who brought her home."

"The children?"

"Dropped them and the governess off at Raleigh Square. Lady Vivian is waiting for you and Lord Deering in the garden, and she's wearing another one of her crazy outfits. Calling herself Mab the Fairy Queen now."

In the mirror's reflection, Cordelia noted Quimsy's disapproving frown.

Cordelia pulled a blue hair ribbon from the drawer of the dressing table and handed it back to Quimsy to tie into a bow in her hair. Then Cordelia donned the blue afternoon dress and white pinafore the maid had laid out on the counterpane.

"What I don't understand," added Quimsy, "is why Lady Vivian ordered tea for eight. I only count six. Are you expecting someone else?"

Cordelia knew whatever she said would travel to the rest of the staff as quickly as the maid could run downstairs. She normally would discourage servant gossip, but she recognized that she owed a certain debt to Quimsy for the information she'd just shared. "Lord Deering's friend, Preston, will be arriving soon."

Quimsy nodded. "That would be Lord Bathers, heir to Lord Stiles. Everyone's heard of him. A handsome devil, they say. And rich. Quite the one with the women," she babbled on as she buttoned Cordelia's dress and tied various bows to perfection. "Doesn't like to be called

Bathers, but insists on being called Preston. I say there's something havey-cavey about his title if he refuses to honor it."

She turned Cordelia to face the cheval mirror. "There you are. Record time and not even Lady Vivian could find fault with your appearance."

"Why do you call her Lady Vivian?"

Quimsy blinked. "Because that's what's proper."

Cordelia remembered Emily saying Granny was listed in the book of peers, but since titles had never been important to her, she hadn't paid much attention. Her curiosity almost got the better of her, but she bit her tongue before asking the maid to explain. Instead she said, "I'm not used to it because we don't use titles in America."

A knock sounded on the door.

"Must make life very confusing," Quimsy muttered as she opened the door. "Yes?"

A footman formally announced that Lord Gravely had arrived and wished to see his great-niece in the garden. Immediately.

"Wait a minute," Quimsy called out the door after Cordelia. "That only makes seven for tea. Who else is coming?"

Cordelia didn't reply. She didn't know the answer.

"You don't look any worse for wear," Uncle Theo said, as he seated Cordelia at the wrought-iron table next to Granny. "In fact, you look surprisingly lovely."

"Thank you, I think," Cordelia said with a smile. "I feel fine. Should I not?"

"It seems adventure agrees with you. Rather like your grandmother, eh?" He nodded toward Granny.

Cordelia started to speak, but no words came to mind.

"Close your mouth, dear. You look like a dead fish," Granny said.

Her jaw clacked shut.

"Unfortunately, the situation demanded I tell Theo the truth, the whole truth, everything."

Cordelia turned to him. "I'm so sorry. I—"

"Aside from the dire news about poor Precious, I'm quite pleased."

"P-pleased?"

Theo looked at Granny. "Perhaps you should tell your granddaughter the whole truth now."

"Everything?" Granny asked.

Theo patted her shoulder. "Leave out the sordid details."

Cordelia was more confused than ever.

Granny took her hand. "This is very difficult for me to say because I'm afraid it will make you think less of me. Shhh, let me finish. When I was quite young, I made a foolish serious mistake."

"Ho, there a minute, I resent being called a mistake."

"Hush, Theo. This is my story. I was very much in love, but because my young man's parents didn't approve of me, they sent him on a Grand Tour of the continent to separate us. He had no choice but to go. Though I knew I'd miss him, I tried to get him to think of it as an adventure he could share with me through letters. We went over his schedule so I could picture him on specific days at particular places. The night before he left, we met in secret and pledged our love. Your mother was the result of that night."

"Granny, I—"

"Please let me finish. When I learned of my blessing, I tried to contact Theo, but my increasingly desperate letters went unanswered."

"Unbeknownst to either of us, my parents charged

my tutor with the job of censoring my mail," Theo said, reaching for Granny's hand. "I thought she had forgotten me."

She smiled up at him with watery eyes. "After three months of not hearing a word from him, yet knowing he was healthy and having a grand time according to mutual friends, I could only come to one logical conclusion. Because I had to act quickly before my condition became obvious, I decided to accompany my twin sister to her new home in America. Once there, I rashly accepted the suit of a man I hardly knew."

"Grandfather," Cordelia said, nodding. "I always wondered why you chose each other."

"Silas Smith was a different person when we met. Intelligent, a bit shy. Kind, I guess is the best word to describe him then. Or, rather, I thought he offered for me out of kindness, knowing I carried another man's child. Only later did I learn a childhood accident had robbed him of . . . of his ability to father children. I was his trophy, his badge of normalcy to be displayed to his neighbors and friends."

"How very sad for you."

Granny shook her head. "Your mother gave me so much joy, and I was busy with the house and garden. I visited my twin sister often, and rejoiced in her happiness and five strapping boys. Big beautiful babies who grew into fine young men."

"But?"

"Over the years, Silas changed, so gradually I hardly noticed it at first. After your mother married and moved to Savannah, I began to see the bitterness eating away at him, turning him snide and cruel. For several years, I tried my best to repay him for his kindness, to help him, but he only grew worse, sadistic."

Cordelia couldn't help but note the similarity of her

grandmother's marriage of convenience to the current situation. All the more reason to prevent Burke from marrying Emily. To prevent her from just such sadness. To prevent him from becoming an embittered old man like her grandfather.

"Why didn't you leave him?" Cordelia asked.

"I might have, eventually. Who knows?" Granny shrugged. "Your mother became ill and came home to die, bringing her wonderful girls with her. You and Emily were my salvation."

"I don't remember much of Grandfather. He was gone most of the time."

Granny nodded. "He was very involved in politics, always in Savannah or Richmond or Washington."

"Then the war broke out, and he joined the army. You grieved for him when he was killed."

"Yes, I grieved. Not for the man he was, but for the man he might have been."

Cordelia hugged her grandmother. "Thank you for telling me. I don't think less of you. I'm proud of you, and I love you as much, if not more, than before." Then the additional implication of the story hit her, and she pulled back. "This means Theo is my grandfather?" When Granny nodded, she jumped up and gave him a hug, too. "I can't wait to tell Emily. Why isn't she here to hear this?"

The older couple gave each other a telling look.

Granny cleared her throat. "Emily is not to know just yet."

"Why? Because it might affect her decision? I should think you would want her, of all people, to know and learn from your mistakes."

"Now even your granddaughter is referring to me as a mistake," Theo said.

"I don't think she's talking about you," Granny said.

"No, of course not. I don't want Emily to make the disastrous mistake of marrying someone she doesn't love."

"Well, it isn't always a disaster," Theo said. "My marriage to Beth was arranged, and we rubbed along quite well. Developed mutual respect and affection over the years. On her deathbed, she said her only regret was that we never had children. I had no regrets whatsoever about our marriage."

"I know a number of such marriages I'd call sucessful," Granny said. "That's not the reason I don't want Emily to know. The situation is complicated."

Cordelia crossed her arms. "So enlighten me."

"Theo has been working for years on a compulsory education bill that will benefit the entire population of England from the ages of six to twelve. Attaching a scandal of this magnitude to a member of that committee could well set the passage back years, if not kill its chances altogether."

"Now, Viv—"

"No, Theo, that legislation is important to you and to the children."

Cordelia was nearly convinced, but she sensed there was more. "What else?"

"Deering's friend is on his way to fetch Ernest as we speak, and Theo arranged for a special license."

"He found Ernest?" A great weight lifted from Cordelia's shoulders.

"Yes. So, if we maintain the masquerade a little longer, Emily will be married before Parliament's summer break."

"Then," Theo said, "we'll travel to Italy for a few months, and return in the fall, with Vivian as my wife and you as my new granddaughter." He gave them both a triumphant grin.

"What about the people I've already met as your great-niece?" Cordelia asked. *Lord Deering, for instance,* she thought.

"We'll explain the situation to those few, and I'm sure they'll understand," Granny said.

"Absolutely," Theo added. "Everyone adores a love story."

He smiled at Granny and she blushed, actually blushed. The truth had given them their long-awaited happy ending. Cordelia wasn't so sure Burke would be thrilled to hear the truth about her, but she would do her part to ensure her grandparents' happiness and pretend to be a young girl for a bit longer.

"I think I'll warn Emily that Ernest will be here shortly," Cordelia said. "She'll probably want to change her dress five or six times." She turned to leave them alone and spotted Burke walking toward her.

Time seemed to slow as if the universe conspired to give her an adequate opportunity to admire his stature and easy grace. His black evening clothes and white shirt contrasted sharply with the colorful garden behind him, resplendent in full summer bloom. The afternoon sun glinted off his hair, sparking it with golden highlights. He looked deep into her eyes, and smiled, as if they shared a secret.

And, oh, how she wanted to share secrets with him— intimate, delicious secrets.

Burke bowed over Granny's hand. "Lady Vivian, you're looking lovely as usual." He nodded to Theo, then turned to Cordelia. "I'm glad to see you've recovered from your ordeal."

Because it seemed so at odds with her previous thoughts, his formal tone irked her. "Hardly an ordeal. I get wet on a regular basis. In America, we call it bathing."

"Precious! That is neither an appropriate subject nor

any manner to thank someone who has been so nice to us," Granny said.

"My apologies," Cordelia said to Burke. "I hear you found Ernest and your friend Preston is bringing him here. I can't tell you how much I appreciate your help."

"You can finally return the book you borrowed. In person."

"The what?"

Burke raised one eyebrow. "The book. The one you told me you borrowed from your friend Ernest."

"Yes. Of course. The book. Yes, thank you. That has been preying on my mind."

"I'm sure it has."

Cordelia couldn't decipher the look on his face. Knowing, yet disbelieving. Smug and distraught at the same time.

Burke turned to Theo. "Lord Gravely, if the ladies will excuse us, I would like a few minutes of your time to discuss an important matter."

"Of—"

"First you must escort me to my throne." Granny stepped forward, took Burke's arm, and led him to a bench beneath a rose-covered trellis in a grassy alcove. "Gardens are such magical places, don't you think?"

"Uh, yes," he stammered.

Granny sank to the seat, her multiple colored scarves floating with her movement. "That's precisely why I have always lived in gardens," Granny said, twirling a daffodil colored scarf. "The sweet flowers make the best ladies-in-waiting."

Burke looked at Cordelia with a confused expression.

"Mab, the Fairy Queen," she whispered. She pointed at Granny, hiding the gesture behind her other hand. It occurred to Cordelia that Granny's so-called spells contained a certain element of convenience. Was the cause really emotional upset, or was it a charade she used to avoid matters she'd rather not discuss? Cordelia dismissed that notion as mean-spirited. Granny had suffered more than her share of heartache.

"Come here, children," Granny said, motioning to both Burke and Cordelia to come closer. "I hear you saved a boy's life today," she continued when they stood in front of her.

"Not really—" Cordelia started to explain once again.

"Actually—" Burke said at the same time.

"Hush. I'm speaking. Now, kneel."

Cordelia hesitated and earned a none too gentle tap on the side of her knee from Granny's cane. She knelt. Burke sank to one knee at her side.

"Heroism deserves recognition, and in this particular case I have the pleasure of addressing you directly." She took a long-stemmed pink rose and touched both of them in turn on the left shoulder with the bloom. "For your heroic actions, I grant you each one wish."

Cordelia simply wished to be away from the awkward situation.

"Be careful what you wish for," Granny said.

Startled, Cordelia looked up at her grandmother. From that odd angle, the roses on the trellis behind her almost seemed to form a crown. The sunshine collected around the older woman, caressing her and giving her an ethereal glow.

"Such a small act," Cordelia said.

"Surely there are many others more deserving," Burke added.

Mab the Fairy Queen nodded. "That may be the truth as you see it, but the magnitude of an act cannot always be judged by the immediate results. That boy, who could be destined for greatness, might have drowned even in such shallow water. You must accept that I can see what you cannot. There are greater acts of heroism, and I give each my blessings accordingly. Oh, yes, I grant many wishes. Unfortunately, I've seen wishes wasted on trivialities. That usually happens when people don't believe in fairies and don't know a wish has been given to them. You have the advantage of knowledge. I advise you to consider your wish carefully."

If Granny were really Mab the Fairy Queen and Cordelia really could have her wish granted, she would want Emily married quickly, to anyone except Burke, and she would want him to see her as a woman instead of a little girl, and she would want—

"Only one wish," Mab cautioned. "Choose wisely."

"I don't need to think on it. I know what I want," Burke said. "I wish—"

"There is no need to say it aloud," Mab said, placing the bloom of the long-stemmed rose over Burke's mouth. "I can see into your heart." She tapped his right shoulder with the rose. "Your wish will be granted, but, be warned: it won't happen as you envision it."

"What is that supposed to mean?" he asked.

Mab laughed. "It's the way of the fairies. Surely, you know that?" She turned to Cordelia. "And now you, child. Have you decided?"

"May I have more time? I wouldn't want to waste a wish."

Mab looked up into the afternoon sun as if consulting a trusted friend for advice. Seemingly satisfied, she nodded and returned her attention to Cordelia. "In one week it will be Midsummer Eve. I give you until midnight on that date to select your wish."

"Thank you."

"Now, don't you have an errand?" her grandmother reminded her.

Cordelia remembered she'd meant to warn Emily that

Ernest was on his way. She scrambled to her feet. Burke jumped up and, with a hand under her elbow, helped her stand. The warmth of his fingers, even through her sleeve, sent her pulse racing. Although she'd rather stay with him, she couldn't be so unfair to her sister. She swallowed a sigh. "Please excuse me. I'll return as quickly as possible."

"Don't worry about us," Theo said, stepping forward to hold out his arm for Granny to take as she also rose. "While you and Emily are upstairs, we'll have tea served in the parlor. You two girls can join us there."

"Sir, I'd like—"

"Perhaps later, Burke," Theo said. "We don't want to leave Lady Marsfield in the parlor alone, do we?"

"No, sir, but—"

"Oh, dear me," Granny said, bustling ahead of the two men and shooing Cordelia in front of her along the garden path. "I totally forgot Lady Marsfield brought Emily home. How could I have been so rude as to leave her with only that girl for company? No telling what Emily has been chattering on about."

"Dresses," Cordelia muttered under her breath, but she picked up her pace just the same. "Maybe hats."

"Let's hope so," Granny said as they entered the back hall.

"Is he here yet?" Emily said, her voice muffled as she donned yet another outfit.

"No," Cordelia said from the window seat in Emily's bedroom. She turned to face her sister. "Relax. It could be another half hour before he arrives. You can probably change outfits two or three more times."

"Don't be looking at me. Keep watch out the window."
Cordelia curled up in the window seat and peered

down at the front door, below her to the right. "I don't know why you're so nervous. He'll be so glad to see you, he won't even notice what you're wearing," she said over her shoulder.

"How do I look?"

"Does that mean I can turn around?"

"Don't be a ninny. I need your help. Now, how do I look?"

Cordelia swung her legs off the seat, and faced her sister, who wore her cream muslin sprigged with embroidered violets. "Lovely, but isn't it a little tight around the waist?"

"Only if I breathe," Emily said with a wry smile.

"Not very practical."

"Fashion rarely considers a woman's comfort."

"You don't want to faint at his feet."

"True. Although it would solve the dilemma of what to say when we first meet again after so many months. Swooning is time-tested and effective."

"You won't need any artifice to gain his embrace."

"Maybe yes, maybe no." Emily pirouetted in front of the mirror. "Good afternoon, Lord Dandridge. Nice weather we're having. By the way, we're to be married today." Her shoulders drooped. "What if he's forgotten all about me? It has been months since we last met. What if . . ." She pulled a lacy handkerchief from her sleeve and dabbed at her eyes. "I don't know what I'll do if he doesn't want to marry me."

This was a different side of Emily than Cordelia was used to seeing. Her sister was usually so confident, so self-assured. Emily might dither over a bonnet or a pair of gloves, but she'd never expressed any doubts concerning her appeal to the opposite sex. Cordelia rose to give her sister a hug.

"Of course he'll want to marry you. You're the most

beautiful woman in the state of Georgia, and London, too. You could have had your pick of dozens of men, and yet you chose Ernest. He should be grateful. He should be the one worried about what you'll say to him."

Emily gave her a tremulous smile. "Thank you. I—"

Cordelia heard a carriage and dashed to the window. She could only see the tops of their hats, but two men disembarked. "It's them."

"He's here." Emily looked around with a panicked expression, as if seeking an escape route. "What am I going do? What should I say?"

"You'll be fine. You look absolutely ravishing, and Ernest is a lucky man."

"Where's my shawl? And the brooch he gave me? My reticule? I may need my smelling salts."

"You're wearing the brooch. Here's your reticule, and it's so warm you won't need a wrap. I'll go down first so you can make a grand entrance."

"No." Emily shivered and she clutched Cordelia's arm. "Let's go down together."

"There's no reason to be nervous."

"It's not the jitters. I just had a premonition."

Cordelia patted her sister's hand as she steered her toward the door. "Leave that nonsense to Granny, and let's go down to meet your soon-to-be husband."

Cordelia practically had to drag her sister down the hall. More than a little strange, since they'd chased the man halfway around the world.

Before they reached the top of the stairs, Emily halted, pulling Cordelia to a standstill. "Whatever happens—"

"Only good things are going to happen. You're going to be married and have a beautiful baby and live—"

"I told you I've had a premonition," Emily said, shaking her head. "I want you to know, whatever happens, I do appreciate what you've done for me."

"Your condition is making you overemotional."

"I am not overwrought. I've seen . . . oh, never mind. You wouldn't believe it anyway."

"What?"

Emily took a deep breath and blew it out. She nodded toward the stairs. "It's too late to do anything about it now. There's no sense keeping our destiny waiting. Shall we?"

She set off at a brisk pace, forcing Cordelia to scurry to keep up.

Destiny? What in blazes was her sister talking about?

Twelve

Burke waited in the entrance hall. He'd heard the carriage arrive and immediately excused himself from the group in the parlor. Anne and Theo had given him a quizzical look, but Vivian had waved him on without pausing in her conversation.

Burke may have failed to take Theo aside for a private chat, but he fully intended to talk to Ernest before he had a chance to see Precious. The bounder would have no doubt that his very life depended on her happiness.

Clasping his hands behind his back to keep from balling them into fists, he balanced on the balls of his feet like a boxer before the starting bell. The man's nefarious deeds should not be rewarded with Precious for a wife. Burke itched to give Ernest the thrashing he deserved.

The butler opened the front door.

To Burke's surprise Preston entered first. He'd rather expected his friend would have to force Ernest at gunpoint, or at least manhandle him through the door.

Behind Preston, a man in his late forties entered. A military man, by his bearing. Not particularly attractive or fashionable. Bushy brown hair with a touch of gray matched his full eyebrows and ample sideburns. Not at all what Burke had expected. The man handed his hat, gloves, and walking cane to the butler, and bowed formally when introduced.

"Lord Dandridge's name is Randall Truebrill," Preston said, with emphasis on the man's first name. "Not Ernest."

"Yes, humph, that's why I agreed to accompany Preston here." Dandridge cleared this throat. "Seems my name has been used to defraud a young woman, and I'm terribly—"

"Your name is not Ernest?"

"Randall," Dandridge said, his voice raised as if Burke were hard of hearing. "Randall Truebrill. Two els in Randall, two els in Truebrill. Preston here explained the situation, and I believe I can clear up a few questions. You see, I was hunting in the American West. Buffalo, mountain lion, bear—you know, quite the sport. Though I must say, I'm not one of those who kill for trophies. No, my Indian guides' families ate well that year."

"What does buffalo hunting—"

"Easy, mate," Preston said, laying a cautionary hand on Burke's shoulder. "Let the man explain."

"Yes, well, humph, to get to the point. In the winter of sixty-one, I was snowbound at a high mountain deer camp miles from the town where I had established my headquarters. When I finally made my way back in May, my valet and all my luggage had disappeared. There was some confusion, due to the fact that the United States was by then at war, and I was unable to track him down. Decided it was best to return home, and had the devil of a time getting here, let me tell you—"

"What does that have to do—"

"Tell Lord Deering your valet's name," Preston prompted.

"Yes, humph, quite. Ernest Klempe, with a silent 'e' on the end. A callow youth, but his father had served under my command in the Fusiliers and I thought to give him a chance to better himself. Learned manners and appropriate speech readily enough, but was not up to snuff when it came to hard work. Never could put a proper shine on my boots."

"Where is your valet now?" Burke asked.

"Haven't the foggiest. If you find him, let me know. I don't care for him using my name, not one bit."

The tension left Burke's shoulders. Oh, Ernest still deserved a beating, and would get one if he had anything to say about it, but at least he wasn't present, couldn't marry Precious today. "I quite agree, Lord Dandridge. I, too, would be understandably upset if my valet usurped my name."

A small moan diverted his attention upward.

For a split second, the attractive tableau seemed frozen for his benefit. Two beautiful women poised at the top of the stairs. A scene worthy of an artist's appreciative eye. Then he noticed their twin expressions of shock and horror. In the blink of an eye, one woman's foot must have slipped, because they shrieked and grabbed each other.

Time became disjointed, seeming to slow for him as he rushed toward them, and yet to speed up for them as they tumbled down the stairs in a jumble of petticoats and flying arms and legs.

Skidding to his knees, he reached the foot of the stairs just as the women came to halt, lying still. Too still.

"Precious!" He reached for her.

"Don't move them," Dandridge barked from behind. He also knelt. "If any bones are broken, you could make it worse by moving them." He leaned over Emily, gently feeling her head and working down to her neck and shoulders. "I've had to check many a man on the battlefield," he said by way of assurance. "Someone should go for a physician."

Burke waved the butler over and instructed him to send a footman.

Precious moaned and opened her eyes. "Burke? What happened?"

"Shhh. Lie still for a moment. You've had a nasty fall."

In spite of his urging, Precious sat up. "I'm fine. Emily? What are you doing?" she cried, slapping Dandridge's back. "Get your filthy hands off—"

Burke grabbed her flailing arms. "It's all right. He's helping her."

Precious let out a sob, and Burke took her in his arms to comfort her.

"I'm sure she's going to be fine," Burke said. "We've sent a footman for a physician. Do you hurt anywhere? Are you sure nothing is broken? Are you dizzy?"

"What is going on here?" Theo demanded as he and Vivian rushed into the entrance from the parlor. Anne and Preston followed a few steps behind.

"There's been an accident," Burke explained.

Precious tried to stand. Burke helped her to her feet, keeping an arm around her because she seemed none too steady.

"It's Emily. We fell down the stairs and she's—" Her voice broke.

"Theo, fetch my medicine chest," Vivian said. He bustled up the stairs as she knelt beside Dandridge at the still unconscious woman's side.

"No broken bones that I can detect," he reported.

"Who are you?"

"Randall Truebrill. Two els in Randall, and two—"

"Are you a doctor?"

"No. Major in the Fusiliers. Retired."

"Well, Major," Vivian said, her tone clearly equating his rank with that of a bothersome gnat, "If you'll move aside, we need to get this young woman upstairs to her bed."

"Been my experience it's best to move the wounded as little as necessary." Dandridge held his ground.

"And my experience is that she can hardly be comfortable lying on this tile floor. Now move aside."

"Are you a physician?"

Vivian looked ready to explode. "I am her grandmother."

Dandridge nodded and stood, gently picking up Emily as he did so. "Then I bow to your judgment. Lead the way."

"Are you sure you can manage?" Vivian asked. She stood and glared at him.

The man smiled through his bushy whiskers. "If I can tote a bear down the side of a mountain single-handed, this little bit of a woman won't even cause me to break a sweat, if you'll pardon my language."

Burke hid a smile. If Emily were on her feet, she'd be of a height with Dandridge, probably look him straight in the eye.

Anne stepped forward. "Is there anything I can do to help?"

"Why are you standing around jabbering?" Precious asked, stepping forward as if she intended to carry Emily upstairs herself. She nearly fell when she put her weight on her right foot. Burke tightened his hold and kept her upright.

"Thank you for your offer of assistance," Vivian said to Anne. "If you would take Precious into the parlor, elevate her foot, and get her a cup of hot tea, I'll take care of her as soon as I've seen to Emily."

When Precious demurred, insisting she wanted to accompany Emily despite her injured ankle, Burke swung her up into his arms.

"Put me down."

He didn't have a chance to respond.

"I think she's coming around," Dandridge said, nodding toward the woman in his arms. "Easy, girl, easy," he whispered to Emily as her eyelids fluttered open. "I've got you, and you're going to be just fine now."

Her eyes widened in shock. "You're not Ernest."

He smiled. "It's all right," he continued, his voice a soothing rumble. "I'll take care of you, little one."

"I'm just a bit light-headed is all," Emily said. "I'm sure you can put me down, Not-Ernest."

His chuckle echoed in the hall. "If it's all the same to you, I'll carry you upstairs."

She wrapped her arms around his neck and tucked her head beneath his chin. "I'm fine, really."

"Your grandmother will feel better if she can determine that for herself," Dandridge said.

With a harumph, Vivian turned and led the way up the stairs. Dandridge followed with Emily.

"I feel rather *de trop*," Preston said in a droll tone, as if to break the tension. "I'm the only man not carrying a woman."

"Well, don't look at me," Anne said. She turned and patted Precious on the shoulder. "It looks as if Emily will be well. Would you like that cup of tea?"

"I'm feeling much improved," Precious said. "If Burke will put me down, I'm sure I can hobble into the parlor."

He let her slip a few inches, and as he had hoped, she gave a yelp of surprise and wrapped her arms around his neck to keep from falling. "And deny myself the pleasure of saving a damsel in distress? I think not."

"That was wicked," Precious said.

But she left her arms in place. Her bashful smile made him feel ten feet tall.

He grinned. "I would never drop you."

"I know."

"Perhaps we should leave these two, and their scintillating conversation, alone," Preston said in an aside to Anne.

"Unchaperoned? Heaven forbid," she replied. "Though I love Burke like a brother and would trust him with my life, Lady Vivian would expect me to act in her place, and rightly so. Oh, I know I was the one who encouraged him to bring her home this afternoon, but that was an emergency situation. This is not. Now, Burke, put the girl down, though you may help her into the parlor."

He reluctantly set Precious on her feet—rather, foot—gratified when she clung to his arm for support.

"We'll have tea," Anne said, "and we shall all behave in a civilized manner, even you, Preston."

"Only if I must."

Her reply was cut off by the sharp tap, tap, tap of the brass knocker on the front door.

"Oh, dear, we forgot to send a footman to tell the physician he wasn't . . ."

As the butler opened the door, Precious' words faded to a halt. Worried about her, Burke turned only to see her face pale to parchment.

"Merciful heavens," she said in a breathless whisper before covering her mouth with her hand.

Thirteen

Cordelia reached out blindly for the newel post for support. Through the open door she could see the caller was not the physician making an unnecessary visit. Instead, a blond, blue-eyed virago, flanked by several men in blue uniforms, stood on the doorstep. It was the real Precious, with a troop of dreaded Yankees. Cordelia wanted to run and hide, but her legs would not move.

"Good afternoon," the butler said. "May I be of service?"

"We're here to see Lord Gravely," the Yankee officer said. "I have also been instructed to inquire after a Mrs. Vivian Smith."

"Whom shall I say is calling?"

"Lieutenant Hadley, United States Navy, and Miss Sarah—"

The girl brushed past the butler and stomped into the entrance hall. "You may tell Lord Gravely that I have finally arrived, no thanks to—" Spotting Cordelia, the real Precious pointed at her and said, "That's her."

"Now, see here." The butler reached for the storming young girl, who shook off his hand with a contemptuous glare.

She rounded on Cordelia. "You and your crazy grandmother and your pregnant sister—"

"I can explain, Prec—"

"Do not call me by that ridiculous nickname. My name is Sarah Louise Cosley, and you'd best remember it."

Cordelia did not dare look at Burke. "Sarah—"

"Hear, hear. What's all the commotion? I'll handle this," Theo said, dismissing the butler with a wave of his hand as he descended the stairs. "I'm Lord Gravely. Who is in charge here?" he asked in the direction of the uniformed men.

"Lieutenant Hadley, United States Navy," the officer said, stepping forward, and clicking his heels as he made a curt bow. "My captain sends his sincere regards and requests—"

"All in good time, young man. Now, if your men would wait outside?"

Hadley nodded and instructed his men to exit.

"If you would step into the library," Theo said to the girl. "We can discuss—"

Suddenly, Precious—rather, Sarah—looked about ready to cry. She placed her hand on Theo's arm. "It was horrible, Uncle Theo. That woman left me stranded in the Bahamas by assuming my identity and my passage on the ship. If the Navy hadn't rescued me—"

"You stayed in Savannah by choice," Cordelia pointed out logically.

"I did; that's true." Sarah looked up at Theo with tears in her eyes. "But my friends made me see the error of my ways, and helped me find passage to the Bahamas. I was on my way here, to you, but . . ." She sniffled. "I almost made a grievous mistake, but that was no reason for her to . . ." Sarah wiped her eyes and turned to face Cordelia. "You're wearing my clothes," Sarah shrieked. She stomped toward Cordelia. "Take off that dress this instant."

Cordelia fought the urge to hide behind Burke, his bulk a seductive bulwark of safety. She deserved whatever censure Sarah hurled at her.

THE NIGHT WE KISSED

"Just a minute here," Theo said, catching Sarah around the waist. "Until I straighten out this mess—"

"No, Theo, I—" Cordelia couldn't let him involve himself in the situation.

"There is nothing to straighten out." Sarah kicked out and tried to pry herself free of his hands. "That woman—"

"You will behave yourself or I'll lock you in a closet until you stop acting like a barbarian baboon."

The girl stopped struggling and Theo put her down.

"Now, young woman, you may wait in the library, over there, until I call you."

Sarah stuck out her bottom lip, but she marched across the hall and entered the library, tossing Cordelia one last glare.

Theo asked Lieutenant Hadley to wait in the breakfast room, and the man excused himself.

"My apologies," Theo said to his other guests. "I'm sorry you had to witness that scene."

"Who is that girl?" Anne asked.

Theo mopped his brow with a large linen handkerchief. "I'm sure I've never seen her before in my life."

"She certainly has some strange notions," Burke said.

He looked at Cordelia with a furrowed brow and questions in his eyes. She wanted to lie, to relieve his mind, but she couldn't. Not even if it meant he would never want to see her again. Her relief that Sarah had survived her ordeal, undamaged and apparently unchanged, was tempered by the heartache her appearance caused. No, that wasn't fair. Sarah hadn't been the one who had lied. Cordelia had only herself to blame for her pain.

"Burke, I—"

"I think perhaps we should go," Anne announced. "It's getting quite late, and I have a dinner engagement.

Thank you for the tea and an . . . interesting afternoon, Lord Gravely. Preston? Burke? Shall we?"

Theo wished them a good day and entered the library. The efficient butler handed the gentlemen their hats.

"One moment," Cordelia said, placing her hand on Burke's sleeve. The others left promising to wait outside thus giving Burke and Cordelia a few moments of privacy. She looked up at him, a plea for forgiveness on her lips.

"It's all right, Precious. Your uncle will get the poor deranged girl the help she needs."

"I want to be the one to tell you the tru—"

"Cordelia?"

She turned to the stairs to see Dandridge on his way down.

"That's you, right? Cordelia? Your grandmother sent me to tell you both Emily and the baby are fine. You can relax now. She said she would be down to tend to your ankle in a few minutes." He continued down the stairs and took his hat from the table on his way to the door. "I'm off to fetch some herbs from the apothecary. Be back in two shakes of a lamb's tail."

When Cordelia faced Burke again, the thunderous expression she feared was absent. His face was a stoic blank, masking all emotions, betraying nothing. He backed up a step, away from her. She couldn't see his eyes because he kept his chin up, and stared at a spot over her head.

"Is that your real name? Cordelia?"

"Yes," she choked out. "You see—"

"And your sister Emily is pregnant?"

"Yes." Cordelia wanted to say many things, explain. "I—"

"Exactly how old are you?"

"Twenty-five," she answered absently, not even considering the rudeness of his question because she was trying to frame a reasonable explanation in her head. "Burke, I—" She took a half-step toward him and he moved another full step back. "I don't have a contagious disease," she said, a bit exasperated.

"At this point, I have difficulty believing anything you say."

"Then look at me. The truth is in my eyes."

He didn't look at her for several seconds, his internal struggle obvious by the rigid set of his shoulders. When he finally relented, she tried to project her feelings for him, to put her heart in her eyes.

"What do you see?" she whispered.

"Trouble," he said without blinking. He'd meant it as a flippant answer to her question, but he knew it was the truth. He could sink into her complex hazel eyes and lose himself there. The need to sweep her into his embrace twitched at his arms. Damn her lies. He remembered too well the feel of her sweet body next to his. With a groan, he jerked his head up, focused on the ridiculous cupids cavorting across the top of the mirror on the wall. "If you'll excuse me, my friends are waiting. Good day, Miss Cordelia."

With that he spun on his heel, and forced himself to place one foot in front of the other, forced himself to put distance between them, to walk away from her.

Anne and Preston seemed to sense Burke didn't want to talk. They carried on a conversation about trivialities, neither including him nor chiding him for not taking part.

As the carriage pulled into Raleigh Square, Anne said, "Come inside," her tone solicitous. "This has been an unexpected turn of events. Talk to Marsfield."

Burke declined the invitation.

Anne patted his hand. She gave Preston a significant look before going in the house.

"I do believe Anne wants me to convince you to talk to Marsfield," Preston said, leaning back against the leather squabs of the seat.

"I would rather not bare my soul to Marsfield just yet," Burke said. "It's still rather painful to admit I've been made a fool by such a tiny slip of a woman."

"If this is the first time you've acted the fool over a woman, you're luckier than most men. You can't allow yourself the luxury of wallowing in self-pity."

"Why not? You've done it often enough over one woman or another."

"True, true. However, I had the good sense never to fall in love with—"

"I'm not in love."

"Of course not."

"Her real name is Cordelia and she's—"

"Emily's older sister?"

"How did you know?"

Preston shrugged. "Only a guess. I thought I recognized the dynamics of the relationship from growing up with three sisters. I said from the beginning that . . . Cordelia, you say? Well, I said from the beginning she wasn't the innocent schoolgirl she claimed to be."

"What am I to do now?"

"Sometimes just explaining everything to someone makes the issues clear."

Burke nodded, but he knew he wouldn't tell Marsfield everything. He wouldn't relate the few private moments he'd shared with Prec . . . Cordelia. The honeysuckle smell of her hair, the way her perfect breasts flattened against his chest, the— He shook himself free of the memories. At least for now. He stood and disembarked from the carriage.

"Come on," Preston said. "I'll pour you a stiff brandy before you start."

"No." He needed to keep his wits about him. "My thanks, but a cup of strong tea would serve me better."

An hour later he'd answered all of Marsfield's probing questions about the strange tableau at Gravely's mansion. He sat back in relief as his mentor paced the floor, deep in thought. At least Marsfield hadn't asked about his feelings. Not that Burke could have answered with any degree of certainty. He knew nothing more except that his body responded to the very woman his mind rejected as an impossible choice.

Marsfield halted in front of Burke. "The human race is inherently logical. That is, after all, what sets us apart from the animal kingdom."

"I beg to differ," Preston said. He lounged in his chair, his feet propped on the table, a brandy snifter balanced precariously on his belt buckle. "The fair sex being my prime example. Rarely rational creatures. Our Anne being an exception, if not an anomaly."

"Where is this line of talk taking us?" Burke asked.

"If I may finish," Marsfield said with a quelling look toward Preston, "it will become apparent. When we accept that humans are logical by nature"—he ignored Preston's disdainful snort and continued—"then deductive reasoning leads us to only one conclusion. Whenever someone behaves in a manner considered irrational, that only means we're missing a piece of the puzzle, missing facts that would make the behavior logical and reasonable in light of that knowledge."

"You are excluding madmen and idiots," Preston said.

"Not at all," Marsfield argued with enthusiasm. "Certainly madness is a factor that should be taken into account when analyzing behavior, as well as lack of innate intelligence, but it's by no means the only reason behind irrationality."

Burke rubbed his temples. "I thought we were discussing Cordelia."

"We are."

"Sorry, sir. I don't see the connection."

"The question then becomes, why did Cordelia reason it necessary to hide her true identity and pretend to be a young girl?"

"And the answer is obvious," Anne said, stepping farther into the room and removing her bonnet.

Marsfield gave her a kiss and took her shawl. "You're home early, my love. I assume that means the meeting with your editor went well."

"Not really. That man is distressingly single-minded where the Aunt Bunny books are concerned. I suggested a family of playful weasels for the next book and he nearly had apoplexy. I simply could not concentrate on ducklings and goslings when I knew all of you would be here, so I rescheduled with Blackthorne later in the week. Now, you were saying?"

The butler arrived with a steaming pot of tea. Anne served Burke and herself while Marsfield refreshed his and Preston's drinks.

"You said the answer was obvious," Marsfield said to Anne as soon as the servant had left and everyone was comfortably settled.

"I heard your statement, and suddenly it made perfect sense."

"I wish . . ." Burke hesitated. His memory of that afternoon and Mab the Fairy Queen saying his wish would not be granted as he envisioned it caused a shiver of unease. "It's not obvious to me," he grumbled.

Marsfield reached over and squeezed his shoulder. "It will be when you have time to reason it through."

"Couldn't you just tell me?" Burke asked. "I'm getting the devil of a headache."

"He wants you to come to your own conclusion that Cordelia must be the foreign agent."

"Why, thank you, Preston," Marsfield said, his tone not at all gracious. "That was most helpful of you."

Preston nodded and raised his glass in an unrepentant salute.

Burke sat back in his chair, the facts buzzing around his brain like so many angry bees. Would he have come to the same conclusion? "What about the notes we intercepted?"

Marsfield shrugged. "Simply ordinary flirtatious notes between Emily and Wilcox. One from Digby with an abominable poem about the beauty of her eyebrows. Painful to read, but no hidden clues or codes that I could see."

Burke nodded, accepting Marsfield's opinion as fact. He was a master at deciphering codes, and if one had been present Marsfield would have detected it.

Yet, Burke would have liked it better if there was room for doubt. He didn't adjust easily to change, and his world had been turned topsy-turvy yet again.

"Your instincts were right," Anne said, touching Burke's hand, rousing him from his thoughts. "You identified the correct group, if not the exact individual. Emily was the obvious choice, maybe too obvious."

Marsfield agreed. "Emily's search for Ernest was the perfect cover for Cordelia coming to London."

"You can't mean she encouraged her sister to get pregnant," Anne said, her expression appalled.

"Of course not," Marsfield said. "She simply capitalized on an opportunity, just as she did when Precious stayed behind. By layering the cover stories, she made detection more difficult. That makes her more clever than we anticipated."

"Most convenient, that dalliance," Preston said. "Could she have arranged the poor girl's downfall? I should think it wouldn't be all that difficult."

Burke stood, fists balled, even before he'd finished speaking. "Take that back. Cordelia would do no such thing."

"Just thinking aloud," Preston said, unperturbed. "Someone had to get it out into the open. We all thought of it, right? Are we all agreed it's not a probability? There, see? You can sit back down, Burke. No need to call me out." Preston sent a knowing look to the others.

Burke sat on the edge of his chair. "You shouldn't say such terrible things about Cordelia."

"Face the facts. We're talking about a covert agent from a war-torn country," Preston said, "a good agent, by all indications. Sometimes unpleasantness is necessary in this business."

Burke looked from Preston to Marsfield and back again as if seeing them for the first time. They were referring to lies and deception and ruining someone's life as *unpleasantness*. Instinctively he knew the list of unpleasant activities did not stop there. "I'm glad I left the Agency."

"But you're back in," Marsfield said. "Even if it's only temporary. And the queen is counting on us."

"Sir, I don't know what you expect—"

"I expect you to do whatever it takes to complete this investigation and bring the case to a successful conclusion."

That meant Burke would have to watch every move Cordelia made, day or night. He would need to know where she went, whom she talked to, and what she said.

Burke wanted to ask that someone else be assigned the task of shadowing Cordelia, a task made onerous by his uncertain emotions. But after what he'd heard, he wasn't even sure he could trust his best friend with the job. What if Preston decided some "unpleasantness" was necessary? Burke was ready to defend his queen and country, but the need to protect Cordelia coursed through his veins with his life's blood.

Burke nodded to Marsfield. "Yes sir."

"If you can get back inside, so much the better. Kelso can only find out so much."

"Kelso? My valet?" Preston asked

"Yes," Burke said. "I arranged for him to meet the upstairs maid, Quimsy. They've been walking out, as he calls it. Seems she's quite the talker, and Kelso is a good listener with an excellent memory. Proving himself quite invaluable."

"I know his worth. Saved my life on three distinct occasions," Preston said with a laugh. "Claims a fourth, but I discount that one, since I had to save his life in return. I just didn't know he was also working for you."

All this talk of risking and saving lives as if it were an everyday matter. Burke was in over his head. Obviously, in his short stint with the Agency, he'd been assigned the easiest jobs. Probably because he wasn't the heroic type. What had ever possessed him to leave the Diplomatic Corps, even temporarily? If he had a lick of sense, he'd walk out right now and never return. But then he would lose his dearest friends, and who would watch out for Cordelia? Who would keep her safe?

It wasn't as if tailing her meant he would have to speak to her. He forced a smile to his stiff lips. "I'll do my best, sir," he promised. And for her sake, he would.

Fourteen

Cordelia gritted her teeth as she laced her boot tightly over her still slightly swollen ankle. Hopefully the regular organist would be at choir practice, and she could deliver the second letter without meeting the odious Mr. Fletcher again. After donning her cloak, she double-checked her derringer and tucked it into her reticule. London was proving more dangerous then she'd expected.

Although it was only half past eight o'clock, the household had settled in for the night. Emily was resting in her bedroom with the latest *Godey's*. As soon as Granny and Theo had faced off across a chessboard, Cordelia had claimed a headache and excused herself. Fifteen minutes later, she slipped from her room to meet Quimsy at the head of the servants' stairway.

"Is the carriage ready? Where's your cloak?"

"We can't go. Lord Gravely gave John Coachman the night off, and no one else dares to harness the horses without his permission."

"Then we'll walk. It's only six blocks. Get your wrap. We must hurry."

Quimsy held her ground, twisting her apron in her hands. "Shouldn't you wait till tomorrow? I could be let go without a reference if Lord—"

"He won't find out if you don't tell." Cordelia turned Quimsy by the shoulders.

"But it's dark and—"

Cordelia pushed the maid toward the stairs. "Let's go."

"The Bogey Man will—"

"I've brought my pistol."

Despite Cordelia's constant reassurances, Quimsy clung to her arm and muttered dire predictions during the entire trip. Once inside, Quimsy fell to her knees beside the first pew. Cordelia approached the altar just as the final crescendo echoed through the empty church. Unable to see into the organist's perch, she checked her reticule before approaching the stairs.

"Hello."

A gray-headed dumpling of a woman rolled away from the keyboard and into Cordelia's line of sight.

"Yes?"

Cordelia heaved a sigh. "Are you the regular organist?"

The woman sniffed into her handkerchief. "Yes. My name is Mary Fletcher. What can I do for you?"

"I'm looking for a particular piece of music. I believe it's called *An Archangel's Tribute.* Have you heard of it?"

"No, but there is a lovely cantata called *The Archangel's Tears.* Would that be what you're seeking?"

"I believe it is." Cordelia withdrew the envelope from her pocket and handed it over.

Mary read it quickly and tucked it into her ample bosom. "I don't have the sheet music with me, but I could forward it tomorrow or the next day if you give me your direction."

Cordelia handed her one of Uncle Theo's cards with her name written on the back. "Thank you."

"No," the woman whispered earnestly. "Thank you for giving us the means to help."

Having completed her second errand for Madame Lavonne, Cordelia turned to leave the church with a light heart. After peeling Quimsy's fingers from the back of the pew, she dragged the complaining maid outside.

"Nothing happened on the way here, and nothing will happen on the way home." Cordelia's ankle throbbed, but she could not show any hesitation or the maid would collapse into hysteria. "Come now, chin up."

As they passed the alley, the wrought-iron gate clicked shut, the sound ominous in the otherwise silent churchyard. Cordelia jumped, and Quimsy nearly leapt into her arms.

"It's only the wind," Cordelia assured the maid, although she felt no breeze.

A rustling noise in the pitch dark alley sent a strange all-over shiver across her skin. "It's only a rat," she said, picking up her pace. They reached the safety of the Gravely Mansion grounds at a dead run.

Burke removed his hand from the skulker's mouth, but retained his hold on the man's arm and forced his hand farther up between his shoulder blades. "I asked you a question, and I would appreciate the courtesy of an answer."

"My—my name is Fletcher, Nathan Fletcher. Let me go before I call the night watchman."

"My other question also deserves an answer." Burke raised the man's hand a fraction of an inch, eliciting a groan from his captive before easing his hold to where it was before.

"I work here. I'm the substitute organist."

"That does not explain why you're skulking about in the dark, or why you followed a young woman into the church."

"I-I intended to offer my services as a piano teacher."

"Really?"

"No more, please. I'm in agony."

"The truth?"

"All right. I was waiting for the woman."

Burke's temper flared and he tightened his grip. "Why?"

"I knew she would come tonight to see my mother," Fletcher said.

"Your mother?"

"She's the regular organist."

"Why would she seek out your mother?" Burke asked, more to himself than to the sniveling excuse for a man he held prisoner.

"She said she wanted some music. Honestly, that's all I know."

"Yet you intended her harm."

"Not harm. I just wanted a kiss or two. I thought she'd be willing. She seemed quite brazen when we met."

"She's not brazen, you fool. She's an American." He shook his head to clear it. The need to follow Cordelia worked in the other man's favor. "I will let you go this time, but remember this: if I ever hear of any misconduct on your part, I'll break every finger on both your hands." He pushed Fletcher away, causing the vermin to stumble to his knees.

"I suggest you pray for your salvation," Burke called over his shoulder as he left.

Blending in with the shadows, Burke hurried after Cordelia. Keeping her safe was beginning to look like a full-time job.

Cordelia picked up her embroidery hoop. With all the time she'd spent keeping her sister company, she'd nearly completed the small sampler, to the detriment of her much-pricked fingertips.

"Why don't you send him a note?" Emily said, reaching for another skein of thread.

Cordelia stood to move the sewing basket closer to her sister. Granny had prescribed a few days of bed rest, but Emily had insisted on coming downstairs to the morning room for at least part of the day.

In the background, Cordelia listened to Sarah play her scales on the piano in the parlor, cringing at her frequent mistakes. Apparently, no one had ever insisted she practice. Cordelia had turned over her entire schedule of lessons to Sarah save one. She'd remembered Burke saying he'd learned to dance by practicing with his sister, and decided to supervise the child's time with the dancing master personally. Though waltzing with the prancing Monsieur Delacorte in his clickity-clackity three-inch heels was less than glorious, especially compared to dancing in Burke's arms. Cordelia walked to the window. Staring out at the garden, she wrapped her arms around her waist, the bittersweet memory of her first waltz a physical pain.

"Don't ignore me," Emily said. "Cordelia?"

"Sorry, I was woolgathering. More tea?"

"I said, why don't you send him a note?"

"Who?"

"You know who. Lord Deering. The man you've been mooning over for days now."

The memory of his cold, distant look stabbed at Cordelia's heart. His blue eyes, icy as the North Sea in winter, had said he never wanted to see her again. If only she could take back the lies and start over. Too late. Too late.

If she saw him again, what would he say? Would he have more questions to fire at her in that curt, accusing tone? Some little piece of the unbridled mess he needed to understand before he tucked the puzzle away in a mental Pandora's box of memories labeled DO NOT OPEN? More likely, the only reason he would even speak to her again was that he expected her to apologize, and, as a gentle-man, would feel obligated to offer her that opportunity.

Cordelia shook her head. The last time she'd seen him had caused enough misery. Only a fool would seek out more torture. She returned to her seat and took up her sewing. "I'm not mooning, and I would prefer not to talk about him."

"Perhaps that's for the best. I never thought him right for you. He's much too large. You're such a tiny thing."

"I like tall men."

"He's too stuffy, pedantic. You deserve someone who appreciates you for who you really are. Someone who won't expect you to act in a certain manner just because you're a woman. Believe me, I've learned that lesson the hard way. You have so much energy; you need someone more lively."

"Burke isn't stuffy. Not at all. Not with me."

"Then why won't you send him a note? Ask him to tea?"

"Because . . ." Cordelia blinked back tears, hoping her sister wouldn't notice them. "He doesn't want to see me again." She focused her attention on her handiwork, try-ing to unknot the strand of tangled cerise embroidery floss.

"Did he say that?"

"He didn't have to. His expression said it all. He said that when he looked at me he saw trouble."

Emily smiled. "That means he's interested."

Cordelia might have argued the point, but a tap on the door interrupted.

The butler entered, carrying a silver tray with a pack-age on it. "This arrived for you, Miss."

"Thank you," Emily said, setting aside her embroidery.

The butler bypassed Emily and bowed in front of Cordelia, presenting the tray with a flourish.

"Thank you," she said. Who would send her a present? She could count the people she knew in London on one hand. Was it an apology from Burke? A fleeting hope flared, and was extinguished when she noticed that the bundle wrapped in brown paper carried the return address of the bookstore she had visited. She opened the attached note. *For Archangel: Put it to good use.* The package contained a thick, heavy book with a curiously plain binding. She opened the front cover. The center of each page had been cut out, and the resulting hollow packed tightly with coins. Four neat rows. Nearly one hundred twenty dollar gold pieces.

"What is it?" Emily asked.

Cordelia slapped the cover closed. The last thing she needed was for Emily to discover the truth. "Just . . . just a book I ordered. *Plutarch's Essays.* In Latin."

"Utterly boring," Emily said. "Didn't they carry anything interesting?"

Cordelia rewrapped the book in the brown paper and set it aside. She picked up her sewing. "I didn't see any fashion magazines."

"Novels?"

"I didn't look." Cordelia followed her sister's glance to the clock on the mantle. Ten minutes to two.

"Not—Ernest will be here soon," Emily said.

"Why do you call Dandridge that?"

"What? Oh, Not-Ernest?" Emily smiled. "That first day I didn't know his name, and when I said, 'Thank you, Not-Ernest, for carrying me upstairs,' he laughed. He has such a nice laugh, don't you think? Robust and uninhibited." She ducked her head. "The man thinks I'm witty when I call him that. You probably think it's silly."

"No, I think it's sweet."

"He's the only man who has ever admired my mind. That's why I agreed to marry him."

Cordelia dropped her embroidery into her lap. "You can't marry a man because he laughs at an inane joke."

"Aha! I knew you'd think it was silly."

"Emily, you can't be serious?"

"But I am. Oh, I'm not marrying him because he laughs at my jokes. All of my jokes," she added. "Although, I admit his sense of humor attracted me to him at first, before I found out we have a number of interests in common."

The idea of the burly, retired major discussing the latest bonnet style brought a snicker. "What interests?" she asked. The idea of Emily discussing big-game hunting or military history was equally amusing, and brought another spate of giggles.

Emily waited for her to calm down, her expression clearly conveying that she was not amused. "Chess, for one. Not-Ernest was quite impressed when I played him to a draw twice and checkmate once."

"You know, as well as I, that a man will let—"

"Don't insult him by saying he let me win. Not-Ernest has achieved the rank of Master and would not belittle himself or me with such underhanded tactics. You can ask Theo if you don't believe me. He's watched several of our matches to gain the upper hand with Granny. He hasn't managed to beat her yet."

"If you say it's so, I believe you. It's just that I never knew you liked to play chess, that's all."

"You were always so busy running around, riding horses, and . . . and whatever it is you did outside all day. I preferred to stay inside. Father used to play quite well, you know. He taught me. Not that I had much chance to play, especially after we moved to Belle Oaks. Although I usually read to Mother when it was my turn to sit by her sickbed, if she wanted to sleep, I'd keep myself awake by playing chess games in my head."

"I'm sorry I didn't know that. I should have."

Emily shrugged. "I would have told you if it had been important. It wasn't at the time."

"I feel like my own sister is a stranger." Cordelia was half kidding, but Emily's smug smile stopped her short. "What else is there I don't know?"

"Oh, maybe one or two things. Nothing important."

"Name one."

"Well, I don't think you know I have a passionate interest in Egyptology, and once had an article on hieroglyphics published in the *Scientific American Journal* under the name E. V. West? Does that count as one or two?"

"Hieroglyphics?" Emily? Just the two words in the same thought boggled Cordelia's mind.

Emily heaved a sigh. "I do wish I'd been born sooner. I might have even been the one to decipher the Rosetta stone."

"Hieroglyphics? Those Egyptian symbols, right?"

"A pictorial language of symbols. Without a spoken version it was more difficult to learn, but once I did, everything fell into place and it just seems to make sense. Much like learning Latin or Italian. At least to me. Father always said I have a natural facility for foreign languages."

At that moment, words, in any language, seemed to desert Cordelia completely.

"Close your mouth, dear. You look like a fish," Granny said as she entered and sat next to Emily. "What are you two talking about that has struck Cordelia dumb?"

"This and that," Emily said.

"You told her you're getting married next week?" Granny asked.

"Next week?" Cordelia managed to squeak out.

"I was just getting to that in a roundabout way."

"Roundabout is right," Cordelia said. "When did all this happen?"

"Then you didn't mention your honeymoon trip?" Granny asked.

"Noooo. Not yet."

"Well, you haven't got all day," Granny said, placing the used cups on the tea tray, then gathering up the scattered skeins of thread. "The seamstress wants to do another fitting in the next hour or we'll never be ready in time."

After the shocks she'd already received, Cordelia was almost afraid to ask, but her curiosity triumphed. "What about your honeymoon? What fitting? For a wedding dress?"

"No, I'm getting married in the sprigged muslin I wore when I first met Not-Ernest. That is, if it still fits in a week," Emily said with a sigh. "The fitting is for the clothes necessary for our honeymoon trip to Egypt. Not-Ernest is going to manage an archeological dig for the Royal Society. Isn't that wonderful?"

"What about the baby?" Cordelia asked.

"Babies are born every day in Egypt," Emily said. "They're called Egyptians."

"She doesn't have to worry," Granny said. "The women in our family have never had problems. Remember your Great-Aunt Genevieve who had—"

"Five strapping boys," Cordelia and Emily finished together.

"And not a bit of trouble," Granny continued without missing a beat. "It's all in the hips, and both you girls have inherited your mother's hips."

Not that Cordelia was as pleased about that as Granny seemed to be. "I mean, how does Dandridge feel about the baby?"

"He's thrilled to be a father," Emily said with a dreamy smile. She looked down at the tiny cap she was embroidering with dainty pink and blue flowers. "He said at his age it will keep him young."

"You need to have a fitting, too," Granny said to Cordelia. "Emily's dress for tonight is done, but we'll have to make do at the last minute for yours. Emily, I want you to take a nap since we'll be out late."

"Tonight?" Cordelia shook her head. Granny moved from one matter to another with lightning speed, and it was difficult to keep up.

"Oh, that's right, you were helping Sarah with her French lesson when the invitation came," Granny said. "We're going to the Asterbules' ball tonight."

"I thought we weren't accepting invitations until after—"

"Your sister's engagement has changed all that. I met with Lady Marsfield this morning, and we agreed Emily and Dandridge need to be seen together before the wedding. Everyone will assume they met last year when he visited America. Then, when they return from Egypt, they can settle down without any nasty rumors surfacing. Dear Lady Marsfield arranged for an invitation to her sister's mother-in-law's event. Wasn't that sweet of her?"

"It will be your first real ball," Emily said to Cordelia, clasping her hands together. "I'm so excited for you."

The prospect was terrifying. Dancing when she didn't know the steps. Meeting strangers when she wouldn't know what to say. "I can't go. I haven't anything to wear."

"The seamstress has promised a dress for you by tonight," Emily said.

Cordelia shook her head. If the invitation came through Lady Marsfield, there was a chance Burke would be there. Cordelia would prefer to avoid him and thereby save herself additional heartache. "I'd rather stay with Sarah."

"I expect we'll run into a few old friends from home,"

Granny said. "As one of the last big balls of the season, it's sure to be a crush, and there are quite a number of southerners in London these days."

"Sounds lovely," Cordelia said, forcing a smile. "But I already have the beginnings of a headache, so I'll just stay home and catch up on my reading."

"Nonsense. We need you," Granny said. "The family presenting a united front at a time like this is absolutely essential."

"It's your duty as my older sister to be there when the announcement of my engagement is made." Emily looked at the clock again and patted her hair. "Four o'-clock on the dot in twenty seconds." She added her embroidery hoop, threads trailing, to the top of the basket and fluffed and adjusted her skirt. "I do love a punctual man. He should be walking in right about . . . now. Hello, darling, I've just been telling Cordelia about our plans."

Dandridge leaned over and kissed his fiancée on the lips, and not a quick peck either, right in front of her grandmother, who said not a word. In fact, Granny moved to the opposite chair so he could sit by Emily with his arm around her shoulders. Cordelia had the sensation that nothing in her world was as she'd thought it to be.

"Congratulations," she managed to stammer out.

"Thank you," Dandridge said. He smiled at Emily as he replied, "I am the luckiest man on earth to have found a brilliant woman to share my life and my work."

"Well, we're not happy that you're taking her away from us so soon," Theo said as he joined the group. He perched on the arm of Granny's chair, took up her hand, and held it, resting their entwined fingers on his thigh.

"Am I the very last person in this house to know about your wedding?" Cordelia asked.

"Of course not," Emily said. "I know how you fret about details, and you do tend to take charge . . ."

"There's nothing wrong with that," Dandridge said. "Shows good moral fiber."

"Yes, dear," Emily said, patting his knee. "But this is my wedding, and I wanted everything set before—"

"Before you told me?"

"Well, you do—"

"Arrange everything?" Heat crept up the back of Cordelia's neck. Just because she didn't like to blow with the wind and let chance determine what would happen. Just because she liked to know what came next, to have a plan. "So you weren't going to tell me until right before the ceremony? In the carriage on the way to the church? Is that what you're saying?"

"Not exactly. Please don't get upset."

Emily's words came a little late. Cordelia stood, clutching the packaged book. "If you'll excuse me, I think I'll take a walk in the garden." She didn't wait for a response but turned and walked to the door with measured steps.

"Cordelia? I'm sorry. I never meant to hurt your feelings. Cordelia? Please, come back."

She heard her sister's plaintive call but didn't pause.

"Leave her alone," Granny said. "She's had a few shocks this week and needs some time to adjust."

Then, thankfully, Cordelia was out of earshot and eyesight of the parlor. She continued on to the garden, avoiding the servants. A shiver racked her body. Feeling as if bits and pieces of her would fly off if she didn't hold herself together, she wrapped her arms around the book, clutching it to her breasts. A few shocks? That was an understatement of monumental proportions.

Not that Emily getting married was a shock. A wedding was the reason they had come to London in the first place. But to Randall Truebrill? And going to Egypt?

If Cordelia was honest, she had to admit that the real
shocks were that she didn't know her sister at all, and
that her sister viewed her actions as busybody interference. Who was it who had kept a roof over their heads
and food on the table, the one who faced reality and
made plans? Why, if she hadn't taken charge, then . . .

Well, she'd only done what had seemed necessary at
the time. Dire circumstances required dire measures.
She refused to regret her actions. How could she? Emily
and Granny had found happiness. Dandridge and Theo
had handled the situation, including the lies, with good
humor. Even Sarah had forgiven them for the masquerade once everything had been explained to her. Only
Burke had refused to see the mitigating circumstances,
refusing to even listen to her side of the story.

"If Burke is that stiff-necked, then he's not a man I can
love," Cordelia said to a marble Greek goddess guarding
the entrance to the formal garden.

She found a bench and plopped down. So where did
that leave her? She would always have a home with
Granny and Theo, the two senior lovebirds who sneaked
off every day for a carriage ride in the park—as if they
were fooling anyone. Both of them were old enough to
know better. Soon they would get married and go off on
the honeymoon already in the planning stages, a Grand
Tour together. Sarah was already talking about spending
the next year at an exclusive girl's school in Switzerland
that Granny had attended as a young girl. Suddenly
Cordelia saw her future as very lonely. Even Thunderation would soon be moved to Theo's country estate.

She didn't want to be the spinster aunt who came for
Christmas with lavish gifts for the children she rarely saw.
She didn't want to be the guest at the dinner table
paired up with the odd man to make it even. She wanted
to go home.

At least back in Georgia she'd have a home of her own. Not much of a home, to be sure, but the war couldn't last forever. The land could be made productive again. She could rebuild. At home she would be useful—and that thought reminded her that she still had one more letter to deliver before she went home.

Cordelia stood, but hesitated. Where would she get the fare to take a ship home? Theo would probably lend her the money, but with the war, it could be years before the plantation showed a profit and she could pay him back. She was already indebted to him for so much. Borrowing from the donations was not an option.

Maybe she could find a real position as a chaperone or companion to someone returning to America. Granny had mentioned there were quite a few Confederates in London, and the season was drawing to an end. Surely someone would be returning home. If she could find one who needed a companion, her problem would be solved. With her plan set, she headed back to the house, her steps resolute. The ball tonight was as good a place as any to start.

She would find a hiding place for the book, then worry about what she would wear to her first public outing in London as an adult. Possibly this would be the first time Burke would see her as a woman instead of as a girl. She crossed her fingers, not sure if she hoped to see him or dreaded to.

Burke stretched and rolled his stiff shoulders before putting the spyglass back to his eye. Watching Cordelia's house was more tedious than reading diplomatic dispatches. From his perch in the attic window of an empty house a block away, he could see the comings and goings at Gravely's, although his meticulous notes had no listings beyond the usual servant activity, tradesman's deliveries, Theo and Vivian's daily drive, and the arrivals of that opportunist Randall Dandridge, who had been received on a daily basis.

At least he knew Cordelia was still there. He'd caught a glimpse of her as she walked in the garden. Had she seemed paler than usual, more subdued, or had that been his imagination?

"I brought you something to eat."

Burke lowered the glass and turned to his friend. "Thank you. I'm half-starved."

"Anything to report?" Preston asked, entirely too cheerfully.

"Twenty-seven birds have visited the birdbath in the side lawn so far today." He looked at his list. "Twelve wrens, three nuthatches, two yellow buntings, three finches, two jays, a magpie, a chiff-chaff, a spotted flycatcher, a swallow, and a raven that seems to have escaped incarceration in the Tower of London."

"Never knew you were a bird fancier."

Burke gave him a glare as he stood and walked to the small table and wobbly chair. "I'm not," he said, handing Preston the spyglass and picking up his sandwich.

Preston wandered over to the window and propped one hip on the sill and one boot on the chair Burke had vacated. As he surveyed the area below, he spoke over his shoulder. "Marsfield says there are definite rumblings in the House of Lords—although, in two instances Cordelia's plans seem to have back-fired. Castleton and Jonesbourough, both on our list of possible targets for the Confederate agent, have publicly voiced support of the queen. Curious, don't you think?"

Burke grunted in agreement. He would add that to the long litany of inconsistencies he'd been turning over and over in his mind the last few days. Lack of activity had left him too much time for brooding. He had re-lived every encounter with the suspected agent, and had found nothing to indicate Cordelia was acting on behalf of her country.

In the process, he was surprised to learn actions he'd once deemed charmingly childlike, now, with the knowl-edge of her true age, had the power to arouse him. The memory of her smile warmed him, and the recollection of her scent tickled his senses. The well-remembered sight of her rising from the water, and the unforgettable feel of her body lying on his chest had both caused acute physical reactions. He hadn't had such uncontrollable and inconvenient stiffness since early adolescence.

Yet he had to ask himself whether or not his response to her had clouded his judgment. Did he not notice any-thing suspicious because he didn't want to see?

"I don't see how Cordelia could be in contact with any-one. She hasn't been away from the house once in three days."

"Letters, messages." Preston flipped through the pages of Burke's notes. "I see she's received a package from a bookstore. Then there's the dancing master, the seamstress and her two assistants, the—"

"You and Marsfield have already checked everyone. Is there a possibility we've made a mistake?"

Preston gave him an assessing look. "Possibility? Yes. Probability? I don't think so. You're the one who brought the letter from Pinkerton to Marsfield in the first place. Are you saying—"

"No, no. I haven't changed my mind about that." Burke dragged his hands through his hair, rubbing his scalp. "I'm still convinced there's a danger. I just have my doubts as to Cordelia's involvement."

"Then let me remind you of a few facts. Within twenty-four hours of her arrival, we followed several exiled

Confederates to an empty warehouse for a meeting of sympathizers and suppliers. Our source says their leader promised not only imminent action, but also a fresh supply of gold for the purchase of arms, ammunition, and medical supplies. By extension, that also means gold for bribes."

"But she hasn't—"

"She's done nothing we can put our finger on, but she did represent herself falsely. For that alone, she remains suspect."

Burke pushed the remains of his meal aside and stood. He shook his head. "In my gut, it doesn't feel right," he said, fisting his hand over his stomach.

Preston laughed. "Either that meat was tainted, or you need to indicate a different portion of your anatomy, my friend. The ability to inspire lust is an underrated weapon. I remember a French agent, Cloe was her name. We met in a chalet in the Swiss Alps and interrogated each other day and night for an unbelievable week."

"Spare me your stories."

"Just a reminder not to lose your perspective."

"Cordelia is different, not like that . . . that Cloe, at all."

"Maybe." Preston examined his fingertips. "I guess we'll know soon enough. Marsfield wants me to offer my services. To see if I can get close to her, find out anything."

Burke took two threatening steps forward before he remembered Preston was his best friend. He forced his muscles and fists to relax. "Why would he suggest that to you?"

Preston shrugged. "He's only trying to be helpful. You haven't been inside the house since the real Precious arrived. If I pretend to court Cordelia—"

"Not necessary. If he thinks that's a good idea, then I can do that."

"Then I can escort her to various functions—"

"I'll do that."

"Where, hopefully, we can observe her making contact, and if the opportunity arises, I'll interrogate—"

"No, you won't. If anyone interrogates her, I will."

"I have more experience in this type of—"

"Your experience be dammed. I'm in charge of this investigation. I'll handle the situation."

Preston shook his head. "So far you haven't—"

"Damn and blast it." Burke stomped to the other side of the room and took several deep breaths, releasing each one to a slow count of ten. He'd spent years learning to control his temper and here he was ready to resort to violence against his best friend. Over a woman. "Damn. Damn. Damn."

"If you will allow me to finish a single sentence . . ."

Burke nodded but remained with his back against the far wall.

"So far you haven't made any progress getting back inside the house; however, Marsfield thinks if you can accomplish it within the next twenty-four hours, your previous relationship as a friend of the family will be an advantage over a relative stranger, *c'est moi*, stepping in."

"Why twenty-four hours?"

"We're not sure, but two different sources named Monday as significant."

"That's five days away."

Preston smiled a wicked smile. "If you fail, that still leaves me time to get in the door and—"

"Like hell it does." Burke grabbed his coat and hat and headed for the door.

"We've learned Vivian has accepted an invitation to the Asterbules' ball tonight. Cordelia is expected to attend."

"Then that's where I'll be."

"Be careful, my friend. Never let your emotions over-rule your reason."

Burke didn't dignify the spurious warning with a reply.

"What about the surveillance?" Preston called after him.

"Count the birds to stay awake," he replied, his voice echoing back up the empty attic stairway.

Burke didn't know what he was going to say to her just yet, but he would think of something, anything, before he would let Preston *interrogate* Cordelia.

Fifteen

Cordelia eyed her mirrored image critically. Her dark rose dress was starkly plain, devoid of ruffles, bows, or flowers. Not by the seamstress's design, but simply because they'd run out of time, basting the last seam even as she donned her petticoats. Still, the moiré silk caught the light in shifting patterns, giving the illusion of complexity that to her eye complemented the unadorned lines. Her long white gloves reached to within the required two inches of her puffed sleeves. Before leaving to help Emily with her finishing touches, Quimsy had done up Cordelia's hair in a twisted chignon, accented with sweet-smelling, barely pink rosebuds from the garden.

The effect of bare shoulders and the deep heart-shaped neckline was quite elegant, but the décolletage was lower than she remembered it being during the fitting. Either the seamstress had erred, or the new corset, trussed an extra inch tighter, had pushed Cordelia's small breasts higher than normal. The wisp of material barely covered her nipples. One good sneeze and she'd pop right out.

Wouldn't that attract Burke's attention?

She shook aside any more stray thoughts of him. She wasn't going to the ball in hopes of seeing him, but to find a respectable position that just happened to include a voyage home. She frowned at her reflection. Not the image of a dependable, mature woman that she wanted to create.

However, it was too late to start dressing all over, and
she had nothing else appropriate to wear. Neither her
old, outdated clothes nor any of Sarah's girlish outfits
would do for the evening ahead. Quimsy knocked on the
door and informed her everyone else was already downstairs, even Emily, who hadn't wanted to keep Not-Ernest
waiting.

Cordelia tucked a handkerchief across her bosom, but
that just looked like she expected to start drooling and
would need a bib. She tore several large roses off an old
bonnet and poked the short stems into her now ample
cleavage. That looked like she'd padded her bodice for
fullness and the stuffing was bursting out. Plus they
itched. Searching for something else, she found a wide
length of lace in the seamstress's tidy stack of material
awaiting the next day's fitting, and wrapped it around
her neck and shoulders, draping it to cover the exposed
tops of her breasts.

A quick check in the mirror assured her that she was
decent, so she grabbed her reticule and fan and rushed
out of the room.

The music swirled around her, but Cordelia wasn't interested in dancing. Her cheeks hurt from smiling so
much, and her neck ached from nodding. Listening to
one matron after another recount the itinerary of her
sojourn in London had tested Cordelia to the limits of
her forbearance. She'd located an elderly widow who
might need a companion in the near future. Mrs. Barse-
worth was hard of hearing and had limited topics of
conversation. Two months confined in a small cabin with
her incessant talk of the aches and pains of getting older
seemed a dismal prospect. Cordelia shuddered. Emily
and Granny may not have been ideal shipmates, but at

least they hadn't bored her to stupefaction. Cordelia intended to continue searching.

Excusing herself with a blatant lie about finding her sister, Cordelia edged around the crowded dance floor and headed for the ladies' retiring room. All she wanted was a few minutes of blessed silence before resuming her quest. She sidestepped around four young dandies who had inexplicably chosen the narrow path between the dancers and the row of chairs lining the wall to compare coats and discuss the merits of horn buttons versus metal ones. She dodged a couple of enthusiastic dancers who apparently misjudged their sweeping turn and nearly crashed into several unsuspecting bystanders.

Now she knew why they called it a crush. Was every peer in London packed into this one overheated ballroom? She knew Granny and Theo had headed for the card room to play whist, but she'd lost track of Emily and Dandridge an hour ago. Cordelia ducked through an archway to avoid being seen by Rutherford Ketters, who, after trampling her feet for an entire country dance, had assured her that he would look her up later for another "go at it." Even if he did have a twin sister who would be returning to Atlanta after an unsuccessful season, Cordelia wasn't yet desperate enough to sacrifice her toes for a position. There were more Americans at the party for her to meet.

The archway led into a picture gallery that ran the length of the ballroom. An errant puff of cool air wafted across her bare shoulders. Although the long, wide hall was also crowded, matching sets of French doors at both ends stood open, encouraging the evening breeze to circulate. Turning her face into the fresh, garden-scented air, she turned right and followed her nose. Without a chaperone, she couldn't promenade along the verandah or walk in the moonlit garden as many lucky partygoers were doing, but that didn't mean she couldn't examine the paintings nearest the doors. No one would find fault in her admiring the art collection, dubious as the hostess's taste might be.

Assuming an expression of intense interest, she paced from sour-faced portrait to dull landscape to insipid still life, edging closer to her goal with studied nonchalance. As she reached the last painting, a portrait of a stern matron and her two frowning black and white French bulldogs, half a dozen men in uniform chose that moment to reenter the gallery. Yankees! Instinctively, Cordelia hid behind a large potted plant in the corner.

She shook her head and chided herself. Silly goose. Yankees could not hurt her here. She let out the breath she'd been holding. Nevertheless, she decided to wait until they passed by her before coming out. Perhaps she ought to consider finding Emily and Dandridge after all. Taking a step forward, she realized the spines on the leaves had caught in her lace wrap, trapping her in the tiny alcove. She struggled to free herself, only succeeding in digging one of the pointed leaves into her skin. She twisted around to reach for the offending greenery.

Cordelia felt rather than heard him. Even before he spoke, she knew Burke was behind her. Maybe a draft had wafted his distinct citrus-woodsy scent her way. Maybe it was his near silent footfalls. Whatever the clue, the pleasant shiver up her spine told her Burke was near. She spun around.

"Surely you could find a better dancing partner than this," he said with a smile, reaching for the bit of lace stuck to the plant. "Perhaps one that wouldn't try to disrobe you?" he whispered, so close his breath fanned her ear.

How was she supposed to forget him and concentrate on her future if he was right next to her?

"What are you doing here?" she asked, also whispering, so as not to attract undue attention. "I'm surprised you're even speaking to me after . . . after telling me I'm nothing but trouble. Why are you—"

"Perhaps I overreacted. I'm willing to—"

"Forgive me? How generous of you Lord Deering. Now if you don't mind, I'll find my sister."

He fingered her lace wrap where it was caught on the plant.

"What are you doing?"

"Apparently I'm rescuing you from a tall, green, overeager admirer." He tugged, and the lace came free in his hand, free of the plant and free of her dress. His gaze widened slightly and his eyes darkened to a deeper shade of blue. "Although, I must say, I can't quibble with the end result."

She looked down. Her breasts, dislodged by her earlier fussing, practically hung out of her bodice. Flipping open her fan, she held it in front of her, shielding herself from the warmth of his gaze. Grateful for the accessory she'd always derided as silly and pretentious, she used her other hand to yank upward on her bodice. "A gentleman would not notice."

He chuckled. "Maybe a blind man."

"A gentleman would refrain from uttering such a tactless comment."

He shrugged. "I'm only being truthful."

"As opposed to my lies?"

"A precious rose by any other name would still have thorns."

"What a charming, and witty *bon mot*. You really know how to sweep a woman off her feet," Cordelia said, giving him a honeyed smile but allowing her voice an acidic edge. She peeked through the plant leaves to see the

Yankees lingering by the door. It was a ball, for Pete's sake; why didn't they go dance?

"I never claimed to be a poet," Burke said. "If I wanted to sweep you off your feet, I wouldn't use words."

"Really? Oh, I remember. Your forte is dancing. How could I have forgotten? The country reel, wasn't it?"

He smiled a wicked grin. "In your own words, a woman never forgets her first waltz."

"Did I say that?" She forced out a little trill of laughter. "You may consider that yet another untruth and count it forgotten. Now, if you'll excuse me?" She stepped forward, expecting him to back away. He did not.

"Excuse me," she said again, nodding toward the entrance to the ballroom that he was blocking with his body. Any gentleman would understand and move out of her way. Instead he took a step forward.

"We danced well together," he said, his voice a husky whisper. "That portends—"

"What? Never mind. I don't think I want to know." She stepped back again.

Burke reached for her left hand, unbuttoning the tiny pearl buttons at the wrist of her glove as he raised her hand to his lips. "Aren't you the least bit curious how I would sweep you off your feet?" he asked, his breath skimming her bare wrist. "I think you are," he said, his mouth against her skin. "Your pulse is beating *prestissimo.*"

"Agitation with your impertinence." She pulled her hand out of his grasp. Dropping her fan to let it dangle by the cord around her right wrist, she re-buttoned her glove.

"I think perhaps you need this." He folded the lace and presented it to her with a slight bow, and a blood-stain on the cloth became visible. "You're hurt. Turn around."

She hesitated and the gentle pressure of his hand

turned her to face the corner. She peeked over her shoulder, but could see nothing.

"The villain plant has marked you, milady," he said, his fierce expression at odds with his light words.

"What? I can't see anything."

"A red welt about four inches long, bleeding a bit at the top." He quickly untied his snowy white neck cloth and pressed it to her shoulder blade. "Unchivalrous plant. Shall I seek revenge in your name?"

The whispered conversation, too intimate, too close, set her senses quivering. "Don't be ridiculous. I'm fine. It doesn't even hurt." She spun around, expecting him to drop his arm and step back. Instead, she turned into the half circle of his arm, her movement causing an increase of pressure on her wound. She winced.

"Liar," he whispered, his voice huskier than before. "Such a lovely liar." Bracing his free hand against the wall, he leaned over her, slowly coming closer and closer.

He intended to kiss her. She knew she should try to escape. Kick him in the shin, duck around him, or even holler for help. But she couldn't. Nay, she didn't want to escape. She craved the taste of his lips, had wished for this in her heart of hearts from the moment she'd first laid eyes on him. Her Viking warrior. Once her plans came to fruition she would never see him again, never have the chance to . . .

Cordelia refused to think about that now. She would seize the opportunity even if she regretted it later. Raising her chin, she stood on tiptoe to meet him halfway. She closed her eyes and puckered up, willing him to hurry.

He chuckled and her eyelids flew open.

"You look like you just sucked on a lemon," he said, his eyes sparkling with amusement. "Haven't you ever been kissed by a man before?"

"Of course I have." If you counted sisterly pecks on the cheek from her father and her male cousins and one clumsy, drunken, slobbery, apologetic kiss from poor Travis the night before he left for the war. Not by anyone she wanted to kiss back, she also failed to add.

He smiled. "That may be so, but there are different kisses. This," he said kissing her on the forehead, "signifies fondness. On the left cheek is simply a greeting. On the right cheek, a kiss means thank you." He demonstrated both with quick efficiency. "A kiss on the tip of your pert nose is only saying that you are adorable."

She looked up at him. "But . . ."

"Oh, I'm not forgetting lips. Although kissing on the lips is a most enjoyable activity in itself, a kiss on the lips is also a promise."

Her blood turned to warm honey. "And pray sir, what would you promise with such a kiss?"

"Many things," he whispered, leaning close to her. "Relax. I won't hurt you."

She knew he couldn't keep that promise, for her heart had already been wounded once, but she tried to relax anyway. Which was difficult, because she felt like a child on Christmas morning facing the biggest, brightest present under the tree with her name on it. He leaned in another inch. Waiting was excruciating.

"Close your eyes," he said.

She did.

"Relax your lips," he said, his mouth grazing hers.

His lips, dry and smooth and oh so warm, gently explored hers, encouraged her to explore his in return. Only their lips and his hand on her shoulder connected them. With the tip of his tongue, he licked at her lips, sending chills across every inch of her skin.

"Open for me," he said against her lips, and she drank in his words.

He tasted of peppermint and brandy and . . . heat; glorious, wonderful heat. Desire balled her stomach and sent honey through her veins. She shivered in the warmth of his body heat. No, that didn't make sense, but she could not stop to puzzle it out. She swayed toward Burke, wanting . . . wanting . . . something; she didn't know what. A mewling moan escaped her.

He pulled back a fraction. She followed, eager for whatever came next.

"Easy," he whispered, slowing the pace of his kisses, each a little less fervent. "You have convinced me that you are quite experienced," he whispered, the lie sliding off his tongue with surprising ease, "But now is neither the time nor the place to indulge our mutual appetites."

What was he saying? What did he mean? Cordelia fought to regain her senses. Suddenly the room came back into focus and she realized she'd been kissing a man practically in full view of half the *ton*. Embarrassment warmed her cheeks. "I . . . I . . ."

"Don't worry. No one can see. Your reputation is safe. From everyone except me." Burke grinned as he handed her the piece of lace.

"Thank you," she said automatically, and draped it around her neck, tucking the edges into her bodice and sleeves.

"Need any help?" he asked with a comic leer.

She did not respond to his attempted humor. "No. I'm finished already."

"Don't say that as if you and I are done. Shall I escort you home tonight or call on you tomorrow morning?"

Cordelia flipped open her fan and plied it with agitated movements, more for something to do than for the cool breeze it created. In fact, she felt decidedly chilled. "I will be leaving with my sister and grandmother tonight." Soon, she hoped. "And I will not be at home to-morrow morning."

How could she face him over a pot of coffee after what she had just done? Why, she'd practically begged the man to kiss her.

"Tomorrow afternoon?"

"Not then either. I intend to tell the butler that I will not be at home to you tomorrow or any day thereafter. In fact, I would prefer never to see you again. Now, if you will excuse me?"

He stepped back, making only a small opening between himself and the wall. "Liar," he whispered in her ear as she squeezed past him.

Burke folded his arms and leaned against the wall, observing her hurry away, her hips swaying in unconscious provocation, skirts twitching with each agitated step. He smiled. Cordelia didn't know it yet, but they had unfinished business. She could not get rid of him that easily.

"Find anything out?" Preston asked, stepping forward with a cheroot in each hand. He gave one to Burke and nodded toward the verandah.

As they strolled toward the unoccupied far end, Burke drew in the smooth smoke and debated with himself how much to tell his friend. "How long were you watching?" he asked, as they found a deserted spot and leaned against the balustrade. The thought of his friend spying on him and Cordelia together made him more uncomfortable than he had thought it would.

"Long enough." Preston shrugged. "It's a thankless job, but someone has to guard your back."

Burke nodded his appreciation. The house could have caught on fire and he wouldn't have noticed, so completely had the woman beguiled him. He turned to face the darkened garden, the sweet taste of Cordelia still on his lips, the honeysuckle scent of her still in his nostrils despite the expensive cheroot between his fingers.

"Did you learn anything?" Preston asked again.

"Nothing of importance to the case."

"Until we resolve the issue, it is difficult to judge the relative importance of any bit of information."

Burke nodded reluctantly. "She's an innocent."

"Or a very good actress."

He bristled. Was it because Preston doubted his judgment or because his friend doubted Cordelia? He suspected it was the latter. "I know an innocent when I kiss one." That had always been a red flag telling him to run in the opposite direction.

"Even that will be helpful, should I be needed to interrogate the suspect," Preston said with a grin.

"You won't."

"You never know. I've always been lucky at cards and with women."

Burke flicked the remainder of his cigar into the flower bed below. He faced Preston with cold fury. "Mark my words carefully, friend. You will never touch that woman. Not even over my dead body."

Burke was unsure where those words had come from yet knew he'd spoken the fearful truth. A truth he wasn't ready to face, wasn't ready to fully admit even to himself. He shook himself like a wet dog. "Sorry about that. Don't know what came over me."

Preston only laughed and slapped him on the shoulder. "My friend, you've got it bad."

"Got what?"

"The dreaded sickness. Love. With a capital L."

"Don't be ridiculous."

"It's written all over your face."

"Nonsense. Intelligent people do not fall in love."

"I know, pap for the unfulfilled masses and all that

rubbish. I've heard your theories before." Preston did not stop grinning. "Nevertheless, you've got it."

"Love is irrational and illogical. I am neither; therefore, it is a foregone conclusion that I cannot be in love."

"I can't believe it took a little chit of a Confederate agent to bring the mighty god of logic and reason to his knees. It's utterly marvelous."

"You are insane. And she is not the foreign agent."

"You haven't proven that yet. She spent the entire evening meeting with assorted Americans, mostly known Confederates or Confederate sympathizers. How do you explain that?"

"Home sickness? Good manners?"

"Hah!"

Burke turned and stomped away, leaving Preston still chuckling. The man really was insane. Love? Rubbish. Bloody insane rubbish. If he had to put a name to his feelings for Cordelia, it would be . . . lust and . . . fair play. That was it. The unjust accusations leveled against her went against his well-developed sense of fair play. Any man, or woman, had the right to expect proof beyond a shadow of a doubt before she was convicted and hanged as a spy.

A feeling of dread swept over him. He would not let them hang Cordelia. In this case he didn't need proof of guilt, but proof of her innocence. The best way to clear Cordelia's name was to find the real spy. Quickly.

Sixteen

Cordelia placed the card back in the silver tray held by the butler. "Thank you. You may tell Lord Deering we are not at home."

Emily jumped up and raced toward the butler, grabbing the card before he could turn away, giving lie to her supposed semi invalid state in which she needed Not-Ernest to carry her up and down the stairs twice a day. "Please tell Lord Deering we will receive him in five minutes. And you may serve tea."

The butler bowed and left before Cordelia could contradict her sister's instructions.

"Why did you do that?" Cordelia put her hands on her hips. "I'm not dressed to receive company." She hadn't expected anyone other than Dandridge and had not seen the need to fuss over her appearance. The man barely noticed anyone else's presence once he'd set eyes on Emily.

"Well, you can't leave. It wouldn't be proper."

"I'll fetch Granny. She can chaperone."

"She's playing the piano for Sarah's dancing lesson, because the regular pianist is ill."

"Then I guess you're on your own." Cordelia rose to leave.

"You can't leave me alone with him. What would Not-Ernest think?"

"That you're a headstrong woman who got herself in a pickle by interfering in her sister's life?"

Emily folded her hands under her chin, and gave Cordelia an overly sweet smile. "And that's *your* usual role, isn't it?"

"You don't understand—"

"Oh, but I think I do. What's the matter? Can't take it as well as you dish it out?" Emily, confident in her new role as Dandridge's soon-to-be wife, was paying back years of big-sisterly advice and interference.

Cordelia knew she couldn't argue her way out of the situation. At least not in the next five minutes. She didn't have time to change out of her plain afternoon dress, either. She gave up and sat down, taking consolation in the fact that Emily would soon be bossing Egyptian tomb diggers around. "I'm only here as your chaperone. You may entertain Burke since you're the one who allowed him in."

"At least put on your gloves."

Cordelia complied, but not without a frown. Sewing was tedious enough without the necessity of stitching while wearing gloves just because they had company. More than once she'd sewn the tip of one finger to the back of a sampler.

"And, you might want to fix your hair. It's sticking up on that side." Emily pointed to a vague spot over her left ear.

She stubbornly ignored the advice and took up her embroidery, determined not to even look at the man. How could she face him after what she'd done, the way she'd behaved? How would he behave toward her? When her sister turned toward the door, Cordelia surreptitiously smoothed her hair. Emily must have caught the motion from the corner of her eye, because she gave Cordelia a knowing smile.

"Gnat," Cordelia said. "I heard buzzing." She gazed into the air off to her left as if searching for the nonexistent insect. "Must have been a gnat. Can't see it now, though."

Emily nodded wisely, but the corner of her mouth twitched. "Of course. Gnats are bad this time of year in London."

Were they? Cordelia had no idea. Then Burke entered, and as much as she wanted to, she couldn't ignore him. His presence seemed to fill the room. His height, his broad shoulders, the panther grace of his walk. He was the epitome of an English gentleman in his gray afternoon coat and striped trousers.

"Good afternoon, Miss Weston," Burke formally greeted Cordelia first, as good manners dictated the eldest sister should be so honored. However, after an inane comment on the weather, he turned to face her sister.

"Miss Emily, I called today to apologize for my breech of manners."

"Good heavens, Lord Deering, whatever for? I didn't notice you being remiss."

Surely Burke wouldn't carry tales of their behavior to her sister. Cordelia clasped her palms together in her lap, braiding her fingers so her hands would not tremble. He never even glanced her way.

"I failed to offer my felicitations on your upcoming nuptials last evening. I hear your family's announcement was quite the hit of the evening."

"How kind of you, though totally unnecessary. It was such a crush, I don't even remember seeing you there."

"Oh, I was there. And I must say, you looked lovely. Not every woman can wear that singular shade of peach, but it is definitely your color. You should wear it more often."

They chatted on, and Cordelia could have been a stick of furniture for all the notice Burke—or her own sister, for that matter—gave her. He really turned on the charm, and Emily lapped it up like a tabby with her first bowl of cream.

Cordelia looked up at the clock. Thank goodness Dandridge was expected at four for tea. Then she could escape the humiliation of being blatantly ignored by the very man who had kissed her just the night before.

However, Dandridge rushed in, grabbed Emily's hand, and drew her to a far corner for a whispered conference before Cordelia could excuse herself.

Burke sat on the sofa next to Cordelia, his back ramrod straight, staring ahead, clutching his teacup in two hands. "Are you enjoying your stay in London, Miss Weston?" he asked loudly, as if he wanted Emily to hear him, rather than Cordelia, who was less than two feet away.

Her temper snapped. "What is the matter with you?" she hissed. "You're as stiff as a board."

Burke groaned and closed his eyes.

"I don't know what I expected from you after last night, but it wasn't being ignored," she continued in an angry whisper. "Say something." She poked his arm. "Are you made of wood?"

If Burke had ever doubted her innocence after last night's kiss, he never would again. Only a true innocent could spout such innuendoes without batting an eye. The problem was, he was as stiff as a board. At least one particular part of his anatomy seemed to be made of wood. One look at Cordelia, one sniff of her unique scent, and memories of last night and the taste of her lips had assailed him, and his body had reacted as if he were an unruly schoolboy. Not that he had ever been unruly, but he couldn't prove that by his current reaction.

His only hope to avoid embarrassment had been to ignore Cordelia, and to distract her sister, the not-so-innocent Miss Weston, so that no one would notice his predicament until he got himself under control. He'd babbled on, inane social chitchat that had become second nature in his job, not knowing or caring what he said, while in his head he recited the multiplication tables.

He'd reached eleven times twelve, and the distraction had been working, as it always had, until Cordelia had made the comment about him being stiff. He took a deep breath and started over again at one times one.

"I give up," Cordelia said, throwing up her hands and slumping back into the cushions of the sofa. Her arms fell to her sides. "I'll never understand men."

Moving with deliberate care, Burke placed his nearly full teacup on the table, turned in his seat and braced one arm on the back of the sofa near her head. Keeping an eye on Emily and Dandridge still in conference on the other side of the room, he found Cordelia's hand, tracing the seams on her glove with one finger.

"Stop that," she said, but she didn't move her hand.

"Don't give up on me, Cordelia," he whispered.

"What is that supposed to mean? I'm so confused."

"So am I. We need to talk. Where are you going tonight? I'll meet you there, anywhere."

She shook her head. "We're dancing attendance on Dandridge's rich relatives. The ones that are helping sponsor his expedition. Very important to make a good impression."

"Then ride with me tomorrow. It's my last morning before Theo ships Thunderation off to the country."

Again she shook her head. "It's two days before the wedding. With everything Emily has scheduled, I'll be busy from dawn till past midnight."

"Then meet me at midnight."

Before she could answer, Sarah stormed into the parlor. She stopped just inside the door, put her hands on her hips, and blew out her breath in a huff. "How am I supposed to learn to dance without music?"

Cordelia sat up. "Granny is playing for you."

Sarah bent forward, shaking her head. "No, she's not. Your crazy grandmother, last seen in the garden wearing that ridiculous Mab the Fairy Queen outfit and talking to the flowers, is nowhere to be found."

Dandridge and Emily rushed over.

"We were just discussing a plan to find her," Emily said.

Cordelia jumped up. "You knew about this? And you didn't say anything?"

"Dandridge just got the news on his way in." Emily motioned toward Burke with her head. "I was going to tell you . . . later."

"I take it this means I don't have a dancing lesson?" Sarah asked. She nodded, answering her own question. "Then I'm sending that mincing fool of a dancing master home. I'll be in my room if you need me," she added on the way out.

A moment's reflection allowed Cordelia to realize Emily had meant to wait until after Burke left to discuss the matter of Granny's disappearance, but time was of the essence. "Burke can help us. Who knows what trouble Granny can get herself into? We have to find her quickly."

"Let's not panic," Burke said. "We'll split up into search parties. Footmen, maids, everyone. If Vivian thinks she's Mab, we should concentrate on the gardens and parks."

"That won't be necessary," Dandridge said. "According to the footman, Vivian had him hail a hackney cab, and she told the driver to take her to Janestown Green. She's headed for that pagan festival. Where else would Mab the Fairy Queen be on Midsummer's Eve?"

"The what?" Cordelia asked, looking from one Englishman to the other. "What festival?"

Burke answered. "It's a throwback to ancient times when druids, fairies, and elves supposedly gathered to celebrate Midsummer's Eve. There are still a few people who sincerely believe in the old ways, but mostly it is just an excuse for—"

"It's an excuse for a drunken org—"

"Party," Burke interrupted Dandridge in turn. "A big, loud costume party outdoors. The Church has been trying to stop it for decades, but . . ." He shrugged. "The designated place is different each year, the location passed on secretly. Hundreds of people manage to find it. Servants, farmers, foreigners . . ."

"Young bucks of the ton," Dandridge added.

"How do you know all this?" Cordelia asked Burke.

He loosened his collar with a finger. "I went to the festival a time or two. In my youth."

"So this Midsummer Festival is at Janestown Green," Cordelia said. "What are we waiting for?" She started toward the door. "Let's go get Granny."

Burke stopped her with a hand on her shoulder. "Dandridge and I can handle this."

"No, Dandridge can't," Emily chimed in. She brushed off her fiancé's protest. "Dandridge and I have a dinner engagement that is very important to his career. If Granny were in her right mind, I know she would want the rest of us to act as if nothing were at odds. Burke has volunteered to fetch her, and I say we let him."

"Vivian's safety is more important than—"

"Actually," Burke interrupted Dandridge, "that may be for the best."

"Not cricket to let you take on the burden," Dandridge said, shaking his head. "Vivian is practically my family."

"Have you ever been to one of these?" Burke asked.

"Can't say that I have," Dandridge answered, pulling on his whiskers. "Never saw the point in dressing up in a silly outfit just to—"

"In that case, I'll move faster and cover more ground on my own."

"I'll go with you," Cordelia said.

"Absolutely not," Burke said with fervor.

"I want to help," she argued.

"You, uh, you can help by staying here in case she comes back early. That way Dandridge and Emily can attend their dinner. If there's new information, you can organize other search parties."

"It doesn't sound like that's going to be of much help," Cordelia said, sticking out her bottom lip. She usually took charge and found Granny, but London was unfamiliar territory and she could just as easily get lost herself.

"Believe me," Burke said, with a gentle squeeze on her shoulder. "It will ease my mind to know you're here."

Cordelia nodded.

"I'll leave right away." Burke pulled out his large pocket watch, and while it played "God Save the Queen," he said, "It's now just past four. An hour to get there, and, say, an hour to find Vivian—two hours tops because the bulk of the revelers won't arrive until dark. I could conceivably have her home before you leave for your dinner engagement, but don't wait. Traffic at these events can be horrific."

"Wouldn't you travel faster on horseback? You could take Thunderation," Cordelia offered.

"I thought of that, but getting a cab to bring Vivian home will be near impossible. And I'd have to leave Thunderation in a stranger's care while I search for her. These types of crowded events are open invitations for pickpockets and horse thieves." Burke shook his head. "I'll take my carriage. My coachman is a good man, dependable."

"Armed, too, I hope," Dandridge said under his breath.

Cordelia walked Burke to the door, taking his hat and cane from the butler and handed them to him.

"Don't worry," he said. "I'll make sure your grand-mother is safe."

"I don't know how to thank you for all your kindness."

He looked around the entrance, noting only the stone-faced butler who stood at the other end, staring off into space. Burke bent over, and, holding his hat so the butler couldn't see their faces, he gave Cordelia a peck on the lips. Straightening, he said, "Perhaps, that's an-other thing we can talk about, later." He put his hat on his head, giving it an extra jaunty tap on the top, and left her with a wink and a grin.

Cordelia stood gazing at the door for a moment. A man had never winked at her before. What was that sup-posed to mean? Emily would know. Yet, for some reason, she decided not to ask her sister.

Six hours later, Cordelia had more questions than an-swers, and no one to answer her. Theo had not returned from his business, but his valet didn't expect him until late. Sarah, petulant in the best of times, had chosen a thick volume from a library shelf and taken herself off to bed after Cordelia had asked for the umpteenth time, "Where can they be?"

As long as Emily and Dandridge were in the room, calmly discussing their trip and names for the baby, Cordelia had not felt the rising sense of panic that threatened to overwhelm her now that she was alone. The past hour had crawled by.

"Where are Burke and Granny?" Cordelia asked the clock as she paced by it, wearing a path in the blue and gold carpet of the parlor. What if Granny had *not* gone to the festival and that's why Burke hadn't found her and returned? What if she was down by the river, wrapped in a bedsheet and looking for Cleopatra's barge? What if she was seated in the corner of an inn, offering to read palms for pennies? Cordelia knew both of those things were possible, based on previous experience.

She decided to check Granny's room, chiding herself for not thinking of it earlier. But the bedsheets were tucked securely in place, and the gypsy outfit hung neatly in the wardrobe. Cordelia stood, debating with herself whether or not Granny's trunk might hold a clue to her whereabouts, and whether or not the curse of all-over boils was still active, when she overheard two of the maids outside in the hall.

Cordelia recognized the voices and reached for the doorknob to announce her presence.

"No one is to know Kelso and me is going to Janestown," Quimsy said. "No one, you hear?"

Cordelia hesitated. The maids were talking about the festival. She leaned toward the door to hear better.

"Except me," Tweeny, the between-stairs maid, answered.

"Not even you. All you know is that I'm called away to my mother's sickbed. Got it?"

"But if you don't even leave till nine—"

"The real party doesn't get going until ten. And don't expect me back before dawn." Quimsy giggled. "If I'm lucky, that is."

"I wish I could go with you," Tweeny said with a sigh. "I hear there's hundreds of eligible men go to the festival."

"More like thousands," Quimsy said. "Free ale brings

the bachelors out of the woodwork. And you can't go, ''cause then who would answer the bells, huh?"

"What costume are you wearing?" Tweeny asked.

"Miss Emily gave me one of her old ballgowns what don't fit her no more. I'll be looking like a fine lady, I will."

"Don't you need a mask?"

"I've got this. Made it myself."

"That's not a real mask. Just a piece of cloth with eye-holes cut in it."

"It'll do," Quimsy said, her voice huffy. "Enough to keep me from being doused with water, anyways. Any disguise or costume is fine. It don't have to be a fancy-dancy one. Though you should see some o' them. Brocades and silks. Jewels and feathers and gold fringe."

"Coo, I do love fringe."

The maids moved out of earshot discussing the merits of feathers versus fringe, but Cordelia wasn't thinking about costumes. "Thousands of people," Quimsy had said. Burke would never find Granny in a crowd like that.

Cordelia headed for her bedroom. She should have told Burke to look for a flower-covered bench, because Mab liked to sit among her "ladies-in-waiting." She should have told Burke to look any place there was card playing or chess games. How could he find Granny if he didn't know her well enough to know where to look? Blast it all, she should have gone with him. Granny was her responsibility.

Cordelia put on a plain, serviceable dress. Discarding her reticule as too small to be useful, she dumped out her sewing basket on the bed. She stuffed it with any-thing and everything that might prove useful: a fat, stubby candle, a box of Lucifer matches, smelling salts, scissors, needle and thread, bandages and ointment, and ammunition. After checking her pistol to make sure it was loaded, she put it in the basket, covering it with a flap of the flowered chintz liner.

She swung a cape around her shoulders and adjusted the hood over her head. One more thing and she would be ready to go. No: two. She needed a mask. Retrieving the sewing scissors, she found a usable scrap of material, two inches wide and about three feet long, and cut two eyeholes near the center before hurriedly stuffing everything back into her basket.

On the way to the front door, she stopped in the parlor and took the money Theo had left in the desk drawer to pay the dancing master, who hadn't given a lesson today and had left without asking for his week's wages. Surely Theo would understand the emergency. She hoped it was enough to pay the cab fare all the way to Janestown Green.

Cordelia's feet hurt, and her arms ached from carrying the heavy basket. Janestown Green was not the rustic village square she'd expected, but rather a pasture, a very large pasture, currently filled with animals of the two-legged variety, most of them falling-down drunk or on their way to reaching that state. A number of bonfires, surrounded by raucous revelers singing bawdy chanteys, dotted the field. In the semidarkness between fires, couples strolled, necking and groping and in some cases rolling on the ground. Cordelia had nearly tripped over one such couple before she'd learned to keep to the newly worn paths between the fires. As for what went on in the darkness beyond the bushes, well, judging by the giggles, moans, grunts, and groans, she would not be looking for her grandmother there.

With determination, Cordelia headed for the next

bonfire. Several tables set off to the side gave her hope that she would find Granny embroiled in a whist game there. A man approached, heading the other way, and doffed his hat. He took one look at her and, shaking his head, gave her a wide berth as he passed her at a near run.

Not that she wanted any attention, but she'd encountered the same reaction multiple times, and, considering the circumstances around her, it was a tad disconcerting. She was prepared to defend her honor, but had only had to reach for her gun once. Even when she'd accidentally pulled out the scissors with a dramatic flourish, that had been enough to scare people off.

Though the scissors had come in handy, she wished she'd thought to pack a bite to eat. The aromas of meat roasting over open fires was torture, but she would not be deterred from her errand. There would be time to sample the wares of various vendors once she knew Granny was safe.

Cordelia noticed a gradual change in the crowd. Gone were the fresh-faced farm boys with pasteboard shields and wooden swords and the giggling dairymaids dressed as fairies. Although she still spotted an occasional person obviously rich enough to have a special costume made, most were replaced by thick-booted pirates with leering eyes, and loud women with low-cut dresses and red-painted lips below their black dominoes.

Cordelia rearranged her basket so that the pistol was within easy reach—just in case, although she would prefer to avoid trouble. A couple, he richly dressed as Henry the Eighth and she dressed as a water sprite, approached on the path. The woman looked directly at Cordelia, and giggled. The man shook his head as he passed by.

Enough was enough. Cordelia whirled around. "Just what is so funny," she demanded.

The other woman stopped and turned. "You won't have any fun wearing that," she said, pointing at Cordelia's face.

She raised her free hand to her homemade mask. "What's the matter with it?"

"Chickies and duckies are better suited to the nursery."

The material Cordelia had grabbed was left from the baby blanket she was making as a surprise for Emily.

The other woman took off her own elaborate mask, blue silk studded with brilliants and tiny white feathers, and tossed it to Cordelia. "Try that one." She smiled up at her escort. "It brought me luck tonight."

Cordelia caught it rather than let such a beautiful creation fall in the dirt. She said, "Thank you, but I can't accept such a gift," and raised her arm to toss the mask back.

"Consider it a loan. Without the need to return it. Besides, I'm not the original owner. It was loaned to me, too, with the instruction to pass it along to someone who needs a little luck."

Cordelia turned the mask over in her hand. She had never held anything quite so exquisite. Even in moonlight and the distant fire's glow, the brilliants sparkled like real diamonds. She shouldn't keep it, but when she looked up to decline and insist on giving it back, the unusual couple had disappeared into the darkness.

Hesitating only a few minutes, she took off her own mask and donned the blue silk one that was constructed in the manner of a pair of spectacles. Now she could see much more clearly than when she'd had the strip of material tied around her head. She resumed her search for Granny.

Within half an hour she regretted leaving her original mask behind and even considered going back to fetch it, trampled and dirty though it might be. Since she'd switched masks, nearly every man she met propositioned her in one way or another, which was worse than being laughed at and avoided.

Cordelia caught a glimpse of someone with her grandmother's build near the bonfire ahead, the last one in the long field. She plowed ahead, ignoring the invitations from the men she passed. Nearing the fire, she spotted a group of three drunken sailors heading her way. Trouble on six feet waiting to happen.

Instinct warned Cordelia the men were dangerous. She looked around for a hiding place. If she ducked into the woods, she had a pretty good idea what she'd find. She'd been raised in the country, but she'd never actually seen . . .

The drunken sailors came closer.

If she ran, could she get past them to the relative protection of the people around the fire? Possibly, but she was tired, and carrying a heavy basket.

She fingered her pistol. She could hold off one, or maybe two, but if the other one circled behind her . . .

Looking over her shoulder, Cordelia spotted some lights off to the right. Hoping it was a group headed for the last campfire, and figuring there was safety in numbers, she gathered her cloak around her and headed toward the lights at a brisk pace, not too fast because of the uneven ground, her clumsy sewing basket banging painfully against her hip.

When she reached the lights, she found a makeshift hut that had been built beneath a giant rowan tree, sheltered under the overhanging branches. Those branches moving in the slight breeze, together with the light shining through the windows of the small structure, had given an illusion of people carrying candles or small lanterns. She hadn't found the group of farm boys and dairymaids she'd hoped for, but if the hut would shield her from the view of the drunken sailors until they passed by, she was thankful for the godsend. Circling around the hut, looking for a spot to hide where light didn't seep through the tiny cracks, she investigated the curious structure.

Not only was it decorated with streamers of fresh flowers, wreaths of dried herbs, and ribbon knots, but the only door was at the back of the little house, facing the woods. Most unusual. Curious, she looked closer at the door decoration, then drew back with a gasp. A fearsome mask hung on the door, the terrifying facial features made from bits of bark, moss, and dried corn and beans. Well! That would certainly keep nosy neighbors away. If there were any neighbors in the secluded spot.

She suddenly realized how far away from the crowd she'd come in her haste, and turned to retrace her steps. Hearing voices, she paused at the corner of the hut. The drunken sailors had followed her.

Seventeen

Burke could hardly believe his eyes. At a table covered with the remains of a feast, Vivian and Theo sat with a convivial group of gray-hairs, laughing and chatting and toasting as if they'd been there all evening. Burke shook his head. He could have sworn they hadn't been there when he'd been by that very bonfire a few hours ago. Prepared to give the unsuspecting couple a stern lecture for giving their friends and family cause to worry, a sparkle of light off to his left caught his attention and he turned.

Cordelia? He blinked, but it wasn't a trick of moonlight. He recognized her stubborn chin and the unruly wisps of hair around her face, masked or not. What was she doing here? When she turned and marched toward the woods, her determined gait and the sweet sway of her hips were unnecessary evidence confirming her identity. His gaze determined her destination, even as he began moving in her direction. Mercy sakes, what was she doing heading to Mab's Bower?

He spotted the sailors following her, and he ran. Cutting across the field at an angle, he intercepted the miscreants a good twenty yards from the bower and blocked their path.

"I fear you fellows have lost your way. The free ale is over there," Burke said and pointed back several bonfires. "Perhaps a roast beef sandwich to go with that? My

treat, of course, in honor of the Midsummer Festival."
He dug into his pocket, pulled out a five note, and held
it out nonchalantly, not wanting to overplay his hand or
reveal his interest.

"We been there," the tallest one said. "We got us another kind a appetite just now, don't we, mates?" he said,
rubbing his groin, which the other two sailors found in-
tensely amusing.

"You betcha, Torky. We got us an appetite," the heavy-
set sailor said, but he reached out and grabbed the
money.

"You got any more o'that?" Torky said, with a swaggering step forward. "We'll be relieving you of the
burden o' your purse, and thank you for it." He pulled a
wicked knife from the back of his belt.

"You can take 'im, Torky," the smallest one cheered.
"He's big, but you're faster and meaner."

"Dibs on his coat," the fat one said.

"I get his boots," the little one said at the same time.

"Yer get nothing unless you help me take him down,"
Torky growled as he sidled to the right.

Burke had never been an *aficionado* of barroom brawling, but being Preston's friend, he'd had his share of
experiences. He sized up his foes and the situation. He
stepped back a few paces, not allowing Torky to outflank
him, at the same time staying between the sailors and
Cordelia, and drawing the ringleader away from his
friends.

"Why don't you fellows just move along?" Burke asked
calmly. "There's no profit to be found here."

"We say different, don't we, mates?" Torky motioned
with his hand for his friends to follow him but didn't
turn to see that they remained where they were.

Burke gave them credit for a modicum more of intelligence than their leader. Holding his cane in front of

his body in a defensive position, he stepped back another two paces, veering to his left, subtly maneuvering Torky into position.

"Yer got 'im on the run," the smallest one cheered.

"Don't get any blood on my coat," the other called.

Burke revised his hasty estimation of their brain power. "This is your last chance to move along and find other amusements." When Torky laughed, Burke let fly with one end of his cane, the gold head striking him on the wrist, just below the bone.

The sailor yelped and dropping the knife, took a step backward, tripped over a tree root, and sprawled on his back.

Burke picked up the knife. "Not bad balance," he said, hefting it in his hand. "Decent steel." As Torky struggled to a sitting position, Burke flipped the knife back to him. The blade stuck in the tree root between the sailor's knees with an audible quiver.

"Perhaps you'd like to try again?" Burke asked, in the same nonchalant tone he'd used from the beginning.

But he was speaking to empty air. The three sailors were already scrambling across the field. Burke chuckled, hoping they wouldn't stop until they were back on board their ship.

Then he turned, and his mirth caught in his throat with a cough. Time to deal with Cordelia. He strode toward Mab's Bower with a determined step. The woman had a knack for trouble, courted it like a lovesick swain. Not that he knew anything about being lovesick, of course.

Didn't she bother to find out anything about the Midsummer's Eve Festival *before* she came traipsing around a field of drunks and miscreants? Not to mention the young gentlemen of the ton roving the festival grounds. Outside the drawing room, they could be dangerous to an innocent young woman precisely because she would expect them to behave as gentlemen.

He reached the door of the hut and hesitated. Cordelia obviously didn't have the slightest idea of the purpose of the bower in the woods. Or did she?

The thought of Cordelia waiting to play a role in the ritual landed like a well-aimed punch in the gut. There wasn't enough light to see his watch, but it must be close to eleven o'clock. Enough time to give her a lecture on her folly before making sure she was returned safely to her grandmother before midnight. As he reached for the latch, his hand brushed the mask. He didn't relish being interrupted by some wandering fool overly eager to play Oberon. With a growl, he grabbed the mask off the door. At least with the mask gone, any man would assume the male role in the ritual had already been filled.

Cordelia deserved more than a lecture for her foolish escapade; she deserved a good scare. Without questioning his motives, he removed his hat and donned the mask. He jerked the door open and stepped into Mab's Bower.

Inside the hut, the walls and ceiling had been covered with flowers. Sweet grasses had been spread on the floor and then overlaid with blankets of the softest wool. Silken pillows were scattered about, and at the foot of the pallet a low table of tempting delicacies had been set, awaiting the Fairy Queen and her consort's pleasure. In the spirit of the evening's expected activities, many of the food items either had supposed aphrodisiac benefits or were made in the shape of certain parts of anatomy.

On her knees in front of the table, Cordelia looked up in wide-eyed surprise, a marzipan apple halfway to her mouth.

"I am Oberon," he said, deepening his voice and making his words boom in the small room—and feeling rather silly, but it was a necessary part of the charade if he was to make his point. "Tonight we celebrate Litha, a time of peace and plenitude."

Slowly, Cordelia replaced the candy on the dish, swallowing visibly.

Burke set aside his cane and removed his gloves, getting into the role. He held out his hand. "Come to me, and we will celebrate the fertility of the earth. By rejoicing together, we will ensure the bountiful harvest ahead."

Cordelia stood, dusting sugar from the candies off her fingertips.

He could practically see the wheels turning in her busy mind, but he didn't see any fear. Didn't she understand the seriousness of her folly? Perhaps he hadn't been blunt enough.

"By joining our bodies as one—"

She stepped forward and took his hand. "I understand." She pulled him farther into the room.

Shocked speechless, he stumbled on the edge of the pallet, falling to his knees.

Gracefully, she knelt beside him. "Tell me what to do, for although I am willing, I do not know—"

"Bloody hell." He ripped off the mask. "It's me, Cordelia. What in the name of—"

She laughed because she'd known all along who was behind the mask, from the moment he'd entered the room. No other man had his height, or his shoulders, or his gait. No other man made her heart hammer in response to his nearness. Her only dilemma had been whether or not to respond to his charade in kind, or to admit outright that she loved him, wanted him to love her.

"You knew it was me?" he asked.

"Of course."

She settled more comfortably into a sitting position.

"Are we supposed to eat first?" She picked up a plate of raspberry tarts made in the shape of lips and held it out.

He shook his head. "You're the one with the sweet tooth. We should be going now."

Unwilling to give up, but seeing nothing else to offer him aside from food, she chose a plate of honey-glazed lady fingers, and held it out. "These are of an unusual shape but delicious." To encourage him, she picked up a lady finger and took a bite. "I can't seem to stop eating them."

"Those are made in the shape of a man's . . . uh . . . privates," he said, his tone of voice matter-of-fact.

Cordelia stopped, and glanced at the items left on the plate and then back to his face. Heat crept up her neck and flooded her cheeks. Then she saw the tic at the corner of Burke's left eye and realized he was trying to shock her. He was not as unaffected by her actions as he pretended. The knowledge bolstered her sagging bravery.

"Really?" she said with a knowing smile. She popped the last of the pastry into her mouth, and licked the stickiness off her fingers.

Burke groaned and focused his gaze somewhere off her left shoulder. "Cordelia, please . . ."

She'd already made up her mind. She wanted to make love with Burke, wanted to know his intimate touch, if only once. If she let this chance pass, she knew she'd never have another. Even if she spent the rest of her life alone, she wanted one night with Burke, one night of memories.

Desperation, and some strange hunger she couldn't name, fueled her to action. He was so serious. If only she could make him smile, find the joy she knew was inside him, the laughter she wanted to hear and share. Selecting a platter with two mountainous puddings, each topped by a candied cherry, she swung the plate to her lap. "I suppose then, these represent a woman's breasts, although I must admit, they make me feel woefully inadequate."

Instead of laughing, Burke planted one foot on the pallet, as if to stand. She had to do something to gain his attention, anything to make him stay. Twisting sideways, she flopped on her back, and raised the platter to rest on her ribcage. "What do you think? Better?"

He looked at her as if she'd lost her mind. Maybe she had. He obviously hadn't found her clowning appealing. Oh, why had she acted so foolishly? She blinked to hold back the tears, but one escaped.

Burke stretched out on his side on the pallet next to her, propped on one elbow. With his free hand he removed the platter of puddings, discarding it over his shoulder without another glance. "You don't need any artifice to make you more desirable," he said, his voice a caress. "Especially not a raisin pudding," he added with a smile. "I detest raisins."

She crossed her arms over her breasts, unsure whether he was trying to be charming or sympathetic. "I think there's a couple of cakes on the table."

He shook his head, and took her hand. "I like honey," he said. "I think you missed a sticky spot." He licked the tip of her finger. "There. And here," he added, running his tongue over the pad of her thumb.

She closed her eyes. And popped them open again, as he laved her palm.

"Sugar," he said, a twinkle in his eye. "I have a sweet tooth after all, but I also have a discerning palate. I crave only particular sweets."

Blindly she reached for the plate of goodies she'd set aside, managing to stick her finger in a tart. Hoping he would repeat his previous performance, she brought her hand forward. "How do you feel about raspberry?"

He took her hand, but instead of licking off the thickened juice, he directed her hand and painted her lips with the red syrup.

"Only this way," he whispered before kissing her, tasting her lips, sharing the sweetness with her.

Raspberry was her new favorite flavor. Breaking to catch her breath, she put the last drop of syrup from her finger on his bottom lip, wanting to kiss it off in the manner he'd taught her so well. Before she had a chance, he sucked the tip of her finger into his mouth, gently grazing her knuckle with his teeth.

"Oh, my," she said, drawing in air as if it would help her light-headedness.

He folded her hand in his. "As much as I'm tempted, we must be going."

"But I want—"

"I know. However, this bower was set up so that at midnight, the couple designated to represent Mab and Oberon are supposed to—"

"I think I figured that out."

"Then you understand why we must leave."

"It isn't midnight yet. Can't we stay a little longer? There are more raspberry tarts."

Burke groaned and closed his eyes. "I'm trying to consider your welfare. I think it would be best if I returned you to your grandmother—"

"Granny!" Cordelia sat up so fast, she bumped foreheads with Burke. Mumbling an apology, she scrambled to her feet. She'd totally forgotten Granny. What kind of terrible person was she that she could forget the very reason she'd come to the festival. "I must find her. She could be hurt or . . ."

As Cordelia gathered her belongings in a panic, Burke considered his options. At least now she was anxious to leave, and although it made his duty easier, it didn't sit well to let her worry needlessly. "Vivian is fine. I found her earlier and she's with Gravely."

Cordelia faced him. "Theo's here, too?"

He nodded.

A knock sounded on the door, and she whirled to open it before he could rise and stop her.

A woman wearing a somewhat bedraggled fairy costume was at the door. "I be Mab, and I'm 'ere for the ritual," she said, her words so slurred it sounded like rish-u-el. She looked beyond Cordelia, and her eyes widened. "Coo-eee. Is he my Oberon?" she said, straightening the waist of her costume. "I likes 'em big," she added, focusing on Burke and moving to step inside.

Cordelia blocked her path.

"What's this?"

"I'm sorry, miss. You'll have to return later," Cordelia said, reaching for the door and pulling it halfway closed before the woman stopped it with her foot.

"Now see here. I'm a virgin, I am. And I'm here to be sacrificed."

"Perhaps later." Cordelia inched the door closed.

"Yoo-hoo, my Oberon," the woman called, waving to Burke and bobbing and weaving her head to try to see around Cordelia. "Here I am, my Oberon. Your virgin."

"He's my Oberon," Cordelia said under her breath, as she gave the woman a shove, slammed the door, and threw the latch. She turned to Burke, to find him kneeling on the pallet and grinning at her. "Why are you smiling?" she asked, putting her hands on her hips.

He shook his head.

"That wasn't funny. I make jokes and you sit there stone-faced, but that . . . that poor deranged sot says *I likes 'em big*, and you grin like an idiot?"

She moved to stand directly in front of him. "Aren't you going to explain?"

He shook his head again. He couldn't tell her the simple possessive words she'd uttered, words not meant for him to hear, had warmed his heart. That his smile had been pure pleasure overflowing. For if he told her that, she would reasonably expect . . . and he couldn't give her what she deserved, what she needed for her happiness.

A tap-tap on the door distracted him.

"Yoo-hoo, Oberon," the woman called from outside.

Cordelia placed her hands on either side of his face and forced him to face her. "Ignore that woman," she said.

For a long moment Burke and Cordelia stared at each other, and the rest of the world receded.

She leaned down to kiss him. Lips melded, he stood and took her in his arms. Long, luxurious kisses. Tasting. Exploring. He cradled her head with one hand. She threaded her fingers into the hair at the nape of his neck, matching his movements, learning. He traced her spine with his thumb, rubbing little circles. She stood on tiptoes, reaching, daring, following her instincts.

With a sigh, he kissed her forehead, cuddling her against his body. "We can't do this," he choked out, his voice guttural with the effort it cost him.

Her head resting on his chest, she felt and heard the pounding of his heartbeat, and it echoed the rapid thumping of her own pulse. Her knees were weak, and she clung to him to remain standing. "I know," she whispered. "It's supposed to be wrong." She looked up at him, her chin on his chest. "But it feels so right."

"It's more than we shouldn't," he said with a tiny shake of his head. "We can't. I don't want to hurt you."

"It's all right." Granny had told her what to expect years ago, she just hadn't wanted to put the knowledge to use before. "It won't hurt after a minute."

Burke looked up at the ceiling as if he would find the words he needed to say written there.

"It's all right," she said again, pulling on the back of his neck, pulling his head down or herself up, she wasn't sure which. She just wanted to kiss him again.

He took her hand from his neck and laid it over his heart. "We cannot do this," he said. "You are so small, and, well, I'm, unfortunately in this case, a bit too—"

"I likes 'em big," she said with a smile.

He groaned at her innocence. "Your body isn't . . . I mean, because you're not used to . . . I mean, because you haven't . . ."

"Are you saying that because I haven't previously known a man you may not fit inside me?"

Burke actually blushed. "I don't want to hurt you."

She stepped back out of his embrace, and he dropped his arms to his side. "You're serious? You won't make love with me because I'm a virgin?"

He nodded. He'd always avoided innocents, and thus had little experience to draw on, but surely even a virgin determined to change her status would listen to reason.

"Well, then." She turned and walked to the door. Her hand on the latch, she looked over her shoulder and said, "You wait here. I have a plan."

"What?" Hopefully she'd ask her grandmother for advice, and the woman would be sane enough to drag the chit home and lock her in her room.

"A brilliant plan, I might add. After I find the smallest man I can, so it will be the least painful, I'll work my way up through the medium sizes, and when I'm sufficiently stretched, I'll return. Considering the availability of candidates, this shouldn't take too long. I'll be back before—"

"Like bloody hell you will," he said, lunging to stop her before she actually tried such a crazy stunt.

She jumped out of his reach, but her dress caught on something and ripped. She twisted away, and slipped on the discarded puddings, her feet going out from under her. In her fall, she kicked the simple plank table, up-ending it and sending food flying in all directions. He grabbed for her, and managed to hug her to him and roll so that he landed on his back, cushioning her fall.

After a moment of shocked stillness, she looked down at him. He looked like he'd been brawling in a sweet shop. A chuck of cake sat on his head like a lopsided hat. A streak of treacle marred his forehead, and a blob of chocolate decorated one cheek. She smiled. "You're a mess."

"You're not in such good shape yourself."

She lay on his chest, her chin even with his nose. She raised her head up farther and looked down to find that her dress had torn and one breast was bared except for a coating of vanilla sauce. She wiggled backward, scrambling for a place to put her hands and knees in order to stand.

"Stop," he said in a fierce whisper, holding her firmly in place. "Before you unman me completely."

She stilled, and he took a deep breath and blew it out slowly.

"May I get up now?" she asked.

"No." He looked up at her. "Have you changed your mind?"

She wasn't sure if he was referring to her brilliant plan, a blatant lie if she'd ever told one, or to making love with him. If it was the first, she didn't want him to know the answer; if it was the latter, she most definitely hadn't changed her mind. She shook her head.

"You're positive you want to go through with this?"

She nodded.

The thought of her with another man twisted Burke's

gut, but he wouldn't risk hurting her. There was another way to relieve her frustration, to sate her curiosity. Not as satisfying for him, to be sure, though he would certainly take pleasure. Would he be able to stop, to control himself? He would have to, for her sake.

"All right," he said. "On one condition. If anything we do is painful, you must tell me."

She agreed. "What made you change your mind?"

He rolled her to her back, ducked his head and licked a long swathe across her breast, sending chills down her spine.

"Vanilla is my favorite," he said.

Eighteen

Now that Cordelia had her most fervent wish, she was suddenly shy and worried. She had so little experience enticing a man, and none in . . . well, none, and no knowledge beyond the basics of which parts went where. "You'll have to tell me what to do," she said, and bit her lip. She settled back on the pallet, arms at her side, gazing up at the ceiling.

Burke choked back his laughter. Gone was the playful nymph, replaced by the virgin's version of *the position*.

Suddenly, she sat up. "Shouldn't we take off our clothes?"

"We will. Later."

"Oh." She lay back down. And sat up again. "Shouldn't we put out the lights?"

"Not necessarily. Unless you would prefer the dark."

"Oh, no. I want to see what we're doing." She leaned back. And sat up again. "Before we start, I must warn you that although I'm willing, I'm woefully ignorant. And a little nervous." She resumed her prone position.

"The first step is to relax."

She took a deep breath and blew it out in a quick puff. "I'm relaxed. What's next?" She sat up again. "Maybe a few of the candles out?"

He nodded and proceeded to extinguish all but three candles, while she lay back on the pallet and watched him. He removed his coat, vest, and boots, making a neat pile in the corner. Then he knelt on the end of the pallet. "Perhaps if I remove your shoes, you'll be more comfortable?"

She shook her head, but he pretended not to notice. If he was lucky, she'd chicken out and solve the dilemma of what to do with a curious virgin. He untied the laces of her half-boot and slipped it off, rubbing the arch of her foot with his thumb.

As he worked his way from her heel to her stocking-covered toes, she moaned in pleasure, and he felt the vibrations of the sound deep within him. She poked his hand with the other foot. He removed her shoe and began to massage that foot, and he started reciting multiplication tables to himself.

When he stopped rubbing her feet, she sat up. "Can I do that for you?"

He shook his head. "I'm relaxed enough," he lied. "Any more relaxed and I might fall asleep." Any more wound up and he would explode.

"Oh. What's next?"

"There is no particular order. What would you like to do?"

"Kiss," she answered immediately, then ducked her head. "I like kissing," she mumbled.

"Me too." Putting his hands on her shoulders, he laid her back with gentle pressure and stretched out beside her, all in one smooth move. "I like kissing you." He nibbled her top lip, and she sucked in his bottom lip. "I like how you kiss me."

"I'm a fast learner." She ran her tongue along his teeth.

He shivered and leaned back a few inches. If he was going to remain in control, he needed to distract her from distracting him. Starting at her chin, he kissed and nibbled his way to her ear, laving the lobe with his tongue and sucking it into his mouth.

"I didn't . . . know you could . . . kiss other parts of the body . . . like that," she said, her breath coming in uneven gasps.

"Mmm, yes." He kissed a line down the swan column of her neck, nuzzling her head aside to give him room, licking the indent at the base of her throat. "I could kiss you all over." Using the wet tip of his tongue, he drew a line from her throat, down to her cleavage, smelling and tasting the remnants of vanilla sauce, smelling and tasting something uniquely Cordelia.

With a deft movement, he freed her breasts from the confinement of her chemise. He licked her nipple with the flat of his tongue, then blew across the wetness, watching the bud pucker tighter. Feeling her squirm next to him, he threw one leg across her hips. Taking the nipple into his mouth, he sucked and tongued the tip at the same time. She arched into his mouth, tiny mewling sounds escaping her lips.

When he released the one, she turned her other breast for attention. He gladly complied, alternately palming and tweaking the first breast with his free hand.

She threaded the fingers of one hand into his hair, her other hand gripped convulsively at his sleeve. "Burke, I want . . . I don't know what I want."

Unconsciously, she ground her hips into his thigh.

"Shhh, my sweet. I know what to do."

"Then do it, dammit, before I—"

"Not yet. There's more."

"I don't think I can take any more."

"Yes, you can." He wasn't as sure about himself. She was so sweetly responsive to his touch, his self-control was already sorely tested. He shifted uncomfortably on the pallet. Five times eleven equaled fifty-five. Five times twelve equaled sixty.

Shifting his body lower, he touched her ankle first,

sliding his hand up her leg slowly. Up on the outside a few inches, then around to the inside and up a few inches, then down and back to the outside. Moving back to her ankle, he brought it toward her, bending her knee. He planted her heel. Cupping her knee he pushed it slightly outward until he could easily reach her inner thigh, though her beauty was still hidden beneath her skirt.

"What are you doing? I liked the other better."

"Bear with me, sweet," he said with a chuckle. "You'll like this, too. I promise." He returned his attention to her breasts and she quickly forgot anything else in the heat of his kisses.

Ever so slowly, he slid his hand from her knee to her hip, gently scooting her skirt and petticoat, baring her legs. Although her squirming helped him rather than hindered, it still seemed to take forever until he knew he'd freed the tight nest of curls.

He wanted to pause, to see her beauty, but he sensed she would cover herself if she recognized her nudity, if she realized she was sprawled open to his gaze and his hands. He would not give her that chance.

Timing his moves to coincide, he took her lips in a searing kiss, and at the same instant, he cupped her Venus mound, thrusting a finger into her slick nether lips and finding her nub of pleasure. He swallowed her cry of passion. Or was it his own?

She lifted her hips, pushing against his hand, undulating to the rhythm he played with his finger. Wet and slick and hot. He slipped his finger inside her, stopping short to leave her membrane intact, yet earning another delicious moan. Working his hand to the tempo she now set, he added a second finger. When he found her pleasure nub with his thumb, she cried out, jerked upward. He felt the ripples begin, tightening on his fingers, milking them. So wonderful. He held her through her orgasm, extending it as long as possible for her, and then welcoming her back to earth with soft caresses and gentle kisses. She looked up at him. Her sated smile was the most beautiful sight he'd ever seen.

Cordelia looked up at him, sure that her smile must look silly and vacuous but unable to offer any other expression. She lay, a boneless heap, a pile of clothing incapable of movement, unwilling to end her glorious experience just yet.

She wasn't exactly sure of everything that had happened, but she knew it was wonderful and amazing and beautiful, and Burke had given it to her, shared it with her.

He kissed her on the tip of her nose and moved away. A sudden chill swept up her side where his warmth had been. He stood and turned his back to her.

"I'll give you a bit of privacy to restore yourself," he said. "Then I'll see you home."

One matter nagged her. She was no longer innocent, but by strictest definition she was still a virgin. That wasn't what she wanted. She'd already accepted she would have only the memory of this one night to cherish for the rest of her life. Burke was grossly unfair to cheat her of the complete experience.

What could she do? He was bigger and stronger, and she could hardly force him to make love to her. Yet, by taking her innocence, he'd given her power, a woman's power.

He started to turn, but she warned him she wasn't ready, so he continued to stare at the far wall. "Do you require assistance?"

"No, thank you," she said, over the rustling of material. "I'm managing just fine. You can turn around now."

He faced her. She was stark naked. She stood in the

middle of the pallet without a stitch of clothes, her long hair covering one shoulder and one breast and one hip.

"Now we can do it again," she said. "The right way this time. Take off your clothes, please."

Stunned, Burke could only gape.

"Don't just stand there," she said with a trill of nervous laughter. "You'll make me think I've made a terrible mistake."

"It is a mistake," he whispered hoarsely, even as he moved toward her, as if drawn by a magnet, Cordelia his true north.

He cradled her face in his hands. "You are so beautiful."

"You make me feel beautiful when you look at me like that." She untied his neck cloth and tossed it aside. She unfastened the top three buttons of his shirt, trailing her fingers in the opening. "I want to see your chest," she whispered, giving him what she hoped was a siren's smile.

He ripped off his shirt and threw it over his head.

She ran her hands over the hard, sculpted planes. Up over his shoulders and down his arms to his hands, she stepped back, holding only his fingertips as she boldly looked her fill. She drew him forward to stand on the pallet with her.

"I want to see the rest of you, all of you."

When he hesitated, she knew she couldn't give him time to think, to resist, or her hopes would be lost. She stepped close to him. He did not lean down, so she kissed what she could reach, his chest, laving his nipples as he had done to her.

Burke shuddered with the effort it took not to toss her to the ground and drive into her. "Cordelia," he pleaded with a groan. "Be reasonable."

"You're the one making this hard."

He chuckled. "No, I believe that would be you."

Oh, how she loved it when he smiled at her like that. Blindly, she reached for his belt buckle. She missed on her first clumsy attempt, but Burke's indrawn hiss of breath encouraged her fumbling around, up and down.

"I'm beginning to think you're a dangerous woman."

He had no idea all she planned for him. "More than you know," she said, undoing his belt buckle.

Burke shook his head. This was the Cordelia he'd suspected existed beneath her controlled exterior. Bold and deliciously wanton. She'd discarded her innocence as easily as she'd shed her clothes. Had he been mistaken? Had she lied to him again?

The specter of her past lies resurrected with his doubts. Was she playing him for a dupe, as Preston suspected? After all, what did Burke know of virgins, having avoided them all his life? He looked down at Cordelia, and his breath caught in his throat. Damn, but she had innocent eyes.

A valuable asset in an agent, his good sense reminded him.

What should he do? Desperate reason dictated that if she was a true virgin, his unleashed passion would scare her, send her scurrying for safety, whereas if she was experienced . . .

Lucky for him, his reason concurred with the raging physical needs of his tortured body.

He swooped her into his arms, searing her lips as he picked her up. He knelt, laid her on the pallet, and paused for a moment to look at her, so beautiful. Touch followed sight, so soft and smooth. Taste followed touch. Sweet, delicious.

Then his senses seemed to jumble together. He touched her sweetness, smelled her softness, tasted her beauty, and heard her little pleasure moans with his heart. And he wanted more. So much more. He wanted to touch and kiss and taste and suck and lick every inch of her, greedily taking pleasure and giving pleasure back in equal measure.

Cordelia, in her boldness, had awakened a sleeping giant, and she gloried in his unbridled passion. Any hesitation on her part was quickly overcome by the unexpected hunger he stirred within her. If she was clumsy in her first attempts to follow his lead, it didn't seem to matter. Enthusiasm apparently overrode skill. She was a quick study, and improvisation was rewarded.

Despite several trips to the stars, by his hand, by his mouth—oh, but that had been glorious—she was still a virgin. As wonderful as Burke had been, she intended to resolve that issue before being reduced to a quivering mass of mindless, needy flesh once again.

She was prepared to demand, if necessary. She pushed on his shoulders, and he obligingly rolled to his back.

"You want to set the pace?" he asked. "Go ahead." He propped his hands behind his head.

She had meant to talk to him, but the opportunity was irresistible. Drawing on her memory of his actions, and her own curiosity, first she looked.

Catching a glimpse of him as he moved from here to there was different than seeing him displayed in all his glory for her avid inspection. She traced his ribs with her fingertips, moving ever lower. When she reached the light pattern of hair pointing lower still, he sucked in his breath and closed his eyes. Did he find her touch as pleasurable as she found his?

Teasing touches, firm massages, dragging her nails across his skin. Moving ever lower toward the most fascinating piece of his anatomy.

She touched him lightly at first, silk over steel. He was larger than she'd anticipated. She wrapped her fingers around him to measure the girth, and he answered with a deep moan. Starting at the tip, she measured the length to the base with her fingertips. The muscles in his thighs tightened, and his toes curled.

A plan formed in her mind. If she could distract him, then she could simply impale herself and the deed would be done. She had no real fear. If her body was designed for a baby to emerge, surely he would fit. Somehow. But since he'd assiduously avoided taking her virginity, first she needed to reduce him to the mindless, needy, quivering state he'd so effectively brought her to. How? Obviously, by the same method.

She leaned forward and tentatively flicked the tip of his . . . his manhood with her tongue. His entire body tensed, his hips convulsed upward. Startled, Cordelia jerked her head back, but then she smiled. She remembered that intense feeling.

He tried to sit up, as if to deter her, but she pushed him back down, determined to give him more of the same pleasure. She experimented with her hands and lips and tongue, easily learning what pleased him most. Also learning, to her surprise, that a warm coil of desire started deep within her, the fire fed by his reactions, spiraling upward and outward until she was breathless, until she ached for the relief of his touch.

Knowing she would lose the ability to think clearly, if at all, she straddled his body. As she raised up and inserted the tip of his penis into her vagina, he caught her around the waist. Though he held her easily in the air, strain was visible on his face.

"Are you sure you're ready?" he asked, his voice low and gruff as if he hadn't used it for a long time.

Burke fought the need to bury himself deeply inside her. Not because he'd given up on the idea of her as a true innocent—only an experienced courtesan would know to use her mouth in such a way as to drive a man crazy with desire—but because he wanted to be sure his path was well lubricated.

"Are you ready for me?"

She nodded, her face solemn, her eyes filled with passion.

He lowered her a few inches, slipping inside her tight sheath, moving up and down a mere inch to test her wetness. She gripped his forearms and threw her head back with an guttural sigh. He felt the ripples begin inside her, needed to feel them along his length.

With a swift move, he pushed down on her hips, and lifted his to meet her.

Her cry of pain shocked them both.

Cordelia had expected a bit of discomfort, but not tearing pain. She scrambled, trying to back away, attempting to escape the stinging and burning.

She was a virgin. The truth barely had time to seep into his muddled brain when he realized she was trying to climb off him. He tightened his grip on her hips.

"Be still a minute."

"Let me go."

"It will be better for you if you're still for a minute. I promise the pain will pass. Relax and let your body adjust."

"Easy for you to say," she said, dashing away a tear.

He grimaced with the effort it took to remain still. "Not really."

They stared at each other for a long moment.

"Better?" he asked.

She was still aware of an uncomfortable fullness, but the stinging had subsided. She nodded and the motion of her head moved the rest of her body a fraction. Burke closed his eyes and bit his bottom lip. The knowledge that she gave him pleasure with the smallest of movements emboldened her to try more. Her small movements lessened her discomfort rather than increasing it.

"Burke?"

He opened one eye and peeked up at her.

"Is this all there is?"

He blinked.

"Because if this is what all the fuss is about, I must confess I'm disappointed."

Burke laughed out loud, and his laughter vibrated up inside her. She closed her eyes and rode the wave of pleasure.

"There's more, my sweet. When you're ready, there is much more." He slid his left hand upward to cup her breast, fingering the nipple between his thumb and finger. He slid his other hand across her hip, downward until he found her nub of desire, rotating his knuckle over it.

She gasped. She squirmed, not sure which instinct to obey. Burke grasped her around the waist, lifting and lowering, helping her set a rhythm. But she could not keep the pace, distracted by his counterthrusts, by his hands, by the look on his face.

He sat up, hugged her to him, and rolled them over. Holding himself above her, he drove into her, slow, slow, slow, then fast, fast, fast. She dug her heels into the pallet and lifted her hips.

The ripples began with an intensity she hadn't yet known. He groaned, feeling them, too. He gathered her in his arms and held her close. His release seemed to go on and on, prolonged and hastened, and heightened by the pulsing of her orgasm. Together, they soared to the stars, awed at the power of their experience.

She, because it was her first time to share the ecstasy, because it was better than anything that had happened before. He, because although he'd known other women, it was his first time to truly share, to make the trip to the stars as one.

They'd shattered, and when they came back together, a bit of each was in the other. Never again to be truly alone.

He collapsed, remembering to roll to his side to keep from crushing her. She snuggled into his embrace. He looked down, and seeing her beautiful, sated smile, he kissed her eyelids and her forehead. Did she know how special their experience was? How precious and rare? Words of love and gratitude and wonder stuck in this throat.

"You were wrong," she mumbled in a sleepy voice. "I knew if a baby could come out, you would fit in."

A baby! In the heat of passion, Burke had forgotten his worst fear.

Nineteen

Burke gently turned Cordelia to her side, cuddling her spoon fashion. He didn't want her to wake and see the expression of fear and horror he was sure the thought of her carrying his baby had put on his face. Just the possibility was terrifying. He spread his large hand across her belly, the span of his fingers reaching from one hipbone to the other. So small, so delicate.

His baby, likely to be large as he'd been, would surely kill her. His mother had said, again and again, giving birth to him had nearly done her in, and she was a substantial woman. By impregnating Cordelia, he could well have doomed her to an early, painful death.

If he had. There was always a chance, a good chance, that he hadn't. This time.

He buried his face in her soft hair, smelling the honeysuckle scent that would always remind him of this night. For her sake, he would have to be strong, resist her charms, maintain his self-control. She snuggled closer with a sleepy, satisfied mew, and he realized resistance was an impossible task. Already his body responded to her nearness.

He reached behind him for his coat and draped it over her like a blanket, tucking it around her. Moving slowly so as not to disturb her slumber, he stood and dressed. Logic dictated his only course of action.

* * *

Cordelia stretched and opened her eyes, aching in places she hadn't known could hurt. She wrapped Burke's coat more tightly around her shoulders, suddenly, inconceivably shy. Although after what she'd done, the way she'd acted, the heat of a blush came as no surprise.

"Bless you, Mab, sweet Queen of the Fairies, for making my dearest wish come true," she whispered. "Thank you for an enchanted Midsummer's Night."

Cordelia sat up, looking around the hut for Burke. The height of the candles indicated she'd slept for several hours and, judging by the condition of the hut, quite soundly. Food and broken crockery had been pushed into the corner. The low plank table had been set back on its trestle legs, and a bowl of water and several folded rags placed next to her clothes, also in a neat stack. Burke's tidiness and forethought irritated her. She would have preferred to wake with him beside her.

Had he left her to fend for herself? She immediately dismissed the thought as unworthy of the man she had come to know and love. He would be waiting outside, protecting her slumber, giving her a chance to put herself to rights. A gentleman, he would take her home.

Humming a little tune, she set about washing up and dressing as best she could, making a quick repair to her torn dress with the needle and thread from her basket. The seam wasn't neat or even, but she was decently covered.

Taking a last look around the bower, fixing it in her memory, she swung her cloak around her shoulders, picked up her basket and Burke's coat, and opened the door.

She located him easily in the light of a lantern set on

a tree stump several yards from the door. Burke stood, one foot propped on the stump, smoke from his cheroot dissipating in the cool breeze. As she approached, he straightened and ground out the thin cigar.

She smiled. He looked at her, his brow furrowed. Confused by his expression and solemn attitude, she fought to keep her smile from fading, knowing she failed.

"Good evening," she said, for lack of anything better to say, forcing a bright tone to her voice.

"Good morrow. It will be dawn in little more than an hour."

She'd slept longer than she thought.

"We should settle a few matters before we leave," he said.

Something in his tone warned her she didn't want to hear whatever he was about to say. She turned, the instinct to flee urging her to run. He stopped her with a hand on her shoulder, but she couldn't look at him.

"Cordelia, I'm sorry. So very sorry."

That was the very last thing she wanted to hear. That he was sorry for sharing the most beautiful experience of her life. That he was sorry he'd shared it with her.

"I would never willingly hurt you."

He was hurting her now. Deep, stabbing pain. She wrapped her arms around her waist. Wanting to curl into a ball, she forced herself to remain upright. She would not cry. She would not let him see her devastation, would not let him see that he had that power.

"I'll call on your grandmother tomor—today, later today. We can be married within a week."

The prospect of marriage didn't thrill her as she once would have expected. He only felt obliged to marry her, his sense of propriety compelling him to salvage her reputation. Damn him and his self-righteous gentleman's code of morality. She might not have his love, but she didn't need his pity.

She shook his hand off her shoulder and turned to face him. "Don't be ridiculous."

He didn't look her in the eye but turned and paced within the space lit by the lantern. "I'll get a special license. Once we're married, you can live wherever you wish. I promise you'll never want for anything."

Except love.

"I have a villa in Italy, near Marsfield's, and it's at your disposal. After the war, returning to America is an option, if you so wish, and, of course, if you can. Or I'll buy you a chateau in France. You'll have anything you want."

Except him. From the sound of it, he intended to marry her and then shuffle her off to some foreign land, unable to stomach the idea of her in the same country as him.

Damn Mab for listening to her dreams, for making this one come true. Fairies were famous, or should she say infamous, for their tricks on humans. Cordelia should have known better than to trust a fairy. Be careful what you wish for, indeed. She shook her head and gave a rueful bark of laughter.

"You find my offer amusing?" Burke asked.

She looked at him and raised her eyebrows. "Not at all."

"Is there something else you want?"

Oh, yes, there was, but she wasn't about to blurt it out. She would not beg for his love.

"I want nothing from you. Not a villa, or a chateau. Not even marriage."

"I'm offering you my name, my protection."

"Then you obviously are placing a higher value on my virginity than I do. I'm quite relieved to be rid of the pesky hindrance."

Burke jerked his head back, disbelief written in his expression.

She'd rather surprised herself with her bold words, but she wouldn't take them back. "However, gratitude can only be carried so far. Marriage for the sake of propriety is not necessary."

"You're suffering from shock. I'll take you home now. You'll see reason in the light of day."

She turned and started walking back toward the area where the carriages were parked, knowing she wouldn't feel different tomorrow. She would still love him—and hate him for being such a cold bastard of a gentleman.

If Burke ever doubted women were irrational, Cordelia was *prima facie* evidence. She confused and confounded him. Innocence personified one minute, wanton siren the following. Demure damsel in distress, then calculating sophisticate. She had more faces than the inconstant moon, and left him chasing moon shadows in her wake. He never knew what to expect next.

He grabbed the lantern and followed. With his long legs, he quickly caught up with her. "The simple fact remains, I am responsible—"

"Do not insult me by implying I'm incapable of making decisions," she said.

"Cordelia, try to see this logically."

Logic? He wanted detached reasoning at a time like this? Oh, she would give him logic, all right. "I am neither a child nor dim-witted. I am, therefore, *logically*, responsible for my own actions." She continued walking, pique at his attitude hastening her pace.

"Your conclusion is based on false assumptions." He lengthened his stride to keep pace.

"Since my age is no longer at issue, are you then questioning my intelligence?"

"In the matter of seduction, yes. Your lack of experience puts you at a distinct disadvantage."

"Exactly my point. I made the decision, premeditated and with forethought, to gain that valuable experience. You simply cooperated, and, therefore, I refuse to hold you to some arcane male standard of . . . of . . ."

"Now you are spouting utter nonsense. That bluestocking rubbish—"

"Has certain merit." Anger raised her voice and quickened her steps even more. She glared at him. "I don't need you to protect me from—"

"From the consequences of our actions?" he shouted back, keeping pace at her side. "Or have you even considered there will be a price for this night of love?"

Cordelia stopped suddenly. Burke was two steps past her before she asked, "Love? Is this what you call love?"

He stopped and turned. "For lack of a better word."

"For future reference, the correct word is lust. Hot, fevered, panting, vanilla sauce and raspberry syrup covered lust. That's all it was. Nothing more."

"And I suppose you're an expert."

She pulled herself to her full height. Her heartbeat pounded in her ears and she told herself it was due to running across the field. She took a deep breath. "I know love is putting another person's benefit above your own, thinking of the other's welfare first."

Burke threw his free hand into the air, the lantern in the other bobbing with his agitation. "Isn't that what I've been trying to do?"

"No," she said, a dead calm seeping over her with the realization Burke did not understand the difference. "You've put the expectations of society first, regardless of the detriment to either one of us."

Burke's shoulders stiffened. "What could you possibly see about marrying me that would be a detriment to you? I've already offered you anything you could ever want."

"Except a family. I want children. Lots of children." She bit her tongue before she added, all of them with your blue eyes and blond hair. "Even as *inexperienced* as I am, I know that would be difficult if I lived in France or Italy and you lived here."

Burke ran his hand through his hair. "I can't . . ."

As far as she could tell, his equipment had worked just fine, but, then, what did she really know about such problems. Perhaps he'd been wounded, or suffered a childhood illness. "Have you seen a physician? A specialist?" she asked him softly, putting her hand on his forearm. "I've heard—"

"I don't need some quack—"

"But if—"

"Stop. As far as I know, I'm physically capable of fathering children. I simply won't allow it to happen," he blurted out, the words torn from his gut.

"But how can you—"

"There are ways."

"What ways?" she asked.

"I hardly think this is an appropriate topic of conversation." He ran a finger around his collar.

"All things considered," she said, "I have a right to know if you—"

"I didn't." He looked down and dug the toe of one boot into the dirt. "I forgot to . . . I mean I didn't . . ."

That she could be carrying his child at that very moment suddenly occurred to her, staggering her. She turned away from him. Wanting children at some time in the future—a nebulous, familiar longing—was quite different from the shock of the very real possibility of a child, Burke's child, being born in nine months. What should be a joyous event, he would view as a terrible accident.

Conflicting emotions washed over her like waves pounding the shore in a storm. She needed time to think, to sort through everything. Time alone, away from him.

"I'm sorry," he said. "I should have—"

She whirled to face him. "Stop saying that. I'd rather you didn't keep reminding me that you regret this night, regret spending it with me, probably wish you'd never met me."

He blinked. "I don't regret this night. How could I? Not for anything in the world would I give back this wonderful, awesomely beautiful night."

The tears Cordelia had managed to stave off welled up, threatening to overflow.

"It is the unfortunate consequences we must face that I apologize for," he said. "As a gentleman—"

"Arrrgh!" Her anger reignited. She held onto her ire, knowing it would salvage her pride if nothing else. "There are no consequences. There is nothing to regret." She stomped around him, willing herself not to cry, not now, not when he would see. "As far as I'm concerned, this night never happened," she shouted over her shoulder.

She sensed his presence behind her, gaining on her.

"But it did, and as such—"

"Nothing happened." She walked as fast as possible on the uneven ground. "Nothing at all."

"You can't just deny—"

"Oh, yes, I can." She began running.

"No, you can't." He kept pace.

"Can."

"Can't."

"Good heavens!"

Cordelia and Burke both pulled up short and spun to the left at the sound of Granny's voice.

"What in the world are you two arguing about at the top of your lungs?" Granny asked as she and Theo approached. "And, Cordelia, what on earth are you doing here?"

"Looking for you," she answered, grabbing her grandmother by the arm. "Now that I've found you, we can leave. Do you have a carriage?"

Granny nodded. "Theo brought his. Over there," she said, pointing to an area with many parked carriages.

"Good." Cordelia marched forward, dragging Granny in her wake, assuming Theo would follow.

Burke appeared on Granny's left. "Mrs. Smith—"

"Vivian. I asked you to call me—"

"Don't listen to him," Cordelia said, picking up speed.

"This is neither the time, nor the place," Burke continued. "However, I beg your indulgence tomorrow, or rather later today, at three o'clock—"

"We won't be at home," Cordelia said, hurrying her grandmother along as fast as the older woman could manage.

Granny looked from one to the other, her gray curls bouncing like springs on a bumpy road around her concerned expression. "Of course, we'll be at home. We don't have any plans for later, do we, Theo? Theo? Where is Theo?"

Cordelia looked back over her shoulder. Theo, struggling to keep up, had fallen several lengths behind. "He'll catch up with us at the carriage."

"Mrs. Smith . . . Vivian—"

"Ignore that man," Cordelia said to Granny. "He has nothing to say that is of the remotest interest."

"Can we slow down?" Granny asked, a little breathless.

"We'll be at the carriage soon," Cordelia said, hoping it was the truth. "Which way?"

Granny pointed to the left. Cordelia spotted Theo's crested bright yellow carriage and headed in that direction without slacking her pace. The sooner she could get Granny in the carriage, the sooner Burke would leave them alone, preferably before he blurted out . . . anything.

Burke raced ahead to open the carriage door and let down the steps.

"Why, thank you, dear," Granny said as he helped her aboard.

"Ever the gentleman," Cordelia sneered. Pointedly refusing his hand, she climbed aboard by herself.

Unfortunately, the basket she carried made the task awkward, spoiling the effective exit she would have preferred. She tried to maneuver the basket in ahead of her. Her hand slipped, and she would have fallen backward out of the carriage door if not for Burke.

He stopped her fall with his body. Her feet were on the top step, her body angled in midair, her shoulders balanced precariously against his solid chest.

"Easy, now," he whispered in her ear. "I've got you."

A delicious shiver traveled slowly down her spine.

"That's what I'm afraid of," she muttered. Gritting her teeth, she stretched her arms forward, reaching for the carriage doorway just beyond her fingertips. "Do something."

"Ever at your service," he said, his lips tickling her earlobe, his breath warm on her neck. He cupped her derriere in his hands, and leaning forward, boosted her into the carriage. She scrambled across the seat, and sat as far away from him as she could.

Before she could think of an appropriately scathing remark, he said, "Why, Miss Cordelia Weston, you seem to have lost something."

He wouldn't dare tell her grandmother now, not like that. Would he? "If I have," Cordelia countered, "it was of little importance. I've forgotten all about it."

"Really?" he asked, one eyebrow raised.

From behind his back he produced her sewing basket. She must have dropped it getting into the carriage and, in truth, had forgotten it, what with the other . . . distractions. He placed the basket on the seat beside her.

"Thank you, kind sir," Cordelia answered with a false smile. "But it truly has no value, unworthy of your consideration."

"It is my pleasure, most certainly my pleasure, to be of service to you," he said with a teasing grin. "And I disagree." His expression turned serious. He looked deep into her eyes. "Should I ever hold any . . . ah, possession of yours, it would be precious to me, and I would cherish it all my life."

Theo arrived and Burke turned to speak to him, their voices pitched so low Cordelia couldn't hear the conversation.

"Do you want to tell me what that was about?" Granny asked, her voice startling Cordelia out of her reverie.

She turned to her grandmother. Should she say something? She hesitated, and the opportunity slipped away as Theo climbed into the carriage and sat next to Granny.

"My sewing basket," Cordelia said in answer to her question.

"In a pig's eye," Granny said, but as Theo had climbed aboard, she let the matter drop with the veiled threat of, "We'll talk later."

Theo tapped on the roof of the carriage with his cane to gain the coachman's attention. "Home, John." He patted Granny's hand. "Well, we had an eventful evening, didn't we? But it's all over now."

Granny nodded and, yawning, laid her head on his shoulder.

Cordelia stared out the window as dawn pearled the eastern sky. Night might be ending, but she was afraid it wasn't truly over.

Twenty

Cordelia plunked her bonnet on her head and, with stiff fingers, tied the ribbons into an awkward bow under her left ear. She jerked on her gloves. "We are going shopping," she said to Granny.

Quimsy awaited in the carriage out front. Emily and Sarah, the other members of the outing, stood by the front door, bonnets, gloves, and capes in place, sufficiently cowed by Cordelia's stormy attitude to wait silently.

"It's Sunday. There aren't any stores open today," Granny argued.

"Good," Cordelia countered. "Then it won't be crowded." She had no real interest in shopping, but it was a creditable excuse to be out of the house when Burke arrived. If he arrived. There was still a chance he would consider himself well rid of the problem and go about his merry way.

Granny shook her head. "But what—"

"We'll window-shop," Cordelia said. "While we are gone, if Lord Deering should call, which he probably won't, but if he should call, you are not, I repeat, not to accept anything on my behalf."

"Like what?" Granny asked.

"Anything. No gifts, no flowers, no notes, no offers."

"You're expecting an offer?" Emily stepped forward with a smile. "Why that's wonderful."

Cordelia glared at her sister, and Emily backed to the door.

"I am not expecting an offer." Cordelia turned to her grandmother. "I'm not even expecting him to call, but if he does, and if he makes any sort of offer, you are to say no in absolute firm terms. No. Not now. Not ever. Not under any circumstances. Do you understand?"

"Did you two have a tiff?" Granny asked. "Sometimes a couple will quarrel—"

"We did not have a tiff. We did not quarrel. Most of all, we are *not* a couple." Cordelia turned and stomped across the entry hall. She shooed Emily and Sarah out of the door ahead of her. "Remember what I said," she called back over her shoulder to her grandmother. "Accept nothing."

Burke dressed with care. After all, he wanted to make a good impression while asking for Cordelia's hand in marriage. Before telling his future grandmother-in-law he'd dishonored her granddaughter.

The knot in his tie was a fraction of an inch off-center. He pulled it out and, not trusting his valet to get it perfect, began the complicated process of tying it all over again.

"If Gravely calls you out, I'll be your second," Preston said as he entered Burke's dressing room and plopped on the chaise. "More likely, Vivian will shoot you on the spot."

"How did you know?"

"The look of desperation in your eyes."

Burke turned back to the mirror and examined his face. If anything, he looked shamefully happy. "I don't see it."

Preston gave him one of those looks that said the answer was too obvious. "My job, assigned by you, in case you forgot, was to track Cordelia and determine whom she contacted." He leaned back on the chaise, put up his feet, crossed his ankles, and propped his hands behind his head. "Last night, she contacted . . . you."

Burke whirled around, his blood suddenly boiling. "You didn't—"

"Watch?"

He slapped Preston's feet off the chaise.

"Whoa, there. Easy, mate." Preston raised his hands as if to show he wasn't armed. "I was just teasing. In fact, you can thank me for guarding your back and keeping the curious perverts away from Mab's Bower."

Burke took a deep breath and blew it out to the count of ten. What was the matter with him? This business with Cordelia had him acting crazy. He returned to his position in front of the mirror, ran his hands through his hair, and rubbed the back of his neck. "Sorry, old friend."

Preston stood, elbowed Burke aside, and took up the ends of his tie. "If your hands aren't relaxed, the bow will reflect your tension." He tied a perfect waterfall knot and turned Burke to face the mirror. "*Voila.* It's all in the wrist."

"I guess I am a bit nervous."

"Any bridegroom would be."

"How—"

"I know you. Even if I didn't, half of London overheard you two arguing last night. I'll marry you. No, you won't," Preston mimicked, alternately using a low voice and a high falsetto. "Yes, I will. No. Yes. No."

Burke glared at him.

Preston grinned. "So, I assumed you'd take the first opportunity to seek out her grandmother, and act the fool."

"I'm only doing what's right and proper."

"It's a little late for noble posturing. If you're seeking absolution for your sin, you should see a priest. If not, why do you want to marry her?"

Burke paused, reflecting on his friend's words. "I suppose because it's expected."

"Not good enough. I suggest you search for the real reason, or both you and Cordelia are doomed to an unhappy life shackled to each other by force."

"Not by force. I'm willing."

"Are you? Do you want to marry her, or are you simply willing to sacrifice yourself for the sake of propriety? And what of Cordelia? Is she willing?"

Burke sank into a nearby chair, dropped his head into his hands. "You heard her. She said she won't marry me."

Preston cuffed him on the shoulder. "Perhaps there is hope. We know she's an expert liar."

Burke looked up in surprise. "You don't still think she's the Confederate agent, do you?"

"If I did, I wouldn't be here. I'd be on the job following her. Probably sitting in that stinking room counting magpies."

"Why are you here?"

Preston dusted off his hands. "Come now. You have an appointment, and I shall be either your best man, or your second."

"Miss Weston is not at home," the butler droned, as if the goings on of the household were of little interest to him.

Burke and Preston stood in the entranceway of Gravely Mansion, hats in hands. Placing their cards in the silver salver the butler held, Burke said, "Please inform Mrs. Vivian Smith that Lord Deering is calling. You may also inform Lord Gravely that Lord Bathers—"

"Preston, please."

"—is also calling."

"Very good, milord. Please wait here."

After several tension-filled minutes, the butler returned. "Mrs. Smith will see Lord Deering in the parlor, and Lord Gravely will see Lord . . . Preston in the library. If you will follow me."

Cordelia plied her fan with diligence but barely stirred the stifling air inside the carriage. She'd chosen to sit alone rather than stroll with Emily and Sarah as they examined the shops' window displays and discussed each item in excruciating detail. The wheels creaked as the coachman led the horses forward another six inches.

She should have brought a book. At least then she would have something to occupy her mind other than Burke and what might be happening back at Gravely Mansion, if he had even shown up. She looked at her brooch watch for the umpteenth time. Not quite four o'clock.

If Burke had arrived at three, add ten minutes for Granny to appear, another ten for the butler to serve tea, and another ten for the usual social chitchat. Cordelia gave Burke twenty minutes to plead his case. He was rather long-winded when he was nervous, a quality she'd once found endearing; today it seemed annoying. Love had blinded her to his faults. Like his archaic gentleman's code. She dashed away a tear. But she wouldn't think about all that now. Once she was on the ship bound for home, she would have plenty of time. She just had to get through today without crying.

She recalculated Burke's speech to thirty minutes. Giving Granny five minutes to say no, and maybe another five to hand him his hat, the shopping party could return anytime after four-ten and be safe.

Then she would have to face Granny. During the long sleepless morning, Cordelia had decided to accept Mrs.

Miranda Severe's offer as a companion. Beyond getting as far away from London as possible, Cordelia's ideas for the future were a bit nebulous, but she was sure she would be able to think more clearly and make some definite plans during the long sea voyage.

Her stomach rumbled, reminding her that she hadn't eaten. Unfortunately, without the usual crowd of shoppers, the street vendors had also taken the day off. She leaned out the carriage window to call to Emily and Sarah.

"Ten more minutes."

A refreshing breeze lifted the damp tendrils of hair from her cheek. No wonder she wasn't getting any air. The wind, what there was of it, came from behind, and the back of the carriage had no windows. She returned to her seat and plied her fan. Deciding it was better to listen to Emily and Sarah than to roast alive, she opened the carriage door and kicked down the little folding step. She looked toward the front of the carriage. The coachman, who was up front holding the horses' heads, was deep in conversation with Quimsy. Rather than disturb them, Cordelia stepped down unaided. The last step was a stretch. She jumped.

Cordelia immediately regretted her hasty decision when she landed on her sore ankle the wrong way and it twisted painfully beneath her. At her stifled cry, Emily and Sarah came running, as did Quimsy and the coachman.

"Stop fussing. I'm all right," Cordelia said, struggling to a standing position with Sarah's help.

"Whatever possessed you to jump like that?" Emily asked.

"Was it something in the carriage?" Quimsy asked, looking inside as if eager to find a rat or some such.

"I didn't want to be a bother, and, besides, I've jumped out of carriages a hundred times as a child."

Cordelia forced a trill of laughter even though her ankle throbbed. "Guess I'm getting too old for that."

"I should think so," Emily said. "Let's get you right back inside. We need to get you home right away and have Granny look at that."

"No," Cordelia cried. They couldn't return yet. Not for at least another ten minutes. "I'm fine. I wanted to see that hat." She pointed to the nearest window and hobbled in that direction, Sarah supporting her arm.

Emily directed the coachman to his seat and told Quimsy to wait in the carriage before trailing after her sister. "Be reasonable, Cordelia. Your foot is probably swelling again."

She knew it was, but would rather stand that pain than endure seeing Burke again. "Just look at the purple plumes on that adorable cap."

"Please get in the carriage so we can leave," Emily said.

"Wouldn't that be absolutely stunning with your yellow pelisse?" Cordelia asked.

Emily turned to look.

Suddenly, four masked men darted from the alley between the millinery and the tobacco shop farther ahead. Robbers! Three of the men each grabbed one of the women.

Cordelia swung her reticule in self-defense and was rewarded with a grunt of pain from her assailant. A burlap bag was thrown over her head and tied securely around her shoulders, waist, and knees. Though she struggled, the man lifted her up and threw her over his shoulder.

The men were not robbers, but kidnappers. Either for ransom or . . . A rivulet of panic snaked down her spine. She couldn't think about the other gruesome possibilities. If she was going to survive this, she must keep her wits about her. Swallowing the lump in her throat, a deceptive calm came over her.

She heard Quimsy scream, and scream, and scream, though how she knew it was Quimsy she wasn't sure.

"Not her," one of the strangers said.

"This one. I got her."

"No, this is the one."

"Take 'em both. Let's get out of here," another said.

The coachman yelled for the men to halt, and she pictured him climbing down from his perch. Too late. The man carrying her ran, his shoulder digging into her stomach with each heavy step.

She was thrown down, and her breath was knocked out as she landed with a thump. Someone else landed beside her. And lay distressingly still. Emily? Or Sarah?

"Giddyup, Mabel. Get on up, Gertie."

From the movement and sound, Cordelia deduced she was lying on the bed of some sort of wagon. The last load must have been cabbages and onions. A farm cart, then. Traveling at top speed on cobblestone streets. She tried to remember turns, but was quickly lost.

As far as she could tell, there were only two of them lying on the bed of the wagon. At least one woman got away, or so Cordelia prayed.

"Can't you go any faster?" a man yelled, as he walked from the rear of the wagon to the front, stepping between the two women, and kicking Cordelia in the hip in the process.

"Watch your feet, you big lummox," Sarah said.

Cordelia smiled. Not because Sarah had received the same rough treatment, but at least now she knew the girl was alive.

"Do you want to drive?"

"I could do better'n you."

"Shut up and pay attention."

From the voices, it seemed all three men were up near the driver's seat. Where was the fourth? Cordelia had to take a chance he would be there, too. She wiggled onto her side. "Sarah," she called in a loud whisper.

"Cordelia?"

"Are you all right? Are you hurt?"

"Bruised and battered, but other than that, just dandy."

She had to give the girl credit for gumption. "Good."

"I think they've ruined my bonnet."

Despite the lighthearted comment, Sarah's voice held a note of panic. "Stay calm," said Cordelia, "and we'll get out of this."

"Do you think someone's following us? They'll save us?"

Cordelia hated to destroy all hope, but realistically the only possibility was the coachman, and she didn't think he could have gotten the carriage in motion quickly enough to tail the wagon. "No, but we'll get a chance to escape."

"How? I'm trussed up like a Christmas goose."

"Me too. I don't know how. We'll just cooperate, and pay attention, and something will come up." At least she prayed it would. "I'm sure of it."

After a long silence, Sarah asked, "Where do you think they're taking us?"

Cordelia sensed the wagon slowing down. "I guess we'll find out soon enough."

Burke sat on the edge of his chair and gulped down his fifth tiny cup of tea. The interview was not going at all as he'd expected. Vivian was very chipper and lively for a woman of her age who had been out all night, and who must have at least some notion of why he was calling. Yet every time he broached the subject of her granddaughter, she poured him another cup, and asked him a question about something totally unrelated to the issue.

"What news have you heard of the war at home?" she asked, offering yet another biscuit.

He shook his head, and she replaced the plate on the tea tray. Even if he had been in his office, which he hadn't for several weeks now, he couldn't share that information. "Nothing that isn't in the newspapers."

"Oh."

"Mrs. Smith—"

"Vivian, please."

"Yes. Vivian." Burke cleared his throat and once again began the speech he'd rehearsed in the mirror all morning long. "I'd like to speak to you on a matter of importance concerning your—"

"Have you seen the Elgin Marbles? I hear they're quite impressive."

"Yes, quite. I'd like to speak to—"

"Then you recommend I see them?"

"Yes. I'd like—"

"Vivian! Gravely!" a man's voice called loudly from the entry.

"Good heavens. What could that be?" Vivian said, as she stood and moved toward the door of the parlor.

Burke rose to follow her.

The door to the parlor slammed open, and Dandridge burst in carrying Emily. She was hatless, her dress was torn and dirty. Tears streaked her face. Dandridge set her gently on the sofa.

Vivian knelt by her side and took her hands. "What happened, my dear?"

Burke noticed the butler, coachman, and maid in the door and ordered a basin of cool water and some cloths. He poured a cup of tea and handed it to the distraught young woman, who looked up at him with tear-filled eyes.

"They got Cordelia," she said with a sob. "And Sarah."

"Who got her? Where's Cordelia?"

Emily buried her face in Vivian's shoulder.

"From what I can gather," Dandridge said. "The three women were accosted while window-shopping. Cordelia and Sarah were carried off by kidnappers."

"Four men, big ones," Quimsy said stepping forward. "I was there. I seen 'em."

"And where were you?" Burke asked Dandridge, undisguised accusation clear in his voice.

"At home."

"I went to his house first," Emily said, raising her head, tears making fresh tracks down her smudged cheeks. "It's all I could think to do."

Burke nodded his apology to Dandridge.

"Tell me what happened," he said to Emily, his voice gentle and coaxing, not betraying his gut-wrenching fear. "It's important for you to tell me everything you remember."

Theo and Preston silently joined the group. Burke didn't have to tell everyone the need for as much information as possible, and the necessity of haste.

"We were window-shopping," Emily said with a hiccup. "Suddenly four masked men ran from the alley."

"Big men," Quimsy said. "Devils, with fangs and red eyes. I seen 'em, I did. Grabbed the gels and flew away."

Burke motioned for Preston to silence the hysterical maid, and he guided her out of the room still ranting about demons.

"Go ahead," Burke said to Emily. "You're doing fine, now. Just fine."

Emily sat a little straighter and swiped at her face with the cloth. She focused on him as if he were the only one in the room, just as he wanted her to do.

"Four masked men . . ." he prompted.

"They ran right at us. At first I thought they were

purse snatchers. Then I noticed they all carried burlap bags, so I figured they must be robbers wanting to break into one of the stores. Everything was closed. That's why we were just window-shopping."

"Naturally," Burke said, nodding his encouragement. "But they didn't go into a store?"

"No. They grabbed Cordelia and Sarah, threw bags over their heads, and tied ropes around them."

"Not you?"

"No, and that was very strange."

"Why do you think it strange?"

Emily shook her head. "No, it's silly. I must have imagined it. I'm as bad as Quimsy and her demons."

"You're being very logical and helpful. Even your impressions are important because they may give us a clue. Why did you think it strange?"

"Well, I can't remember the exact words, but I seem to recall them arguing about which girl was the right one." She blinked up at Burke. "That doesn't make any sense, does it?"

"Not at the moment." He smiled at her. "But that's all right. It may prove helpful later." Vivian moved aside to speak to Gravely, and Burke slid into her place, keeping his attention on Emily. "What happened next?"

"A cart came racing down the street and stopped at the corner."

"What sort of cart?"

Emily shook her head. "I don't know. A farm cart."

"Describe it."

Emily closed her eyes and massaged her temples. "High wooden sides. Unpainted. No, red paint that was almost all worn away. Open in the back, like the drop gate was missing. Dray horses. One dapple gray, one tan with a black mane."

"Good girl." He wasn't sure any of this would be of

value, but it meant she was observant. "Then what happened?"

"The two men carrying Cordelia and Sarah over their shoulders ran after the cart. They dumped them into the back and climbed on, and the wagon took off."

"Which direction?"

"East, I think."

"Go on."

"I was still struggling with the man holding me from behind. I tried to tear off his mask." Tears filled her eyes. "He threw me down. They waved their pistols at us, told us to stay where we were for the count of one hundred. Then they disappeared down the same alley they'd come from." She shook her head. "I heard horses leaving, so they must have left mounts in the alley."

"Then you went to Dandridge's?"

"I didn't know what to do. Quimsy was hysterical, and the coachman was too terrified to move because he couldn't count that high."

"You did just fine. And Dandridge did the right thing bringing you directly here." Burke stood.

Emily grabbed his coat sleeve. "You will find them, won't you?"

Burke patted her hand, gently removing it. "I'll find them." It was a promise and a vow.

"One more thing," Emily said. She bit her lower lip. "I hate to have to say this, but I think they were Confederates." She took his hand, and laid a button still attached to the bit of cloth in his palm. "I tore that from the coat of my attacker."

The brass button had the insignia CSA. "They were soldiers in uniform?"

"No, not in uniform, but he's a Confederate, isn't he?"

Burke curled his fist around the button. He turned to face the room. "Dandridge, you notify the police and get a Bow Street runner or three. Preston . . . Where the hell is Preston?"

"No police," Vivian said, entering the parlor. She wore her traveling cloak, and dragged an obviously heavy carpetbag. "I know who they are, and this is what they want."

"What are you talking about?" Burke asked.

"Gold," Vivian said, indicating the bag with a flourish. "Not all of it, but enough of what's left to convince them to release the girls."

Twenty-one

Cordelia's intention to cooperate with the kidnappers while waiting for a chance to escape was sorely tested as they pushed her, pulled her, carried her, bumped her head against something hard, smacked her knees, and dumped her into a chair.

"I'll thank you to remember I am not a sack of potatoes," she complained in a loud voice, more to signal Sarah of her location than in any expectation it would make a difference.

"Me neither," Sarah said, from approximately the same level, and to Cordelia's right.

At least they hadn't separated them.

"Why are there two of them?" a new male voice demanded.

"We couldn't tell which one was which, so we brought 'em both." Cordelia recognized the man's voice from the wagon, the clumsy man with the big feet.

"The commander is not going to be pleased," the new voice said.

By contrast, his clipped enunciation pointed out a startling fact. The men who had kidnapped her and Sarah were southerners. Cordelia chided herself for not noticing earlier.

"Excuse me, gentlemen," she said in the sweet belle-of-the-ball voice Emily always used when she wanted a beau to fetch her a glass of punch. "It's mighty warm inside this bag. I'm about to purely die of suffocation."

"I'll cut them each a tiny airhole," Clumsy said.

"Might as well have a look at them," the Englishman said. "Cut the bags so we can see their faces."

"No. If we can see them, they can see us. They can identify us to the authorities."

"Not if you have your mask on, you imbecile. If we have the wrong woman, the commander will have our hides."

Cordelia blinked in the sudden light, dim as it was. She and Sarah were seated in chairs in the center of an empty warehouse. The late afternoon sun came through a row of dirty windows high up on one wall, making pale squares on the floor around them. Directly ahead, in the relative shadows, stood three men.

In the foreground, immaculately dressed in gray from his felt campaign hat to the tips of his snakeskin boots, the apparent leader saluted them with his cane. "Good afternoon. I trust you are not too uncomfortable."

"I've been better," Cordelia said. She looked around with a disdainful air, orienting herself as much as possible without seeming to look for the nearest door. "This isn't exactly the palace drawing room?"

"If it is, the queen needs a new decorator," Sarah said.

The Englishman laughed. "Touché. As much as I would enjoy exchanging witty repartee, time is of the essence. Now, if you would reveal which of you has my gold?"

How could they have known about the gold coins the bookseller and the organist had collected to aid the runaway slaves? Confused, Cordelia turned to Sarah, only to find Sarah facing her with a shocked expression.

"Come, come. I haven't got all day."

Cordelia decided playing dumb was the best tactic.

"Neither of us has the slightest idea what you're babbling about."

"That's her," Clumsy said. "I seen her in the park." He leered at her. "Got a real eyeful, too."

"Nah, it's the other one, I tell you," the man on the left said. "I seen her back home, lots of times, riding around in her fine carriage, her nose in the air."

"Tell me which of you charming creatures has the gold and the list, and I give you my word of honor, I will let the other one go," the Englishman said.

Silence was their answer.

He tucked his cane under one arm and rubbed his hands together, cracking his knuckles. "Do not force me to become, shall we say, unpleasant. Which one of you is Precious?"

"I am," both women said at the same time.

"Close your mouth, you look like a frog waiting for a fly," Vivian said.

Burke clacked his jaw shut. "You're the Confederate agent." He smacked his palm on his forehead. "I should have seen it."

"I was afraid you'd figure it out sooner. If you hadn't been so distracted—"

"You can tell me everything later," Burke said. "Where are they?"

"A warehouse by the London docks. Number seventeen. The Confederate sympathizers have used it in the past to store goods."

He grabbed the heavy bag and headed for the front door.

"I'm going with you," Vivian said.

"No, but I'll take your coachman." He stood in the

middle of the entrance hall and hollered, "Preston." He turned in a circle. "Where the devil is he?"

"I sent Gravely and Preston for reinforcements. They'll join us at the warehouse. The men who have Cordelia and Sarah are dangerous, and quite serious about their mission."

He nodded. She followed him out the door.

Burke set the bag on the floor of his carriage. "I'll send you word as soon as—"

She elbowed him aside and climbed in. "Young man, that is my granddaughter they have, and I know more about these men than you." She planted herself on the forward-facing seat, her large reticule in her lap. "I am going."

Burke quickly weighed the effort it would take to dislodge her against the time Cordelia had already spent in the villains' hands. He hopped aboard and gave the direction to his coachman. "And don't spare the horses."

Vivian grabbed a strap and braced herself as the carriage picked up speed and careened around corners.

Burke looked out the window to get his bearings. He checked his watch. "At this rate we should arrive in twenty-seven minutes, barring any unexpected traffic."

Too slow. Too slow, Burke's heart seemed to beat. He forced himself to remain calm. Panic would not help Cordelia.

Burke rapped on the ceiling with his cane.

The extra coachman riding atop opened the trap.

"Stop a block short of the warehouse," Burke said. "Find an alley where we can pull off the main street."

The coachman nodded his understanding.

As soon as the trapdoor clapped shut, Burke crossed his arms over his chest and looked across at Vivian. "Now, Mrs. Smith, how long have you been a double agent?"

She gasped, then shook her head.

"No more charades. Your shenanigans have put your granddaughter and an another innocent young woman in danger."

"What makes you think I—"

"The truth, Mrs. Smith. All of it."

She pulled her cloak around her and glared at him. "You can't know—"

"Let me tell you what I do know. You have a large quantity of Confederate gold, sent to London to bribe members of Parliament into supporting the southerners' cause. Also, presumably, to purchase additional weapons and ammunition. Correct?"

"Not weapons, medical supplies. But that doesn't make—"

"Yet, according to all accounts, popular support is swaying to the queen's position of abstaining from taking a side—either side."

"But—"

"That means you're a very poor agent, which evidence denies, or you're a double agent, in fact working for the Federals. I think your true mission is to lead the Confederates in London on a merry chase whilst denying them the use of the gold to garner support." He did not need her confirmation to know he was correct. "The flaw in your plan—"

She looked up at him sharply.

"The flaw was not taking your granddaughter into your confidence."

"She wants nothing to do with the war. It's taken almost everything she's ever known from her. Her father, her home."

"Her grandfather?" he asked gently.

Vivian waved away his sympathetic tone. "Cordelia and her grandfather were not close. She was a lively child, bit on the bossy side, and he was critical of everything she did."

Burke swallowed the longing to have known her then, to have seen her develop into the person she'd become. He forced himself to stay focused on the matter at hand. "We have some time. Is there anything you can tell me that may prove helpful in rescuing Cordelia and Sarah?"

"Such as . . ."

"Who are these men? How did you get involved?"

Vivian took a deep breath. "Silas Smith, my late husband, was a harsh man, totally dedicated to the Confederacy. As he got busy with his succession efforts, he asked me to run some errands for him. I agreed because it gave me a chance to get out of the house for a bit, travel. If I'd known I was passing military information, I wouldn't have done it. My sympathies are with the abolitionists."

"Go on," Burke said, ducking to take a quick look outside for a location check.

"After Silas was killed, a friend of his, Marcus Delaney came to see me. He'd heard I was making a trip to Washington for personal reasons and asked me to deliver some papers to a business acquaintance of his. As a favor, I agreed. Upon investigation, I realized the documents were written in code." Vivian grinned. "I deciphered them, and I took them directly to Alan Pinkerton."

"So then Mr. Pinkerton convinced you to act as his agent."

She snorted. "Not exactly. Oh, he was suitably grateful for the information and Delaney's identity, but he was against my active participation in his network. I finally wore the man down, a major feat I want you to know," she said, shaking a finger at him. "He finally agreed to give me a chance."

"And you were successful?"

"Admittedly, not at first. I was nearly caught several times."

"And that's when you developed the ruse of pretending to be mad?"

"How—"

Burke shrugged. "Just makes sense. You seem to be in excellent control of your faculties."

"Thank you," she said with a gracious nod. "Though I must say, you're one of the few I haven't fooled."

"You did, for quite a while, actually. Then I noticed the manipulative character of your so-called spells."

Vivian laughed. "Let's just say it has come in handy. There were those who remembered I'd always expressed strong opinions against slavery. I had to convince them I was a staunch supporter of state's rights and therefore with them in spite of the other issues. To make them think I had good reason to hate the Yankees, I burned down my plantation and blamed it on the Bluebellys."

"Perhaps I should reassess my earlier opinion?"

"It seemed the only way. At least I was able to move out everything of value first, and hide it in some caves on my property." She sighed and looked down at her hands. "Some of my neighbors have lost everything."

"So you carried messages for the Confederacy . . ."

"Delaney's group was loose and disorganized. Local boys working for their hometown regiments. Once I gained their trust, I encouraged them to act professionally, standardize their codes, widen their network. We became quite efficient, and I have to give credit to Pinkerton: he always made it seem as if the information he received from me logically came from another source, so my position was never compromised. As a result, a representative of Jefferson Davis contacted me about the London mission."

"Which was?"

Vivian stared at him critically for a few moments before she answered. "I was given a list of names. I was to convince, bribe, blackmail, whatever it took to garner their support in Parliament for the Confederate cause."

"A poor example of information gathering if Marsfield was included."

Vivian laughed. "Marsfield was never on the list. That was an invention by Pinkerton. His way of watching my back."

"Where was Cordelia while you were—"

"Spying?"

He made a semi-bow. "As you prefer."

"While I was working as a Federal agent, Cordelia took care of her sister and her crazy grandmother. Life hasn't been easy since we had to move to the cabin. Cordelia knows nothing about my activities."

"Surely, she knows—"

"Nothing," Vivian said, and her voice hissed with the rasp of steel. "I don't want her suspected of treason. She knows nothing."

"It seems to me, Mrs. Smith, that by keeping her ignorant of the desperate characters you're dealing with, you have already put her in danger. Maybe a much greater danger than the hangman."

The man in gray approached the chairs where Cordelia and Sarah were seated, still wrapped and tied in the burlap bags like two Egyptian mummies, with only their heads free.

"Two such lovely young women." He ran his knuckle down Cordelia's cheek. She jerked her head away, which only made him chuckle. "And both with the unusual name Precious. What a startling coincidence."

"I'm Precious," Cordelia said. "Let her go." If she could convince them to release Sarah, she could stall for time while the girl went for help. "I'll tell you whatever you what to know, after you release her."

"No, I'm the real Precious. Let her go."

Cordelia turned toward Sarah, who grinned proudly. Obviously, the girl thought she was helping the situation by maintaining the confusion.

"No," Cordelia said, glaring meaningfully at Sarah. "I am Precious."

"Enough." The Englishman reached inside his coat sleeve and pulled out a long, thin knife. He pointed it at one woman and then the other. "This is not a parlor game, and I am quickly losing patience."

Burke pulled a box from beneath the seat and methodically checked the loads on the two pistols inside. As the carriage neared the warehouse, he cautioned himself to maintain a cool, logical mind. Going off half-cocked could only increase the danger to Cordelia.

"Tell me about these men," he said to Vivian.

"They belong to a pseudo-military group that calls itself Sons of the South." She made a spitting motion.

Burke raised an eyebrow. "I take it these aren't your friends."

"They're exiles and expatriates, trumped-up pirates and gunrunners who seek only profit. An affront to brave soldiers."

The carriage slowed and made a sharp turn before coming to a shuddering stop.

"Wait here," he said, shoving the pistols into his pockets.

Before his hand reached the latch, the carriage door slammed open.

* * *

Cordelia gave the Englishman a haughty look, hoping her fear didn't show in her gaze. "How very brave you are, threatening helpless women."

He drew back his hand to strike her, only to have his arm grabbed by one of the other men, the one she called Clumsy.

The Englishman swung around. "How dare you lay a hand on me, you mealy-mouthed cretin."

Unfazed, Clumsy removed the knife from his opponent's hand. "Calm down, Selkirk. We can't have you accidentally killing Precious before she turns over the gold. The commander wouldn't like that."

"It's my gold," Selkirk countered, pulling his arm free. The Englishman turned to sneer at Cordelia. "I think I'm going to enjoy coaxing the information from you."

"It's not your gold until the commander says so," Clumsy said, returning to his position by the door. "And he ain't gonna say so until we get the guns."

"You'll get your guns," Selkirk said over his shoulder. Leaning close to Cordelia, he whispered, "And when they have no use for you, I'll get what I want." He looked sideways at Sarah, reaching out to finger a long golden curl. "Twice." He laughed wickedly as he turned and walked to the door. "I will return with your shipment. Make sure your illustrious commander has men waiting to unload."

In the alcove by the door, the two remaining men arranged boxes and crates, lit up cheroots, and pulled out a well-worn deck of cards, obviously settling in for a lengthy wait.

Cordelia tested her bonds. The rope crisscrossed around the burlap bag covering her body from her shoulders to her knees, holding her arms at her sides.

Her reticule, with her pistol, still hung from her wrist. If she could reduce the bulk of her skirts, she could create some slack.

Using her fingertips, she scrunched up the material, pulling it underneath the rope and bunching it on her thighs. She tried to work quickly, hoping the men wouldn't look up and see her rising skirts. The process seemed to take forever. Suddenly the front hem of her skirt broke free and fluttered back to reach the floor, over the top of the rope, which immediately slackened.

By wiggling her arms she worked the slack in the ropes upward.

"Hey there, what are you doing?" Clumsy yelled.

"This burlap itches," Cordelia said.

"Yes," Sarah added. "It's chaffing my limbs."

"Hear that, Mickey," Clumsy said. "Shame on us for not using silk to protect their delicate skin." The kidnappers chuckled and went back to their card game.

Cordelia peeked at Sarah, who bunched up her skirt in imitation of Cordelia's actions. Perhaps there was a chance they could escape after all.

Burke stepped out of the carriage, meeting Preston, Marsfield, Gravely, and Lieutenant Hadley, the Yankee Lieutenant who had escorted Sarah to London.

Marsfield spoke first. "We have completed a reconnaissance of the situation. The girls are in warehouse seventeen." He pulled out a scrap of paper with a sketch of the layout. "Two guards inside, two more outside. Here and here," he said, pointing to the side and back door. "They seem to be waiting for someone, presumably their leader."

"They're probably waiting for dark to make their move," Burke said.

"Lord Deering, my men are at your disposal," Hadley said with a smart salute. "We would very much like to catch these gunrunners."

"Thank you, Lieutenant. My first concern is the two young women. I'll take in the gold and make the offer of an exchange. Once they are safe—"

"No," Vivian argued, as Gravely helped her from the carriage. "It's me they want. They won't harm me, because without me the coded list is useless. I'll make the exchange."

All the men argued, and Burke held up his hands and called for silence. Something about the situation didn't set right, but he couldn't put his finger on it. He turned to Vivian.

"If they've taken Cordelia and Sarah with the intention of exchanging them for the gold and the list, that would mean they've identified you as the agent."

"That seems obvious." She took a step to move past him.

"But if that is so, why would they take Cordelia and Sarah and not Emily?" Burke asked. "Why wouldn't they take your two granddaughters, instead of specifically excluding one in favor of a friend?"

Vivian stopped and turned.

"I don't see your point," Gravely said. "We're wasting—"

"Let him finish," Marsfield said, laying a hand on the older man's shoulder.

Burke pinched the bridge of his nose, urging speed to his deliberations. The answer popped into his head. "They don't know Vivian is the agent. They think it's Precious, and they chose Cordelia and Sarah because each one has been known as Precious." A small measure of welcome relief surged through him. Cordelia was safe until they learned she wasn't the agent.

"The fools got the code word wrong," Vivian said. "No wonder they haven't been able to decipher the list. Still, this means one of my men sold me out. The bastard."

"Harsh words from a double agent," Preston said in laconic tones. At Burke's questioning glance, he explained, "Obvious, since she's discussing such matters in front of Lieutenant Hadley here, who, I suspect, reports directly to Pinkerton."

Hadley neither confirmed nor denied the statement.

Burke looked to his mentor.

"You're in charge," Marsfield said. "Give us your orders."

Burke nodded. "Here's the plan. Hadley, disperse your men in a loose circle around the warehouse, concealed, waiting for the signal to close in. Marsfield, you take the front door, Preston the back, and I'll take the side door. Vivian will make the exchange."

Gravely protested.

"I'm counting on Vivian's experience and knowledge to bluff these men into releasing Cordelia and Sarah. Gravely, as soon as the girls come out, take them home. We'll wait until the rest of the party arrives; then Marsfield will give the signal to Hadley, and we'll all close in."

Twenty-two

Cordelia had wiggled the ropes loose around her arms, but her hopes of breaking out took a severe setback when a knock on the door sounded. Her guards scrambled to either side and pulled their weapons before opening the door.

Vivian Smith walked through the opening with the aplomb of a duchess entering a ballroom. "Good evening, gentlemen. If one of you would get my bag?" She motioned to the carpetbag sitting on the threshold.

What in the world was Granny playacting at now?

Granny spared them a quick glance and a nod. Cordelia was reassured, not by her grandmother's actions, but by the realization that if she could find them, others must be close.

As Mickey scrambled for the bag, Clumsy waved his gun to stop Granny. "Who are you, and what are you doing here?"

"I should think that would be obvious," Granny said. "I've brought your gold."

"It's sure heavy enough," Mickey said.

"Open it," Clumsy directed his cohort, without taking his gaze or his gun off Granny.

"Woo-wee, Danny-boy, there's enough gold here to buy us—"

"To buy the Confederacy much needed weapons and ammunition," clumsy Dan countered.

"Ah, I didn't mean nothing by that," Mickey whined. "You know, I'm a loyal Son of the South."

While Dan directed Mickey to put the carpetbag of gold in the corner, Granny motioned to Cordelia and Sarah to remain silent.

"Now, madame," Dan said. "Explain yourself."

Granny removed her cloak, folded it twice, and placed it on a crate before she sat. "Since you seem to have the preposterous idea that either of those two young women have any remotely useful knowledge, I found it necessary to come myself. And I do not appreciate the inconvenience one bit." She removed her traveling bonnet and patted her hair. "Since I'm here, you may release those women." She waved a negligent hand in their direction.

Cordelia shook her head, trying to catch Granny's eye, but the older woman refused to acknowledge her.

Dan seemed to consider Granny's words for a long moment. "How did you find us?"

"Young man, I am not in the habit of having my words ignored. Release those women, and as soon as your commanding officer arrives, I will explain everything to him."

Dan holstered his gun and moved toward Cordelia and Sarah.

"Hey, I know who she is," Mickey said. "She's that crazy old woman what thinks she's Cleopatra. I came up on her once down by the Savannah River, wrapped in a bedsheet. Said she was looking for her royal barge." He laughed. "Crazy as a loon, that's what she is."

Dan, looking confused, returned to stand before Granny. "Is that true?"

"'Course it is," Mickey answered for her.

"No," Granny said.

"What do you expect her to say?"

Dan shook his head as if to clear it. He pulled his pistol back out and pointed it at Granny. "The commander can sort this out. He'll be here soon and since you're willing to wait, I'm sure you won't mind joining our other guests. Mickey, find another chair and some more rope."

Hunkered in the dark near the side door, Burke bound the guard with his belt and gagged him with his neckcloth. And questioned his sanity. He hated this clandestine mucking about. That was another reason he'd left the Agency and joined the Diplomatic Corps. Letting the unconscious man slump against the brick wall, he dusted off his hands. Once Cordelia was safe, he intended to give her a piece of his mind. Not that she was responsible for the situation, but she somehow made him want to act like a hero against his nature and better judgment. He checked the alley for additional guards before approaching the door. Putting his ear to the wood, he heard nothing.

He wished there were enough light to check the time. The stars were not out yet, but the sky had darkened. His instinct told him that he should have heard some activity out front by now. The silence was distressing. Flattened against the door, he forced himself to wait. In the murky darkness, he spotted a rickety stairway to the upper reaches of the warehouse. He groaned and shook his head.

"If there was ever a doubt in my mind, I now know you're crazy," Cordelia hissed to her grandmother as soon as the guards had returned to their card game. Then Cordelia turned her head away, refusing to even look at her reckless relative, who now sat between herself

and Sarah. Her grandmother had not only put herself in
danger, but when the guards had come close, they'd noticed her bonds were loose and had tightened the knots.
The chances of escape had plummeted to near zero.

A prickle along Cordelia's spine told her Burke was
near. Telling herself not to get her hopes up, she slowly
checked out the room, peering into the dark corners
without reward. She tried to shake off the feeling that
Burke was somewhere close by, but it persisted, grew
stronger. Glancing heavenward in exasperation, she
spotted him, moving gingerly along a rickety balcony
near the ceiling, three stories up. The foolish man. He
could fall and kill himself.

Burke edged along the catwalk, willing himself to
move without making a sound, willing the old wood to
hold his weight, cursing his foolishness. Yet, his heart
was lighter, knowing Cordelia was all right, seeing her
for himself. When she looked up at him, he blew her
a kiss. He motioned for her not to give him away by
looking at him; he pointed to her, his eyes, and then
to the men in the alcove by the door. She nodded her
understanding.

He eased forward. If he could make it to the end he
could reach the ladder that descended to the floor out
of sight of the men. What he would do then, he hadn't
the foggiest idea, but at least he'd have his two big feet
on solid ground. He took another step, and the wooden
catwalk creaked loudly. He froze.

Below, Cordelia wiggled frantically in her chair, creating a fuss to cover the noise he'd made. Burke hastened
forward. When he was parallel with the women, one
guard shouted for Cordelia to stop making such a
racket. Burke stopped, waiting for her to do the same.

She continued thumping her chair around, stomping her feet, and yelling.

The guard came running from the area by the door. Burke flattened himself against the wall and stood motionless.

"I told you to be quiet," the guard said.

"I'm tired of sitting here. My arms hurt. I'm thirsty." Cordelia yelled her litany of complaints. "I want—"

The guard slapped her across the face, knocking her off the chair.

Burke's blood instantly boiled. Without thought, he launched himself against the guard, splintering the flimsy railing of the catwalk.

The guard turned and looked up, his expression flickered surprise, amazement, and horror. He raised his gun.

Burke landed on the man and rolled to the left, pulling the man with him so that his gun pointed away from the women. A gunshot echoed loudly in his ears. The shouts of the women and the other guard became muffled and faded.

Burke fought the searing pain in his head and the encroaching darkness, and struggled with the guard for possession of the gun, pinning his opponent's gun hand to the floor. Pandemonium broke out around him. Shots. Shouting. He saw everything as if from a distance, yet he recognized Preston's voice, and Marsfield's. Suddenly, everything was quiet.

"Don't shoot," the guard said, his voice muffled. "I give up." He pushed at Burke. "Get this big lug offa me."

Burke felt himself being rolled to the side. He lay on his back.

"Open your eyes," Cordelia demanded.

He struggled to obey, if only to see for himself that she was truly safe.

Cordelia knelt beside him, tears streaming down her

cheeks. "Burke, look at me. Please open your eyes." She struggled with her bonds, needing to touch him. Someone cut her ropes, and she ripped off the burlap bag, wadding it up to cushion his head. She reached for Burke's hand, touched his cheek, smoothed back his hair. The quantity of blood on his head chilled her heart, as did his stillness.

Granny knelt by his other side, examined his wound, checked his pulse, looked under his eyelids.

"He's going to be all right, isn't he?" Cordelia asked, trying to sound positive and brave and failing miserably. She ripped a strip of cloth from her petticoat and used it to staunch the blood.

"I think so," Granny said. "A deep crease, but, then, head wounds bleed a lot. I'm more worried about a possible concussion." She stood. "Let's get him home, so I can clean that wound and stitch it properly."

"No," Burke croaked, trying to rise.

Cordelia laid her hands on his chest, and he relaxed. "Be still," she said, tying another strip of material around his head to hold the bandage. "We're taking you home."

Burke blinked as if trying to focus his eyes. "Not yet," he mumbled. "Guns. Gold."

"What is he talking about?" Cordelia asked.

Marsfield answered. "He's reminding us the others are still out there. A minimum of two more kidnappers, and the man illegally selling guns to them. Most likely more. They aren't going to give up on the gold easily. If we can catch them red-handed with the guns, the charges will be ironclad."

Burke nodded, then groaned with the pain the movement caused. "I'm fine. Apprehend them, or she won't be safe."

Worried about Burke, Cordelia wanted to protest, but

she knew they spoke the truth. Sarah and Granny would be in danger if they didn't catch the rest of the kidnappers.

"He's coherent," Granny said. "That's a good sign." She checked under the makeshift bandage on his head and gave a satisfied nod. "Bleeding's just about stopped. Let's make a pallet in the corner for him."

"No." Burke struggled to stand, and his friends, Marsfield and Preston, helped him.

"Burke, you need to lie down," Cordelia said, her breath catching when he stumbled forward. "You're dizzy."

"I'll be fine." He put his hand to his head. "Just help me as far as that wall," he said to Preston.

Cordelia followed them across the room.

Levered against the wall, Burke leaned his head back and closed his eyes. "Tie up those two fellows and see if their coats fit you and Marsfield," he said to Preston. "In this dim light we can fool the others long enough to get them inside."

Preston left, and when Burke started to slide to the side, Cordelia stepped forward to prop him up. He leaned over and kissed the top of her head.

"Take Vivian and Sarah, and find Gravely," he said, his voice a hoarse whisper. "Have him take you home. I'll send word when we're done here."

Cordelia had no intention of leaving him, especially in this condition. "You need me and Sarah to take our places in the chairs, or they'll know as soon as they walk in that something's wrong."

"It's too dangerous."

"More so without us. I don't think you have the strength to prevent me from helping you."

Burke leaned his head back against the wall. "I could ask you to leave as a personal favor."

"But you won't, because you know I'm right."

"I'll take Sarah's place," Granny said, donning the girl's half-smashed bonnet. "I need to know the name of the person who double-crossed me. No one will be safe until he's caught."

"We'll wait for your signal, but as soon as Preston and Marsfield reveal themselves, I want the two of you to dive for the floor and stay there until I tell you to get up."

Cordelia didn't argue with Burke because he was obviously in pain. Yet his thinking seemed clear, and his words weren't slurred. She made sure he was balanced against the wall before she slipped away.

Granny moved the chairs several yards back, deeper into the gathering shadows before she and Cordelia sat and arranged the burlap bags and ropes to look as if they were still tied. Preston and Marsfield, wearing the kidnappers' coats, their borrowed hats pulled low on their brows, hunkered over the makeshift card table. The real Sons of the South were bound and gagged in the far corner of the warehouse. Burke stood to the left of the entrance alcove, out of sight unless someone came well into the warehouse. The one lamp gave only a feeble light, but Cordelia could see him. Despite his injury, his presence steeled her nerves. She would not let anything else happen to him.

Once all the actors were in place, they waited for the drama to begin.

Twenty-three

Burke fought the seductive darkness, refusing to let his body give way, refusing to leave Cordelia without his protection. She was his lodestone, his *raison d'être*. He knew it now.

Unreasoning anger had surged through him when she was hurt, followed by unrelenting despair at the thought of her life being in danger. He did not want to face a future without her, could not face a world bereft of the golden light of her smile, the warmth of her laughter. He loved her.

His knees started to buckle, and he pressed his back against the wall, pushing himself upright, willing the darkness away. When Cordelia was safe from the gold-hungry gunrunners, then he would have to save her from the threat he himself presented.

Cordelia watched Burke struggle to remain standing. He flashed her an encouraging smile, and she had to blink away tears. Let the poets write of glorious sword fights and pitched bloody battles, her Viking showed his stubborn warrior's heart by not giving in. And by trusting her to do her part. She swallowed the lump in her throat and vowed to be worthy of his trust.

The door burst open, and the man in gray stormed in. "Where is your commander?"

"He's not here yet," Preston mumbled, not looking up from his cards.

"I can see that. I do not have all night."

Marsfield shrugged. "He'll be here when he gets here."

The man in gray paced several steps forward and then back. "You two go and help my men unload the guns. That will save some time once your commander finally graces the premises with his august presence."

"We're guarding the prisoners," Preston said, dealing a fresh hand.

"Why? Do you feel two girls, bound as they are, constitute a threat? Go, before I decide to report your disrespect to Commander Ketters."

Preston and Marsfield shuffled out. Beneath the burlap covering, Cordelia slipped the pistol from her reticule.

Selkirk turned and looked at Cordelia. She returned his stare with a steady gaze. Granny sat slumped in her chair, the brim of Sarah's bonnet concealing her face.

Selkirk sauntered across the warehouse floor, stopping mere feet in front of Cordelia.

"Did you really expect to keep the gold for yourself?" he sneered. "I can see how you might think to outwit the Sons of the South, but me?" He smiled. "No matter. I shall have my recompense soon enough. The gold . . . and some amusement." He reached out to touch her cheek.

She jerked her head away.

He simply laughed, the evil sound causing her stomach to flip-flop and sour bile to rise in her throat.

"You and her," he said, looking over at the other chair's occupant. "What's the matter with her?" He poked Granny in the shoulder. "Wake up, you silly chit."

"Leave her alone," Cordelia said. "She's fainted."

He turned his attention back to Cordelia. "So you're the feisty one," Selkirk said, one eyebrow raised. "I shall remember that."

Though Cordelia's insides quaked, she did not shrink under his leer. "And I shall remember you—to the authorities."

Any response he might have made was forestalled by the entrance of four workers carrying two long, obviously heavy boxes, followed by Preston and Marsfield with a third crate.

"Where do you want these?" the first man asked with a grunt.

Before Selkirk could respond, Preston answered, "Over here," directing the men to the side of the warehouse away from Burke and the captured kidnappers. They stacked the wooden shipping crates against the wall and shuffled back toward the door.

Rutherford Ketters, wearing the same nonuniform as the kidnappers, but with ostentatious gold epaulets, strutted into the warehouse. Two aides, marching in lockstep, followed him. Cordelia found it difficult to believe that someone she had once danced with could be the leader of the nefarious group. She counted heads. Eight enemies against the five of them, including herself, Granny, and Burke, who was injured. Cordelia hoped her friends were armed with better weapons than the small derringer she held in her sweaty palm.

Ketters went directly to the crates and motioned for an aide to open one. Then he removed one of the guns, fondling it with an appreciative whistle. "Very nice."

"I told you I deliver quality goods," Selkirk said as he joined the group around the boxes.

Ketters and Selkirk shook hands.

"You're early," Ketters said. "My message clearly stated I would make the exchange tomorrow night."

"You're late," Selkirk countered. "Our deal was to conclude three days ago."

"A minor setback."

"A major inconvenience. One that will cost you a premium."

"Now see here," Ketters blustered.

"Don't get into a snit. I'm sure my *price* is within your means, and may even rid you of a potential risk factor. Once you have the gold to pay for the shipment, I'll take the girls as recompense for the delay."

Ketters turned, and Cordelia knew the instant he recognized her. "Miss Weston. Frankly, I'm disappointed. If you had told me the other night that you were masquerading as Precious, I would have known you had the gold and the list, and we could have concluded our business amicably."

"I haven't the slightest idea what you're talking about."

"She wants to keep the gold for herself," Selkirk said. "If you require my services, I have ways of extracting information."

Ketters approached her and stood looking down at her with his thumbs stuck behind his CSA belt buckle. "I'm sure that won't be necessary, will it, Miss Weston?"

"You're making a mistake." Cordelia raised her chin a notch.

Selkirk rubbed his hands together.

"There is no mistake," Ketters said. "And no escape. I have your name directly from Delaney. Now turn over the—"

"That's all I needed to know," Granny said.

Then, everything seemed to happen at once.

Marsfield and Preston drew their guns on the workers. "You're under arrest in the name of the queen."

Granny kicked Selkirk in the knee.

"You bitch." Selkirk slapped Granny, knocking her to the floor.

Ketters jumped behind Cordelia and grabbed her up,

causing her to drop her gun. Using her like a shield, he held a knife to her throat. "Stand back or she dies."

A low, angry growl came from the shadows. Selkirk and Ketters turned, the latter dragging Cordelia around with him. Only an indistinct outline of Burke was visible in the gloom.

Raising a large pistol, Selkirk aimed at the shadows. "Come out with your hands up."

But Burke couldn't walk unaided, hands up or not. Would Selkirk start shooting? Cordelia didn't wait to find out. She grabbed Ketters's wrist and pulled his hand away from her throat. At the same time, she stomped on his foot. Twisting free, she dove for her gun.

Cordelia fired, the sound of the little derringer a weak echo of the boom of Selkirk's pistol. Ketters fell on her, though she'd aimed at the other man. She struggled, kicking and scratching, anything to prevent Ketters from getting a confining hold on her.

Suddenly, he was lifted off her. With a roar, Burke tossed him aside. Then Burke separated Granny and Selkirk, sending the man after his cohort.

Cordelia sat up, and then helped Granny to her feet.

After reassurance from Preston that he and Marsfield had everthing under control, Burke turned to Cordelia.

"We're fine," she responded to his unspoken question. She stepped toward him, needing to touch him.

He collapsed in her arms.

Burke woke slowly, with only vague memories of the night before. He remembered the fight at the warehouse but not much else. Other than that Cordelia had always been at his side. He reached for her now, knowing before opening his eyes that she would be sitting in a chair at the bedside. Dressed in a simple green day dress, with her hair pulled back in a chignon, she looked serene and lovely. If not for the hint of dark smudges under her eyes, he could have imagined her presence there all night.

"Hello," he said, his voice raspy.

She closed her book and smiled. "Good afternoon, sleepyhead."

"Where are we?"

She scooted her chair closer and took his hand. "Uncle Theo's best guest room. How do you feel?"

"Like Thunderation kicked me in the head."

"Granny said you'd have a whale of a headache for a day or two. The less you move around, the faster it will pass."

"You should not be here. It isn't proper."

"Some might say I've already been thoroughly compromised," she said with an unrepentant grin. She rose to place her book on the nightstand and then sat on the bed by his side. "You shall have to marry me now."

"Does this mean you've decided to accept my proposal?"

"Definitely not."

He put his hand to his forehead. "Have pity, Cordelia. Your convoluted logic is making my headache worse."

"It's very simple. I do not accept the proposal you made, with those ridiculous conditions; however, I will marry you and be your wife in all respects. We will live in the same house, sleep in the same bed, have children, and—"

"Cordelia—"

"I understand your hesitancy on the matter of children."

"No, you—"

"But I do. Did you know you talk in your sleep? Well, it may have had something to do with the medication Granny gave you, but you were quite garrulous, even answered questions."

"If you will not leave, then I must." He sat, but the pain in his head multiplied a hundred times over. When Cordelia pulled him back down, he was too weak to resist.

She climbed on top of him. "Now see here, you big oaf," she said, bracing her hands on his shoulders. "You made me love you, and you must deal with the consequences. We will be married immediately, and if I'm not pregnant already, I intend to be before Christmas."

"But Cordelia—"

"For a logical man, you've got a few crazy ideas imbedded in your brain. If bearing you was so horrendous, why did your mother then have another child?"

"I—"

"You may not know this, but my family has a history of birthing big, healthy babies. Granny had only one child, but her twin sister had five strapping boys without a bit of trouble. It's all in the hips." She began to disrobe.

"What are you doing?"

"I'm going to prove to you that I have wonderful, wide hips. Made for—"

"That won't be necessary." Burke took her hands in his. "I remember every sweet inch of your body." He pulled her down and gently kissed her.

"Now, if I may have a chance to say something." He tucked her to his side, cuddling her close. "I realized last night that I love you beyond all reason, and that I do not what to live apart from you. Even though I may never stop worrying about you, Cordelia Weston, will you be my wife, live with me, and share my love?"

When she didn't answer, he looked down. She was sound asleep in his arms, right where she belonged.

Epilogue

Cordelia propped her feet on the footstool as she watched her husband extinguish the last of the candles on the Christmas tree. She patted the prominent mound of her belly. Next year there would be toys under the tree.

"It was a lovely party," Burke said as he joined her on the loveseat by the fire. "It's nice that our families and friends get along so well."

She rested her head on his shoulder. "I missed having Emily here."

"Did I hear Vivian say she received a letter?"

"Yes. Emily is so busy with the dig, she only writes on alternate weeks to one of us. Her son is already a handful, but she has three native nurses to help. They've nicknamed him Tut. Can you imagine?"

Burke chuckled. "I can imagine Emily's son being spoiled rotten."

She slapped playfully at his arm. "Like you have no intention of spoiling your children."

"Me? I should say not. I shall be strict as can be."

Cordelia hid a smile, keeping her knowledge secret: inside her Viking warrior beat a heart of marshmallow cream.

"I rather expected Preston to return in time for the holidays," she said. "You don't suppose he ran into trouble in Savannah?"

Cordelia had finally delivered the third letter, with Granny and Theo's help, and the generous donations for the welfare and education of former slaves had astounded her. Since neither she nor Granny could return to the Confederate states without putting themselves in danger, Preston had volunteered to deliver the donations to Madame Lavonne.

"I expect he'll send word when he's able."

Something in his voice caused a shiver down her spine. "He's on another mission for Marsfield, isn't he?"

"Don't worry about Preston. He can take care of himself."

She knew better than to ask for more than that.

"When are Vivian and Theo leaving for the Continent?" he asked.

She knew he'd changed the subject because he didn't like to discuss his work since he'd transferred back to the Agency fulltime. There was too much he could not reveal, not even to her.

"Granny said they'd decided to wait for their honeymoon until spring and better weather. I think she wants to be here when her great-grandchild is born. She really hated it that Emily was so far away."

"Speaking of babies, I think it's time we get you up to bed, little mother," Burke said. "You shouldn't get overtired."

"You worry too much."

"I'm a blissfully happy nervous wreck."

Cordelia smiled as she wrapped her arms around his neck. She would wait until later to tell him Granny's prediction. The prediction of twin girls was going to be quite a shock for her mighty Viking warrior.